Dark In Different Ways

J.D. Patterson

SPELLBOUND
BOOKS

Cover: Jem Butcher

To M-d,

I hope you like this.

Chapter 1

Sydney, Australia – May 2004

Thom fled Australia on a sunny afternoon. He drove Craig's jeep to the airport where he knew he'd have to dump it. Inside the multi-storey carpark he got out the car, sobbing uncontrollably and bleeding. He slammed the door shut behind him, leaving the keys in the ignition.

He clutched a passport but had no luggage. As he hurried towards the lift, consumed by his own grief, he barely noticed the craggy attendant he passed. But he stopped when he heard the attendant call out to him.

"You okay, mate?"

Thom turned and regarded him with red-raw eyes. He was still shaking, almost hyperventilating. He just nodded, as if unable to speak, and took off again.

"You should do something about that hand," the attendant persisted.

Thom stopped again. He looked down at his left hand and saw blood seeping from several small cuts. He took a deep breath in through his nose and made the effort to be polite.

"I will," he murmured. "Thank you."

He regretted attracting this attention. Rushing away, with his back turned, he was aware of the attendant watching him.

Thom made his way to the Qantas desk, where he checked in in business class.

The young woman behind the counter scrutinised his passport. She radiated efficiency and a chipper Aussie breeziness. "Mr Allerton," she said, staring down at his photo. "You're going to London, aren't you?"

He nodded.

"Any luggage?" She looked back up at him.

He struggled to answer. "No," he managed to say in a whisper. His face contorted as he stifled a sob. He bit his lip to stop any further sound escaping.

"Are *you alright*?" she asked. She was looking at him with an expression that was maybe concern, maybe distaste.

Thom saw her properly for the first time. She wasn't much older than him, perhaps in her late twenties. Her blonde hair was pulled into a tight updo and she was carefully made-up. She made him feel embarrassed and dishevelled.

"Fine," he said, a tear streaking his face. He swallowed hard. *Get a grip*! "I just hate flying. That's all."

"Oh, okay." The young woman seemed reassured. "Just let us know if we can help."

Thom went to the nearest restroom and ran his hand under the cold tap. The bleeding had stopped, more or less. After inspecting his reflection in the mirror, he splashed more water over his face.

Christ! Everybody in the airport must be staring at me.

The redness and blotchiness subsided a bit. He looked almost normal; a pale, slightly-built young man about to begin a long journey home. He closed his eyes for a moment and took a couple of deep breaths.

Back in the terminal, he decided to kill some time. Soon he would have to run the gauntlet through the departures gate, and he needed to steel himself for the extra scrutiny. As a distraction, he went into a convenience store. He was browsing the newspaper rack when he saw the headline screeching at him from the *Sydney Morning Herald.*

'Hit and Run Death Cop was Murdered'

Thom pulled the paper from the rack and began reading.

'Last week, Detective Sergeant Rob Morton (35) died after being struck by a vehicle in Redfern. Police were unable to establish the identity of the driver. They now believe that Morton's killing was premeditated...'

"Fucking hell!" Thom hissed under his breath. He threw the paper back without refolding it. Then he looked around to see if anyone was watching him. Not as far as he could tell.

They know! Time to get the fuck out of here.

He hurried to departures. At the metal detector, he was handed a tray. He had nothing to put in it: no wallet, no keys, and no phone.

"You're travelling light," said a security guard with suspicion.

Thom walked through the scanner holding his passport, his boarding passes tucked inside. He almost breathed a sigh of relief when he was allowed to go.

Striding towards the business class lounge, he had e-mails to send, people to get back in touch with. When he got back to London, he would need somewhere to stay.

His train of thought was abruptly interrupted; a police officer stepped into his path. Thom's heart lurched violently. He knew he was turning a guilty shade of white or red.

The officer was staring at him intently: a tall man, middle-aged with sandy hair and a moustache.

He gestured to his left. "Can you come over here, thanks. I want to talk to you."

"Is there a problem?" said Thom apprehensively. It occurred to him that he should, by now, have been surrounded by a whole phalanx of police. They should have handcuffed him and dragged him off to a cell.

"I'm sure it's all good, mate," the officer replied. "I just want a chat."

Thom was led to a partitioned zone, rather than a room. There was a small table and two chairs. He was motioned to sit down.

"I'm Steve Jefferies," the officer told him, taking the seat opposite. "I'm with the Australian Border Force. And we're a bit concerned about you."

"Really?" said Tom coolly. "Any particular reason?"

He doubted he'd been stopped out of concern. He wondered if Jefferies was just playing a game. This could be a psychological tactic. In his experience, it was best to act cool when questioned by police. The less said, the better.

He'd put his passport down on the table. Jefferies now picked it up, without asking, and began flicking through it.

"Well, you seem upset," he said probingly. "And you're in a bit of a hurry to leave. How long have you been in Australia?"

"Two years," Thom replied. "More or less."

Jefferies carried on studying the passport. "So, you came here on a working holiday visa. For twelve months."

"That's right."

"And you're still here."

"Legitimately. I am...I was in a relationship with an Australian citizen. And I'm a student here too. At the University of New South Wales."

"Ah, yes." Jefferies looked at the logo on the front of Thom's hoodie. "That's where my daughter wants to go to uni. What are you studying?"

"Journalism. I'm on their graduate programme."

"Very good," said Jefferies approvingly. "But you have a one-way ticket back to London. You're not coming back?"

"No," Thom replied.

He decided the officer had to know more than he was letting on. Still, he couldn't understand the point of his *faux* interest.

Jefferies looked at Thom's boarding pass, which he'd picked out from inside the passport. "Business class," he said raising his eyebrows. "You have expensive tastes. Who paid for it?"

"Craig," said Thom awkwardly. "My...partner."

He thought this might bring out Jefferies' prejudices. The officer looked up and stared at him with narrowed eyes.

"Craig what?" he asked.

"Huatere," Thom replied. "Craig Huatere."

He began to suspect that Jefferies didn't yet know about Morton. He was suspicious, no question. But had he made the connection with the dead cop?

"Sounds like a Maori name," Jefferies observed.

"It is. His father was Maori. He's a New Zealander, but he has Australian citizenship."

"I see." Jefferies tossed the boarding pass back onto the table. "It's very generous of him to pay for you to fly home business class."

At that moment, Thom saw an opportunity for escape. He realised that being monosyllabic wasn't going to work. He had to reach inside himself and show some emotion.

"We've split up," he said allowing his voice to tremble just a little.

"That's real sad, mate. But he could've got you an economy class ticket. They're a lot cheaper."

"Craig doesn't care about stuff like that."

"Well, he must have deep pockets. Or he must *really* want you out of here."

It was at this moment, Thom allowed himself to cry in front of Jefferies. "But he does!" he wailed. "After everything, all he wants to do is fucking get rid of me!"

He let out a few more bitter sniffling sobs and slammed his fist on the table, as if frustrated with himself for losing control. Using his sleeve, he wiped his eyes.

For a moment, Jefferies was silent, his face giving nothing away. Then something softened in his eyes.

"I can see you've been through the wringer, mate. But think how it looks to us. You turn up here in this state with nothing but a business class ticket. It all seems a bit drastic."

"I didn't feel I had a choice."

This was partially true.

Jefferies' expression had now become kindly. "I'm guessing this Craig is a bit older than you."

His perception was clear. An older man had tired of his younger lover and sent him packing. Thom decided he had to encourage this.

"Yes," he confirmed. "He's forty-five. That's twenty years older than me. It was never going to work, was it?"

Jefferies smiled ruefully. "That's not for me to judge, mate. You might be hurting now but I know you *will* get over this. Time heals."

Thom was touched by this fatherly compassion. Still, he had to hope the officer wouldn't call Craig to check out his story. He could just imagine Craig's uncomprehending silence on the phone. He wouldn't yet know Thom had gone.

"What are you going to do when you get home?" Jefferies asked. His body language signalled this interview would soon be over.

Thom shrugged. "I don't know yet. I'll probably stay with some friends in London."

"Where are your folks?"

"They live in Lymington, in Hampshire."

"Can you go and stay with them for a while?"

Thom supposed he might have to. He had lost touch with people he'd known in London. Still, the idea was imbued with a sense of defeat.

He offered Jefferies a diffident nod; and the officer, with a small, consoling smile, handed back his passport.

Thom boarded the aircraft an hour later, without being menaced again. When the plane took off, he was overcome by melancholy, but he couldn't cry any more. He leaned back in his seat and stared listlessly out the window.

He kept telling himself that he'd had to go, that he had no choice. Still, he began to wonder about that. Until recently, he'd had a life and a home with a man he loved and the chance of a career he'd always dreamt of. This was all before he'd been consumed by the death of a stranger.

The skyscrapers shrank into the distance, and he thought of Craig, who couldn't now come after him and persuade him to stay. It was too late, and there was no going back. They were in too much trouble – Thom knew that. But as he watched Sydney disappear beneath the clouds, his longing to be home - with Craig - seared through him.

Chapter 2

Sydney, Australia - February 2004

On the night TJ Hickey died, Thom and Craig rode home across the Harbour Bridge on Craig's Harley Davidson. Thom was perched on the back with his arms clasped firmly around Craig's waist. He was relieved when the traffic on the bridge slowed them down. Before them, in the distance, the central business district, with its glassy towers, glittered and sparkled beneath the darkening sky.

Once they were over the bridge, Craig picked up speed and Thom clung tighter as they tore through the business district, stopping intermittently at red lights. Soon, they turned onto Oxford Street, thronging with Saturday night revellers. Neon signs reflected in Thom's black visor. The bars and restaurants along the strip were not so much busy as positively bursting.

The towering apartment block where Thom and Craig lived was close by. Craig slowed the bike as he rode down into the underground car park. The cantilevered gate rolled up. Inside, he manoeuvred the Harley into the parking spot next to his silver jeep. Thom was glad when he heard the engine subside. Gingerly, he got off, pleased to be back on solid ground. Craig pulled off his helmet as he dismounted. He grinned wolfishly at Thom, his dark eyes glinting.

"Did you enjoy that, Tommo?"

Thom looked steadily back at him. "We could have taken the car."

Craig guffawed. In truth, Thom had found the ride exhilarating *and* terrifying. The raw power of the Harley was undeniably impressive. Until he'd met Craig, he'd never been on the back of a motorcycle. Craig, however, had been riding one since he was a teenager.

They walked up into the main building, carrying their helmets. In the foyer, Craig casually greeted the concierge. Once in their apartment on the thirty-ninth floor, he took Thom's helmet and jacket from him to put away.

The apartment enjoyed whitewashed walls and an angular open-plan layout. The tinted windows were full height, from ceiling to floor, and there was a balcony outside. From there, they could see the whole of western Sydney.

When Craig came back up the hallway, Thom told him he was starving.

"Well, we can have leftovers for tea," he suggested, going into the kitchen. "I'll heat up that fish stew you made yesterday."

"That will be perfectly good for supper," Thom said agreeably.

"Yes, it will be *perfectly good for supper,*" Craig echoed, mimicking him.

Thom sorted out the bowls and cutlery while Craig cooked.

"Do you think they liked my sales pitch?" Craig asked.

He was referring to his new clients, a young couple they'd visited on the North Shore that evening.

"Yes," Thom replied. "I think they've totally bought into the property dream."

They ate their reheated stew in front of the TV. Craig relaxed into his recliner chair. Thom sat straight-backed on the leather couch. They were watching an episode of *the Bill*. Thom had always marvelled at the popularity of this British cop show in Australia. One line of English-accented dialogue made Craig laugh out loud. Onscreen, a character said, "Good".

"*Gid*!" Craig exclaimed, pointing at the screen. "That's how you say it, Tommo. Gid."

"No, I say *good*," Thom retorted.

"That's right, Tommo. You say gid."

"Well, at least I don't say *fush n chups*."

As they carried on watching, the screen on Thom's Nokia mobile lit up with a text. He picked it up off the coffee table to read. It was from Lars, his friend and classmate.

"Oh god."

"What's up?" Craig asked, his eyes still fixed on the screen.

"It's Lars. There's been some sort of incident in Redfern, near his house. He says there are police everywhere."

He replied to Lars and had another text back. After *the Bill* finished, he asked Craig to switch over to the news.

"What does Last Chance reckon is going down?" Craig asked, picking up the remote.

"He's not sure. But he thinks an Aboriginal kid has been killed."

"Whoa. That's heavy shit."

It wasn't the first item on the news. But he featured early on. According to the reporter, the boy, Thomas Hickey, known as TJ, had been cycling to visit his mother. Along the way, he'd somehow lost control of his bike and been impaled on spikes on a railway fence. People were speculating he'd been followed by a police patrol.

"He was seventeen," the reporter informed viewers.

Thom was struck by the image of the boy that appeared on the screen: a dark-haired, smiling child. It must have been an old photo because he only looked about thirteen or fourteen.

"I thought the police were supposed to protect children," Thom muttered, staring at the screen. "Not kill them."

Craig glanced at him. "You don't know what happened. The police must have had a reason for following him."

"Yeah, the reason is he was Aboriginal."

"You don't know that either."

"Oh, I think I do. Every time the police kill someone from an ethnic minority, there's always a *reason*. And the right-wing media then spins the *same old* narrative, and nobody ever questions it."

"It's got nothing to do with the right-wing media," growled Craig. He was clearly annoyed. "Everybody knows Redfern has a heroin problem. And the local Aboriginal kids get caught up in it. It might not be politically correct to say it out loud but it's the truth. Sorry if that offends your lefty sensibilities."

"The *truth*, Craig? Well, the truth is that a child has been killed. By police. And because it is an Aboriginal child, because it is a child from a deprived area, everybody is rushing to blame the victim as per fucking usual!"

"For fuck's sake, Thom!" Craig snapped back. "There's no talking to you when you get on one of your rants. You're always on about little Johnny Howard or George Dubya or Tony Blair or whoever it is pissing you off that week. I wouldn't mind but you're not a fucking expert on anything."

Thom's jaw clenched, and he seethed as they sat in acrimonious silence. After a pause, he said: "That could have been you, Craig."

"What do you mean?"

"Well, you're Maori, aren't you? To all intents and purposes. Y*ou* certainly had plenty of trouble with the police when you were young."

"Yeah, that's true," said Craig evenly. "But I'm not a kid anymore. And I know how the world works. You're gonna have to get real too."

Thom sprung up off the couch. "This whole thing completely fucking sucks. I don't know how you can sit there like that and tell me I should just accept it."

He stormed off outside onto the balcony. For a few minutes, he contemplated the city lights. He could hear the hum of the traffic on William Street down below. In the distance, a breeze fluttered across the ocean.

Eventually, he heard Craig get out of his chair and step onto the balcony behind him. He carried on staring at the view as Craig's arms slid around his shoulders.

"Tommo," Craig murmured. "I don't want us to fight over this."

Thom relented a little and allowed himself to relax into Craig's embrace.

"I can't just accept stuff like this, Craig," he said still looking ahead. "I can't just smile and pretend everything is fine. It's just not in me."

"I know." Craig turned Thom around to face him. "All I'm saying is get your facts right. You're going to be a journalist, Tommo, and a good one."

"Do you think?" Thom felt tired now, and sort of defeated. He buried his head in Craig's shoulder and wrapped his arms around his waist.

"I absolutely do," Craig insisted. "You just need to qualify. And *then* you can bring down the government."

"Yeah well, I might just do that," Thom muttered.

Craig squeezed him tighter.

They went back inside. As Craig had cooked, Thom washed up the dishes and left them to dry. Craig closed the blinds in the bedroom and lit his oil burner which he did most nights before they went to bed. Soon the whole apartment smelled of Eucalyptus oil. Thom found it comforting. He associated the aroma with feeling loved and safe.

Craig was now undressed and in bed with his lamp on, reading. Thom was about to join him when his phone buzzed with another text. It was from his twin sister, Charlotte who was back-packing through Vietnam with her best friend, Allie. For the next twenty minutes, he tapped away at his phone exchanging news across the world.

About a year earlier, she and Allie had passed through Australia, and met Craig for the first time. Impressed by the apartment, she jokingly called Thom a gold digger.

"You don't really think that!" Thom exclaimed.

"Well, it's a very nice set-up you have with him. He must be the one paying for it."

"That's *not* why I'm with him," Thom said firmly. He smirked as something occurred to him. "What do you think Mum and Dad will think when they meet him?"

Charlotte sucked in her lips. "Hmm. Let's think. He's a hairy, tattooed Kiwi bloke with a criminal record, and he's old enough to be your father. They'll be just fine about it. Eventually."

"*Imagine* the scandal at the golf club," Thom said clearly relishing the idea.

He finished texting Charlotte and switched the lights out. Craig had fallen asleep by the time he retired to their bedroom. His exposed torso was covered by the tattoos from his youth in the Mongrel Mob. Thom's eye fell on the snarling bulldog with the studded collar, an insignia of a life in which violence was currency. Craig had worked hard to leave his past behind, but it was still indelibly etched on his body.

Thom's bedside lamp was still on. He undressed, climbed under the sheets, and switched it off. On the other side of the bed, Craig stirred, turned over and flung his arm over him. He kissed the back of Thom's neck and dozed off again.

Wrapping his fingers around Craig's wrist, Thom closed his eyes hoping sleep would envelop him, but it didn't. The photo of TJ Hickey floated into his mind. And his eyes flicked back open. He found himself wondering what the Aboriginal boy had been thinking at that moment the picture was taken. What sort of future had he imagined for himself?

Who knows? There's probably no point dwelling on it.

Thom decided to try again at sleep. He closed his eyes and let his mind wander. The smiling boy reappeared but Thom dismissed him this time. Then, he was visited by another image of him, even more unwelcome. It was of his bloodied, mangled corpse next to the fence.

Chapter Three

The Aboriginal boy lingered in Thom's thoughts the following morning, as he rode the bus to campus to meet his friend Lars at the library.

Gazing out the window at the Centennial Parklands, he found himself picking over the latest developments in the story. Hickey's death had already become the subject of rancorous debate, which Thom had watched play out on breakfast TV before he left. He found the politics of it interesting enough. But he was rather more preoccupied by the thought of TJ himself: the obscure, anonymous life that had led to this furore.

He wasn't entirely sure why he cared. All that he and this boy shared was a first name. Their lives couldn't have been more different. He imagined that the Aboriginal boy would have experienced a very different Australia.

But I know what it's like to be chased by the police.

Thom was well aware he'd come to Australia to escape his past. He'd known almost nothing about the place when he'd arrived two years ago, and everything had felt bright, shiny, and new. He believed that Australia was different to Europe, fundamentally. It seemed to him that, unlike Europeans, Australians weren't weighed down by such darkness in their history.

Still, this history seemed to ignore the Aboriginal natives, about whom there was perceptible denial. Thom decided to ask Lars what he thought about it. He'd be sure to have an interesting view, given his patrician background.

After hopping off the bus, Thom made his way through the leafy walkways of the campus. The University of New South Wales, with its grey modern blocks, was like a small town of its own.

He waited by the library lawn for Lars, who was running late as usual. To kill time, he looked at his reading list which he fished out of his backpack. He and Lars had to read about 'phenomenology', whatever that was, for a seminar. Lars often complained about all the theory they had to study but, Thom noticed, he got his best marks for it.

This train of thought was interrupted when Lars finally arrived, looking flustered, and a little dishevelled.

"Sorry!" he called out to Thom as he approached. "I've had a nightmare morning with Cady."

"What happened?"

"Oh God!" Lars cried raking a hand through his red hair. "She lost her bank card and threw one of her scary tantrums. And she was screaming about wanting to kill herself. I think she's been doing too much coke at work. You know what she's like."

Thom had never seen Cady as anything other than the picture of serenity. Still, he'd heard many of Lars' anecdotes to the contrary.

Lars looked up at the library tower, his face a picture of reluctance. "Do you mind if we get a coffee first?"

The campus was quiet because it was Sunday, and they found a table in the café easily. Lars ordered a large cappuccino and a blueberry muffin; Thom had a single espresso.

"I just don't think I have the mental space to deal with Cady's issues," Lars mused as he poured a third sachet of sugar into his cup.

Thom was always amazed by how Lars stayed stick-thin despite consuming vast quantities of sugar. He looked much younger than his thirty-two years, and he dressed like a scruffy, struggling artist. Still, there was something about the way he carried himself that gave away his expensive education, even before he opened his mouth.

"Partners always come with issues," Thom offered, finally. "I think it's important to recognise they're not always about you."

Lars raised his eyebrows. "You're quite the relationship expert all of a sudden. Things must be going well with Craig. How is he?"

"He's good. He's very focused on building up his business, as usual. In fact, he's out seeing clients today."

"He's certainly very *driven,*" said Lars dismembering his muffin with a fork.

"Hmm." Thom decided to segue into what he really wanted to talk about. "We had a bit of an argument last night."

"Really? What about?"

"That Aboriginal boy who died..."

"Oh my God!" cut in Lars. "There were sirens *all night*. I'm wondering if that's what set Cady off. Just be glad you don't live with a psycho-bitch."

"No," Thom said ruefully. "Craig's at the other extreme. No emotional reaction whatsoever."

"Did you expect one?"

"I expected *something*. You know, he's half-Maori and he was always in trouble with the police back in the day."

Lars smirked at this. "Yeah, those Mongrel Mob boys were pretty hardcore."

"That *was* a long time ago, Lars," Thom said firmly. "But still..."

Lars changed tack, diplomatically. "Craig is like a lot of self-made men. He doesn't like people he thinks are losers. Do you remember that time we had dinner in Chinatown, and he went into one about beneficiaries?"

"Oh God..."

Lars performed a perfect impression of Craig: "I'm fucking sick of dole-bludgers stealing money from *my* wallet!" he growled.

Thom began to shake as he tried to suppress giggles. He often found himself doing this when Lars and Craig made withering comments about each other.

"And then," Lars continued in his own voice. "You went into one about "neoliberalism". Honestly, you guys have such a clash of world views. Fuck knows what he makes of your radical past."

"Our relationship is based on mutual antagonism."

"Is that what it is?"

"I guess." Thom took a sip of his espresso. They'd gone off-topic. Trying again, he said, "You know, I've been thinking a lot about that Aboriginal kid."

"*Okay,*" Lars said surprised. "What's the interest?"

"I've lived in Australia for two years," Thom began. "But I have no experience of Aboriginal people. I only ever see a few rolling around drunk on the street. I feel like there's this whole *other* Australia nobody ever talks about."

Lars finished the remains of his muffin. "Well, I think this story has potential and it's obviously got to you. You could make a name for yourself if you did something with it, maybe for an assignment, to begin with."

"That's not a bad idea..."

In fact, it had been germinating in Thom's mind since the small hours. He just hadn't thought of it as a project.

"Seriously" said Lars. "It's all about tapping into the zeitgeist. You just need to find some angle while the story's still relevant."

"Any ideas where to start?"

"Talk to the local community. There's this project called 'Aspirations' or 'Aspire', near my house? It does something with local Aboriginal kids. It's run by this Aboriginal pastor."

"Well, *they'd* have the inside scoop."

"Exactly. You just need to swoop in there and show a bit of killer instinct."

"Fine," Thom said purposefully. "I'll go today. Is that killer enough for you?"

"Yeah, getting there."

The prospect of this adventure felt too exciting not to be shared. "Do you want to come with me?" he suggested to Lars.

"I can't today. I'm working later, *and* I suppose I should make sure Cady's alright, the mad cow. Anyway, this is *your* project."

After they finished in the library, Thom took the bus back home. Craig was still out when he let himself back into the apartment. He opened the sliding door out onto the balcony. The warm afternoon air wafted in.

Still, all Thom could smell was Craig. Even in his absence, he seemed to pervade everything. Every particle in the air, every fabric was somehow imbued with him. For some reason, Thom savoured these quiet moments alone in their home. It was like he was able to absorb the intimacy they shared.

He made himself a sandwich for lunch. After he'd eaten, he opened up Craig's laptop on the coffee table. The modem made its usual grinding, whirring sound. Once he was online, he found the Aspire website.

He called their office in Redfern from his mobile. To his surprise, he found himself speaking directly to Archie Henderson, the pastor who ran it.

"Hello, my name is Thom Allerton," he said introducing himself. "I'm on the graduate journalism programme at UNSW."

"How can I help you?"

"I've been reading about your work on your website," Thom heard himself gabble. "And I would really like to hear your thoughts about the very tragic death of TJ Hickey."

He waited for a response from Henderson but there wasn't one. To fill the silence, he added, "I was wondering if you might have time to talk to me today."

There was another awkward pause before Henderson replied. "Alright. Come by the office at 6pm. I'll be here."

Thom thought carefully about what he should ask the pastor. He had to drill down into what it was he found intriguing about the story. He was sat on the sofa, writing a list of questions, when the front door opened. Craig arrived home carrying his leather briefcase, which he dropped in its usual place. He was dressed in black jeans and a fitted white polo shirt which revealed his tattooed forearms.

"Tommo," he said by way of greeting. He leant over the back of the sofa to plant a kiss on Thom's lips.

"How was your meeting?" Thom asked.

"Good." Craig went into the kitchen to put the kettle on. "Did you and Last Chance get any work done?"

Earlier, he'd predicted that Thom and Lars would go straight to the coffee shop to bitch about him and Cady.

"Loads," Thom lied. "We were in the library for hours."

"Well done, Tommo. Do you want a tea?"

"I'm okay, thanks." Thom continued scribbling away on his notepad.

Craig came back in carrying a mug. "What's that you got there?"

“I’m writing a list of questions. I’ve got an interview with this Aboriginal pastor later.”

Craig looked at him with slightly narrowed eyes. “Really?” he said suspiciously. “What about?”

“That kid who was killed yesterday. TJ Hickey.”

“*Where* is this interview?”

There was a hint of something in his voice; it might have been demand or anxiety, or both. Thom pretended not to notice.

“It’s at an office on Lawson Street. Near Redfern Station.”

There was a pause. Craig stared at him, his mouth a straight, closed line.

“You’re not serious.”

Thom looked up. “What?”

“You can’t go walking around Redfern today,” said Craig incredulously, his voice rising. “A skinny Pommy white boy surrounded by angry blacks! You’ll get bashed!”

“I’ll be fine,” Thom insisted. “I looked at the news earlier and the police are *expecting* trouble. The place is *crawling* with them.”

Craig didn’t appear mollified. “I don’t like you doing it. It’s not safe.”

Thom put his pen down. “Look. You know that I’ve had plenty of experience of civil disturbance. I’m not totally naïve.”

“This isn’t going to be like one of your new age hippy anti-globalisation marches. Anyway, I thought you didn’t believe in any of that shit anymore.”

"I don't," said Thom firmly. "I am well and truly over it. But it taught me that life can be dangerous."

He picked up his pen and began writing again. Craig regarded him for a moment before sitting down next to him on the couch. He put his mug down and slid his arm behind Thom's shoulders.

"I know. But I just don't want you getting into any trouble. I know what you're like. Do you want me to come with you?"

Thom was tempted to say yes. He didn't like to admit it, but he wasn't entirely relaxed about going to Redfern that evening. Craig's presence would have been reassuring.

Instead, he declined: "No, it's fine. I think you should go for a ride on your bike."

"Are you sure?"

"Absolutely. But there is one thing I'd like to ask though."

"What's that?" said Craig warily.

"Can I take the car?"

Craig sighed with reluctance. "Oh alright. But there's one condition. Park it well away from the action because I don't want it getting smashed up. In fact, park it on Last Chance's street. It's pretty safe there even if his house is a rat-hole."

Thom raised his eyebrows at this.

"Don't look at me in that tone of voice," Craig chuckled. "You *know* that Last Chance lives in a rat-hole."

"It's a little on the Bohemian side," Thom said deciding not to argue the point.

"I'm sure pest control would agree," snorted Craig. "Even the cockroaches left in disgust."

A few hours later they look the lift down to the foyer and crossed over the marble floor. Craig had changed out of his corporate casual ensemble into his leather jacket and boots. He carried his helmet in one hand.

"Yo!" he shouted out to the suited concierge, raising his free palm in greeting.

Thom just smiled politely. They walked past the gym that Thom used most morningsand went down into the underground carpark.

As Thom unlocked the jeep, Craig mounted his Harley. He stopped for a moment and looked meaningfully at Thom.

"Just be careful, Tommo."

"I will," Thom assured him.

"I *meant* with my car." His grin flashed like a blade. Then he pulled on his helmet. There was a thunderous roar as he started up the bike and rode off.

Chapter Four

It took Thom about twenty minutes to drive to the edge of Redfern. He took a circuitous route to avoid heavy traffic and parked on Lars' street as Craig told him. He only had a five-minute walk from here to the Aspire office.

He'd got to know this part of Sydney through visiting Lars and Cady. Initially he'd been struck by the contrast between its narrow Victorian terraces and the skyscrapers in the distance. At the time, it seemed exotic and mysterious even though it reminded him of London. He smiled to himself when he saw some graffiti on the side of a house. It read: 'KILL JOHN HOWARD'.

He was startled by a loud bang in the distance; a projectile hit its target. As he turned onto Lawson Street, he sensed danger. There was a commotion nearby. The loud jeers of angry youths speared through the air, promising violence. It sounded like there were hundreds of them.

His heartrate quickened and he pulled a note from his pocket to check the address. He groaned inwardly when he realised that he had to go further up the street, towards the noise.

As he got nearer Redfern Station, he saw the police. They'd sealed off Eveleigh Street which led to the Block, where most local Aboriginals lived. Thirty or forty cops were struggling to contain the mob of teenagers in front of them as their jeers reached a crescendo. It felt like any moment now the line would buckle, and they would be swept aside by a tide of adolescent rage.

The Aspire office was in an old shop with frosted windows. A sign on the door read: "Aspire: The Next Generation of Aboriginal Achievers'. Thom pushed it but found it was locked. Instead, he knocked. It was soon answered by a middle-aged Aboriginal woman.

"Can I help you?" she asked looking at him suspiciously.

"Erm, yes," said Thom awkwardly, pushing his sunglasses up into his hair. "I'm here to see Pastor Archie Henderson."

Inwardly, he cringed at how English and overly formal he sounded.

"You mean Archie," the woman grimaced. "You'd better come in then."

She stood aside to let him past. Inside, Thom found himself facing a group standing around a table. There were three women and two men immersed in an urgent confab. They stopped when they saw him.

"I'll just get Archie for you." The woman who'd answered the door disappeared into the back.

As he waited, Thom found himself the object of attention. He had this notion they would recognise him as a fellow activist. The two men smiled and nodded, but one of the women stared with overt hostility. She seemed about sixty, and she was tiny. Her white-blonde hair was scraped back into a ponytail.

Feeling the need to make conversation, Thom gestured at the door behind him: "Is that some sort of vigil going on out there?" he asked.

Outside, the angry roar was getting louder. It was accompanied by the shattering of glass.

The hostile woman carried on staring. "I'll tell you what it is," she said icily. "It's my people telling you white fellas that we've had a gutful of you killing our kids."

"Knock it off, Ellen," demanded one of the men. "The young bloke doesn't mean any harm."

Before Ellen could saying anything else, Pastor Archie Henderson came in.

He looked like Thom's idea of an Aboriginal elder with his unruly black hair and lined face. But his cream chinos and short-sleeved shirt lent him the air of suburban dad off-duty from his middle management job.

"Young Thom." He sounded friendlier than he had on the 'phone. "Thanks for coming. We'll do this in my office. Come this way."

In the back office, Thom took out his notepad and Dictaphone. "I have a few questions. I want to talk about TJ Hickey and the impact on the local community."

"Okay," Archie nodded.

"But can you first tell me a bit about what you do here?"

"Sure. We're a non-profit organisation, and we do outreach with local Aboriginal kids. Our programmes are about getting them into work or helping them start-up businesses."

"I guess TJ Hickey was like your...target market," Thom ventured.

He instantly regretted saying this. His words were clumsy, and he knew it.

Archie looked pensive. "Yeah, we knew TJ here," he said quietly. "He was a good kid."

There was a moment of silence as the pastor seemed to withdraw into himself. Thom looked down at his next question. He tried to think how put it tactfully.

"It's been suggested TJ was afraid of the police. I know relations with the local community have been...*difficult*. What's your view about this?"

Archie leaned back in his chair and puffed out his cheeks. "Difficult doesn't even come into it. My own kids have asked me why the police pick on them. They don't pick on the Asians. They don't pick on the white fellas."

Thom could hear years of pent-up frustration in his voice.

"Do you want to know how they feel?" Archie went on, becoming more agitated. "They feel that the police hate them. And the *worst thing* is that I think they might be right. And I don't want to think that. I don't want to have to believe that my kids are hated and not welcome in their own country."

He stopped and looked away, perhaps embarrassed. Thom noticed the pastor's eyes were watery. He decided to leave it a moment before moving onto the next question.

They were interrupted by a brusque rap at the door. Ellen came in and scowled at Thom. She was followed by a tall man wearing suit trousers and a white shirt.

"Cops are here for you, Archie," she hissed. Then she left, slamming the door behind her.

Archie acknowledged the newcomer. "Detective Sergeant Morton. How can I help you?"

"G'day, Archie." The detective's tone was affable. "We could use a little help. And you're just the man."

"What *sort* of help?"

It was clear to Thom that the two men knew each other well. Still, there was a certain inscrutable coolness in Archie's manner. Morton, however, seemed to have the languor of easy familiarity.

Thom thought he looked like a cartoon superhero. He had the Gladiatorial physique of a professional rugby player, and he was boyishly handsome.

"We need you to come and talk to your boys," Morton said to Archie. "Things are going to get ugly unless you calm them down."

Archie snorted in derision. "Mate, it's gone way beyond that. I'm not going to be able to get through to them. Do you have any idea how angry they are?"

"Look, mate," pleaded the detective. "I'm on your side. I totally get the anger, but if this turns into a riot, the media will crucify this community. And I don't want that."

Thom could see an inner conflict etched on Archie's face. But Morton, despite his emphatic words, seemed relaxed, almost dispassionate. Thom took a closer look at him and noticed his hazel eyes. He guessed this detective was in his mid-twenties. If so, he was young for his rank.

The door suddenly swung open again and Ellen put her head around. She hadn't bothered to knock this time. Behind her, an urgent hum of voices could be heard.

"Archie," she called. "Your wife's on the phone. Can you take the call?"

Archie got up. "Excuse me," he said wearily. "I have to take this."

The door slammed shut behind him and Thom was left alone with Morton. The detective gave him a wide smile, exposing symmetrical white teeth.

"What's your name, mate?"

Thom stood up and extended his hand. "Thom. Thom Allerton."

Morton didn't respond with a handshake. Instead, he took the back of Thom's hand in his palm, turned it downwards and squeezed. He didn't let go.

"Tell me, Mr Allerton," he said looking into Thom's eyes. "What's a good-looking boy like you doing in a place like this?"

Thom was astounded. In another context, he might have been flattered. But here and now, it was just brazenly inappropriate. More to the point, he understood instinctively what this flirtatiousness was really about: power. The guy was doing it because he knew he could get away with it.

This guy thinks he's untouchable.

"I'm here as a journalist, Detective Sergeant," he said recovering himself. He was determined to act cool now.

"Call me Rob, babe," insisted Morton. "What are you writing about?" He tightened his grip on Thom's hand. Thom tried not to wince.

"It's about TJ Hickey," he replied. "I'm interested in the impact on the local community."

"Wow," said Morton almost in a murmur. "That sounds amazing. I can't wait to read it."

He carried on staring into Thom's eyes but dropped his hand as soon the door swung back open.

Archie came back in looking harassed. "Sorry about that. Family stuff."

"It's all good," Morton assured him. "Look mate, I've got to go. But can you please try to talk to those boys out there? It could save us all a lot of pain, trust me."

"I'll see what I can do, Rob," Archie said resignedly. "But I don't think it's going to be much."

"Thanks, mate. I appreciate it."

As Morton made to leave, he clasped Archie's shoulders from behind.

"This is one of the good guys," he said looking at Thom. He gave them both another broad grin. "See you, boys."

With that, he left. Thom was relieved, but also a little intrigued. He'd never met a cop quite like this man before.

"I'm really sorry, young Thom," said Archie regretfully. "But can we finish this some other time? I've got to go out there and talk to those kids."

"Of course," Thom replied. "I understand. Shall I e-mail you to rearrange?"

"Yeah, do that mate." Archie reached into his pocket. "Here's my business card. I'll see you out."

Thom was led back into the main office where the front door was now wide open. His senses were instantly assailed by the pandemonium outside. He could see the sun was setting, and he smelt something that reminded him of bonfire nights in England. Inside, Ellen and the others stood around, in a huddle, muttering anxiously to each other.

"I'm going out," Archie told them, his voice stern. "And I'm going to shut this door."

He went to step outside. Thom followed only to be stopped in his tracks when the pastor turned back around.

"How did you get here?" he asked Thom.

"I drove," Thom told him. "I'm parked about five minutes away."

"You need to get out of here. And fast."

"I wasn't planning to hang around."

Thom peered anxiously out at the street. He'd have to make a run for it while it was still clear. Almost directly opposite, the police cordon across Eveleigh Street was about to collapse. Once it did, he'd have no protection. The cops were grossly outnumbered by the teenage mob whose fury had only intensified.

He and Archie paused, as if to steel themselves, and then stepped out closing the door behind them. At that very moment, the crowd on Eveleigh Street surged forward causing the police to scatter in retreat.

"Shit!" exclaimed one of the cops.

Thom found himself disoriented by chaos as the crowd surrounded him. Youths and cops seemed to be running in all directions, and there was a cacophony of animalistic cries and shrieks.

A cop bellowed at Thom: "GET THE FUCK OUT THE WAY!"

Thom stepped aside. He turned and collided with a teenage boy who screeched something in his face before darting off. He looked around for Archie but couldn't see him. His whole body felt heavy with anxiety, and his vision was blurring. He frantically looked around for an escape route that would take him back to the car.

Windows shattered as heavy objects were lobbed at them. Thom was alerted to fireworks being thrown by loud bangs and hissing flames. One landed only metres in front of him and exploded.

"Fuck!" he exclaimed, recoiling in shock.

As he turned, someone barged into him, knocking him to the ground. He felt his elbows graze as he landed on his front, the gravel biting and the knee on his jeans tearing.

He pushed himself back up and decided to make a run for it towards Lars' house. He could hear more objects being thrown.

Suddenly, he felt a hard blow to the side of his head. He stumbled. For a moment, he thought he was going to black out. He might have been struck by a bottle, but he wasn't sure. He knew he was bleeding though.

Then he heard a familiar voice shout "Young Thom!"

Archie swam into view. He put his hand on Thom's shoulder to steady him then looked at his face.

"Jeez, mate," he gasped. "We need to get you to a hospital."

"How?" mumbled Thom.

"I'll drive you to St Vinny's. We'll have to take your car though, mine's at home.

"But how do we get out of *here*?" Thom asked, looking wildly around him.

"Just stick with me and you'll be fine," Archie told him. "I'll see you right."

There was a blare of sirens as more police arrived, and the crowd started running towards the railway station. Against the throng, Archie propelled Thom in the opposite direction. It didn't take them long to reach Lars' street which was strangely undisturbed by the riot nearby.

Archie looked at the silver jeep. "It's a slick set of wheels you've got here."

"It's not mine." Thom handed him the keys. "It's Craig's."

"Who's Craig?"

Thom opened the passenger door. "My partner."

"Oh," said Archie uncertainly.

Thom didn't take in much of the drive to the hospital. He was vaguely conscious of traffic and night lights. The sound of sirens wailing seemed to reverberate in his head, but he could have been imagining it.

Archie found a parking spot near the hospital and took Thom to the emergency room. He stayed with Thom during the wait to see the triage nurse. Just as he was called, Thom's phone rang in his pocket. He pulled it out to see who was calling.

"Oh God!" he fretted. "It's Craig. He doesn't know where I am."

Archie glanced at the impatient triage nurse hovering nearby.

"You need to get seen to," he said firmly. "Look, I'll talk to your mate for you. Just give me your phone."

An hour later, Thom was in a cubicle sat on a bed. Archie had gone. A nurse was removing fragments of glass from his wounds. He'd been told that he would be checked for concussion.

He was still being tended to when the curtain opened, and Craig walked in. He just looked at Thom and shook his head.

"Tommo. You're a flaming liability."

Thom was delighted to see him. "I don't mean to be," he said, a smile spreading across his face. "Have you heard what's happened in Redfern?"

"Yes, Tommo. I have. It's all over the news and it's still going on. Trust you to be right in the middle of it."

"All over the news? Wow!" Thom murmured. He winced as another splinter of glass was removed. "Did you speak to Archie?"

"That pastor guy who brought you here? Yeah. You were bloody lucky he was around to help."

"I know! And he's given me some good material for a story. It's all been quite inspiring, really. I've got loads of ideas."

In the car, on the way home, Craig made an appeal to Thom. "I don't want visiting you in hospital to become a regular thing. Can you please just stay out of trouble from now on?"

"I'll try," Thom said distractedly. He contemplated the darkened streets outside. Never had Sydney looked more mysterious, and more promising of new possibilities.

He was onto something. Craig wasn't going to approve. But there was no point arguing about it tonight.

Chapter Five

"Oh my God, you're famous!" cried Charlotte, a couple of days after the riot.

Thom laughed. "I didn't think you'd see it in Vietnam."

He was standing outside the library with his phone pressed to his ear. Charlotte was calling him from the departures lounge in Hanoi. She'd been waiting for her flight to be called when Thom popped up on the news.

He'd been interviewed by the BBC for a feature about the riot. When he watched it back, he realised, to his annoyance, they'd focused on the injured police. Still, he was rather pleased by the way he came across. As he spoke about police harassment, he looked like a dogged campaigner for truth and justice. Or at the very least, he managed to answer the reporter's questions.

"Mum and Dad are just beside themselves. They couldn't believe it when they saw you on TV. You should call them."

"I will. At some point. But they weren't massively impressed last time I was in the news."

"That was different."

"I don't see how."

"Well for a start, you didn't get arrested this time. Anyway, how is everything else in your world?"

"Good. I'm just here having lunch with Lars, and Craig's fine. We're going to see *The Quiet American* tonight. *That's* set in Vietnam."

Before Charlotte could reply, there was a tannoy announcement at her end.

"Ooh! Our flight's just been called. Gotta go. Allie sends love. Give our love to Lars and Craig. Love you! Bye. Bye. Bye."

Thom returned to the spot on the lawn where he and Lars were eating takeaway sushi.

"Charlotte sends love." He sat back down on the grass.

"How is she?"

"Good, I think. She and Allie are on their way home. They're going to earn some money and then go back out on the hippy trail."

"Sounds like a nice life." Lars tore open a sachet of soy sauce. "Oh fuck!"

He'd spilt the soy sauce all over his white t-shirt. Thom, laughing with his mouth full, handed him a paper napkin. Lars dabbed away at the stain, trying to limit the damage.

They had been to a seminar, that morning, where Thom was the centre of attention after his interview. Dr Holly Mailman, their lecturer, had smiled at him indulgently and joked that journalists should never be the story.

Lars gave up on the stain and resumed eating with his chopsticks. "What did Craig think of you appearing on the BBC?"

"I don't think he was wildly impressed."

Lars pulled a face. "Really? Why not?"

"Oh, the usual. He didn't approve of me *shooting my mouth off* about the police. Especially before I've got my residency."

"Oh well," Lars muttered. He put down his sushi box and stretched his arms out. "You know, the one thing I've been amazed by is all the international interest."

"I know! I've been thinking that if I write a story, it's going to be very sellable."

"Well, you've got the inside scoop. Is *that* what you were talking to Holly about?"

"Sort of. I'm interviewing her this afternoon."

"Really? What's *her* interest, apart from being Aboriginal herself?"

"She's written books about Redfern. Her grandfather was one of the Stolen Generation of Aboriginal kids."

"Wow. There's some dark history there." Lars shook his head and stared into the distance as he contemplated this. "Those kids were taken away from their homes and their families and everything they knew. And our fucking government *still* hasn't apologised. Can you believe that?"

"Do you think they will?"

"Not while John Howard's in charge."

"Well, that might not be forever," Thom suggested.

He chewed thoughtfully on a nori roll before changing the subject altogether. "How's Cady?"

Lars winced, as he often did when asked about Cady. "Oh alright. She's calmed down a lot. But she says she wants us to stop having group sex and threesomes."

This made Thom squirm with embarrassment. Sometimes, he felt Lars shared too much about their relationship.

But Lars failed to notice his mortification and just carried on. "The thing I don't get is that it was all her idea. When we met, she told me she didn't believe in monogamy."

"Sounds complicated," Thom murmured, wishing he hadn't asked.

Thom knocked on Holly's office door and waited for an answer.

"Come in!" he heard her call from inside.

When he went in, he found her talking to a delicate Chinese girl who was seated. He felt like he'd interrupted a counselling session.

"Oh, I'm sorry. Should I come back?"

"Can you give us just a minute?" Holly said in a confiding voice.

"Sure."

He waited awkwardly outside in the corridor for a few minutes. Eventually, the door opened when Holly showed her visitor out.

"Let me know how you go with that, Daisy," she said to her. Once the girl had disappeared down the corridor, she turned her attention back to him. "How're you going, Thom? Come on in."

Holly's office was a long, narrow room overlooking another concrete building. Thom noticed that a whole shelf in the cabinet behind her chair was dedicated to her own books.

She smiled broadly at him once he was sat down. "*So,* you've been sprinkled with a bit of star dust."

"Oh, well." Thom attempted a modest laugh.

Her smile tightened. "Don't let it go to your head. Anyway, how can I help you?"

She was a tall, striking woman in her late thirties with dark curly hair cut just beneath her jaw. She cultivated an easy going, effervescent persona which made her seem very approachable. But Thom sensed that she was actually very driven and tightly wound. She'd had successful careers as a journalist and as an academic. He could only guess at the obstacles she might have faced as an Aboriginal woman.

"I want to talk to you about Redfern." He pulled his Dictaphone out of his backpack. "I understand you know a lot about it."

"Yes, I do."

Thom switched on the Dictaphone and began. "After the riot, the Sydney Morning Herald ran an editorial. You might have seen it."

"Uh-huh," Holly nodded.

"This editorial described Redfern as an *Aboriginal ghetto*. Do you have any comment about that?"

"Hmmm." Holly looked into the air and inhaled deeply. "That statement is *just very* inaccurate. Maybe it was true twenty or thirty years ago. But you have to understand that, for the Aboriginal community, Redfern is more symbolic than it is real."

"What do you mean by that?"

"Well, *historically*, Redfern has been a place for Aboriginal people to reconnect with their families. It still sort of is. But it's been gentrified, like a lot of inner-city suburbs. Most of the remaining Aboriginal community live at one end, in the Block."

"Interesting. You mention gentrification. Do you see it as a community under siege?"

"I think the real story here is about *the place* of a community. *That* has to be your angle. Have you heard about the Pemulwuy Project?"

She proceeded to explain it to him in some detail. Thom nodded and tried not to look bored as she delved into the intricacies.

When she finished talking, he tried to change tack. "That's all really useful. I just want to touch upon the role of the police. Some people say that TJ Hickey was followed because he'd been racially profiled."

Holly frowned at this. She looked hard at him for a moment. "Sorry. Can you..."

She gestured at the Dictaphone.

"Oh yes, of course." Thom switched it off.

Holly leaned forward, lowering her voice. "You should know, there were people around TJ Hickey involved in the heroin trade. That's why the police were following him."

There was a moment of silence between them.

"I see," said Thom disconcerted. He wondered how she knew this, and if she would elaborate.

Holly continued. "Journalistically, I just don't think the police harassment angle works."

"Okay."

He thought she might qualify this with an explanation. But she didn't.

"I think you've got the bones of a great story here," she told him. "There's gentrification. You've got a community facing uncertainty. It's all very topical."

Thom smiled and nodded. But he wasn't enthused by any of this. The story she wanted him to write just didn't resonate with him.

"If that's the direction you want to go in, I'll really be able to help," offered Holly. "I could line up some interviews for you. Maybe at the Aboriginal Housing Company, or with people in the state government.

"That would be great." Thom tried to sound pleased.

Holly smiled brightly. "And, if you write something worth selling, I know people at *the Sydney Morning Herald, the Daily Telegraph, the Melbourne Age,* you name it. This could be such a great opportunity for you."

Thom sensed this interview was now over.

"Well, thank you so much for your time. I really appreciate it."

"Anytime. If there's anything you need, just holler."

When she saw him out afterwards, she put on a display of bonhomie. Still, Thom intuited a coolness beneath it. As far as she was concerned, they had made a deal. She would only help him if he did what she wanted. That was clear enough.

Chapter Six

"I just found it a bit weird," Thom fretted. "Why is she trying to tell me what to write?"

"Maybe you should listen to her." Craig took a swig of his Corona beer. "She probably knows what she's talking about."

They'd met for dinner in a Thai restaurant, in fashionable Paddington, before their movie.

"But why did she say all that about TJ Hickey?"

"Because it's probably true. Look, Tommo. I really think you should just quit this obsession with that Aboriginal kid..."

"I'm not obsessed," Thom insisted.

He leaned back and stared, tight jawed, across the table.

"I don't mean *obsessed,*" said Craig trying to row back. "I just want you to be more careful, at least until you get your residency. There's no point making enemies in the government."

"What? You think my residency might be in jeopardy?"

"I don't know," Craig said wearily. "I just don't want anything to stop us staying together."

"Me neither."

Craig looked at him intently. "There's something I want to talk to you about, Tommo. I've been thinking."

"Oh? Sounds ominous"

"No. Hear me out! Do you remember when we met? I said that I didn't want to be a city slicker forever."

"Yes, you did." Thom wondered where this was going.

"Well, I've decided I want to go back to New Zealand."

"But we went last year."

"I don't mean for a holiday! I mean to live. Permanently. How would you feel about that?"

This was unexpected. Thom was in no hurry to leave Sydney. He was happier here than he'd ever been anywhere. But he also knew he didn't want to be separated from Craig. He'd decided that a long time ago.

He reached for his drink. "What's brought this on? I thought your franchise was doing well."

Craig sighed. "It's doing *alright*. But it's not spectacular and I've got no passion for it. Anyway, we wouldn't be going for a while yet."

Thom found, to his surprise, that the idea appealed to him. He had this vision of him and Craig living in a weatherboard house at the edge of the world. He saw himself sat at a vast kitchen table, typing away at a laptop, while Craig tinkered in the garden. They were a picture of contentment.

On their holiday to New Zealand, Thom had been mesmerised by the low-hanging cloud. They'd visited Craig's mother, a retired social worker, in Lower Hutt. She was a proud, aloof woman. Thom knew from Craig that her choice to marry a Maori man had come at a cost.

As he contemplated their future, something occurred to him.

"Aren't you worried about going back? After everything that happened."

Craig helped himself to more rice before answering. "No, Tommo, it was over twenty years ago. I served my time in that lousy, stinking jail and I paid my debt to society then."

"But what about your old friends in the Mongrel Mob?"

"Aagh!" Craig grunted dismissively. "All taken care of. They won't bother me, Tommo. The past is the past. Anyway, we just need you to get this residency. It will make things easier for us in the long run. You'll have to keep your head down for a bit though. I know that doesn't come naturally to you."

"Honestly, you make me sound like so much trouble."

"You know you are, Tommo."

After dinner, they went to see *The Quiet American*. Thom saw all sorts of parallels with the Iraq war. At the time, he and Craig had gone on the march, in Sydney, against the invasion. It was surprising Craig wanted to go given his distaste for all things left-wing, and he hadn't looked entirely comfortable.

Craig yawned. "I'm gonna hit the sack. I've got an early start tomorrow."

They hadn't been home long, having walked back from the cinema. It was now late but Thom was still feeling restless.

"I'll be in in a bit. Just need to decompress."

"Righto, Tommo."

When Craig went off to bed, Thom switched on the TV and absently channel-surfed for a few minutes before switching it off again. In the kitchen, he made himself some Sleepytime tea hoping it would induce tiredness. He took it out onto the balcony.

Sinking into the garden chair, he wrapped his fingers around the warm mug and thought back to dinner. He was aware that he hadn't actually *said* he would go to New Zealand with Craig. But already, they had this unspoken understanding it was decided.

Soon after they'd met, they'd gone to the Blue Mountains for the weekend where Craig had booked them into a luxury hotel. On the drive up, it occurred to Thom how little he knew about Craig's past. As they rolled up the freeway, he picked his moment to find out more.

"What did you do before you bought your franchise?" he asked.

Craig kept his eyes fixed on the road. "I used to build swimming pools for rich folks. I made a good living from it too."

"How long did you do that for?"

"About fifteen years, I guess. I started the business up soon after I came over here."

"What made you stop?"

"Ah I dunno really. I suppose I turned forty and decided there was more to life. And so, I sold the company for a good price."

"Was that like your mid-life crisis?" Thom said deadpan.

Craig turned to look at him in mock disdain. "No, Tommo. *You're* my mid-life crisis."

On the Sunday, there was a serious moment when they were stood at the Echo Point Lookout. Craig stared ahead at the view of cliffs and eucalyptus trees, his hands in his pockets. He seemed distant.

"How long are you going to stay with me?" he asked.

Thom took a moment to answer. "Indefinitely and forever. Obviously."

He looked at Craig and smiled.

"I'm old enough to be your father," Craig cautioned.

"I know. But I really don't care."

"Well, is there anything you want to know before you hitch yourself to my wagon?"

"Like what?"

Craig shrugged. "I dunno. Just anything."

Thom realised Craig felt he had to tell him *something*. But it was mildly irritating that he didn't just come straight out with it.

"Don't tell me. You're secretly married with kids?"

"Ner-oh."

"You...run the Sydney branch of Al-Qaeda?"

Craig rolled his eyes. "Be serious."

"Okay," Thom said dropping the facetiousness. "I think your gang tattoos are a bit of a clue. I'm guessing you've been in prison at some point."

A slightly embarrassed smile appeared on Craig's face. "Yes," he conceded.

Thom raised his eyebrows.

"It was a *long* time ago," Craig insisted.

"I'm sure it was."

"Does it bother you, Tommo?"

Thom shook his head. "No, not at all. In fact, I think I've always sort of known."

"How?"

"It sounds mad. But I when I first saw you, I could just tell you'd had a chequered past."

Craig looked sceptical. "Can you really tell something like that just by looking at somebody?"

Thom nodded. "Yeah. I think you can."

In the library, late in the afternoon, Thom finished an email to Archie. He thanked him for his help on the night of the riot and tried to rearrange their interview. To his surprise, a reply swiftly pinged into his inbox.

'Good to hear from you, Young Thom. Saw you on the BBC. You came across well. Happy to talk more if you want to drop by the office at 5pm tomorrow. I'm going to TJ's burial out at Walgett in the morning but should be back in time. Archie.'

Thom typed a brief reply to confirm. He then logged out, gathered up his things and left campus. When he was waiting at the bus stop, on Anzac Parade, a shiny black car drew up and the driver wound down their passenger window.

"Hey mate!" a man's voice called out to him. "Do you have a minute?"

Thom craned his head to see Detective Sergeant Rob Morton. He wondered what he could possibly want. More to the point, how had he known where to find him?

"I'm just on my way home," he said tersely.

"Not a problem, mate. I'll drop you off. Jump in."

He leaned over and opened the passenger door.

Thom felt conscious of curious glances around him. He couldn't think of a valid reason to say no, and so he reluctantly got in. Morton waited for him to fasten his seat belt before driving off.

"How are you, bro?" he asked, briefly glancing in Thom's direction. His shirt sleeves were rolled up revealing enormous biceps.

He must spend hours in the gym pumping those.

"Erm, fine, thanks," Thom replied.

He noticed the car smelt of coffee and hot doughnuts. On the backseat, there was a tray with polystyrene cups and a paper bag.

"Are you on the coffee run?" he asked.

"Yeah, mate. I'm just like the mother hen back at the station. I always like to make sure everyone eats and drinks."

Thom tried to imagine this. He could see the detective backslapping and gladhanding. But the solicitousness seemed a bit of a stretch.

Morton drove up a few blocks before turning off onto a side street where he parked. Switching off the ignition, he turned to Thom and grinned.

"How do you like your coffee?"

Thom didn't especially want to drink one. "Just black."

Morton stretched his arm into the back and grappled around for a cup which he then gave to Thom.

"Here we go. Long black. Stevo will just have to go without."

"Thanks."

"You're welcome, mate." Morton took a cup for himself, eased the lid off and blew at the liquid inside. "Do you want a doughnut?"

"I'm fine, thanks."

"Well you don't look like the sort of boy who eats much sugar," the detective said, guffawing at his own private joke.

Thom ignored this.

"How can I help, Detective Sergeant?"

"Call me Rob, please," insisted Morton. "There are a couple of things, actually. I heard you got bottled on the night of the riot."

"That's right. It was a bit of a shock but, amazingly, I didn't need stitches."

"Did you see who did it?"

"No. What makes you ask?"

Morton's bonhomie suddenly vanished, and he glowered. "I'm a police officer, mate," he said sharply. "And I'm investigating a crime. *That's* what makes me ask."

Thom was taken aback. In the brief silence that followed, he decided to tread carefully. "I didn't see who threw the bottle. I don't even think it was aimed at me. I was just in the way. I was very disoriented by all the chaos."

The detective pondered this for a moment. Eventually, he nodded: "Yeah, I can understand that." His expression became friendly again. "If you remember anything, just let me know."

"Sure. Is there anything else?"

"Yes, there is." Morton looked sheepish. "I'd like to apologise for my behaviour the other night. It wasn't appropriate."

"Okay," said Thom uncertainly.

"I didn't mean to act like I was hitting on you or nothing..."

"It's fine." Thom was finding this conversation awkward.

Still, Morton persisted. "It was just stress. Redfern was like a tinderbox that night. I have to tell you that I was pretty fucking scared."

This didn't quite ring true to Thom. "You seemed very...self-assured to me."

"All a façade, mate." Morton gulped down the rest of his coffee. "Let's get you home."

He put the empty cup back on the tray and started up the engine. Reversing out of his parking spot, he drove back onto Anzac Parade where the rush hour traffic was just starting.

He checked his windscreen mirror. "How's your story coming along?" he asked.

"Good, I think. I've done a couple of interviews."

"What are you going to write about? Last time, you said it was about TJ Hickey."

Thom thought he should be as vague about this as possible. "That's just part of it. I'm interested in Redfern more generally."

They stopped at a red light.

"I'd like to help," Morton offered.

You really are full of surprises.

"Really?" Thom said dubiously. "What's your interest?"

He wondered about the detective's motives. Still, whatever they were, he might be a useful source.

"I was at high school in Redfern," Morton told him. "My mates were all Aboriginal boys. It's always been a tough place, but it was even tougher twenty years ago."

Thom made a quick mental calculation. If Morton had been a teenager twenty years ago, he would now be in his mid-thirties. It was about a decade older than he looked.

Those long gym sessions must be paying off.

Outside, the lights turned orange, and Morton drove off.

"That's how I know Archie," he told Thom. "He used to coach the high school cricket team I was on."

"I didn't realise."

Thom decided he would ask Archie about Morton. That might help him gauge how far to trust him. Archie was probably a good judge of character, he felt.

As they drove up towards Taylor Square, Thom saw that Oxford Street was busy with shoppers and tourists, mingling with office workers who were leaving for the day. He drank what was left of his coffee.

"I have to ask, Rob," he said tentatively. "Wouldn't you helping me be a conflict of interest for you? As a police officer?"

"Not at all. We've got a lot of fences to mend with the Aboriginal community. I reckon this riot has set us back ten years, and it breaks my heart."

He turned onto Thom's street, and drove down towards the end, stopping outside the apartment building. Thom unfastened his seatbelt.

Morton turned to face him. "I meant what I said. If I can help, just give me a call."

"Do you have a business card or something?"

"I've got something better than that. Give me your phone."

Thom hesitated.

"Come on," Morton urged, holding out his left hand.

Thom took his phone out of his pocket and handed it over. Morton tapped away for a minute and gave it back. He'd added himself to Thom's contacts list as 'Rob'.

"Thanks" Thom stuffed his phone away. "And thank you for the coffee and the lift home."

"Anytime, bro. See you later!"

Thom got out and closed the car door. Morton waved at him before quickly reversing and turning around. His shiny black car roared back up the street.

As Thom swiped his card to get into the building, he was unsettled by a realisation. Morton had driven him home without being told the address.

Chapter Seven

The gym was empty this morning, just before 7am, and Thom was pleased to have it to himself. He got up at six every day to cycle vigorously on the stationary bike for an hour. It drove Craig mad. He couldn't understand why Thom would choose to rise so early.

As he pedalled, Thom wondered how Morton had known his address. Had he got it off a police computer? And what else did he know about him? He'd nearly mentioned this to Craig, but some instinct discouraged him.

It will be interesting to see what Archie says about him.

After forty-five minutes, his t-shirt was drenched with sweat. At that moment, he glanced at the mirror in front of him and saw Craig come in, suited and booted for a breakfast meeting, and wearing a small smile. Craig walked up to the bike and looked at the console to inspect Thom's time and speed.

"Keep going, Tommo," he urged with just a hint of mockery. "You're nearly there."

"You should join me one morning," Thom panted, his eyes stinging.

"Don't think so," Craig chuckled. "Look, I'm going out to Parramatta this afternoon. If you want, I'll get some of that coffee you like."

"That would be lovely. I should be home by seven."

"Seven? I thought you didn't have any classes today."

"I don't. But I'm interviewing Archie again at five."

"Really? I heard they're having the memorial service for that Aboriginal kid today."

"Yes, Archie's going. It's out of town at Walgett this morning."

"Yeah, I know about that. But there's some other service going on this arvo in the Block as well. The cops are expecting trouble. You're not thinking of going, are you, Tommo?"

It was the first Thom knew of it, and he was intrigued. He decided that he was definitely going.

"No, of course not."

About four hundred people had converged on the grass in Pelmulwuy Park when he got there. Many of them carried banners and placards and wore t-shirts with slogans. The police were also visible but keeping a discreet presence. Thom thought the scene looked like an activists' carnival. He was reminded of the many demonstrations he'd been on in London. They'd always culminated in a park like this.

He didn't totally ignore Craig's appeals to stay out of trouble. That was why he hung back on the edge of the park. He tried to listen to the speeches. But it was difficult to hear because of the soft breeze blowing in his direction.

While he stood and watched, a pale girl in a tie-dye top approached him. She was selling copies of a newspaper called *Green Left*. He bought one just to be polite and put it in his back-pack. He turned his attention back to the vigil.

The girl carried on hovering. "It totally sucks what's going on, eh?"

She clearly had him down as a kindred spirit. Thom turned to look at her. She was a bit younger than him with freckly skin and ratty little dreadlocks. Her manner was shy and diffident.

"Absolutely," he said wanting to be agreeable. "I just hope lessons are learnt from all of this."

"Yeah, but have you heard?" the girl gabbled, clearly wanting to talk to somebody. "The cops arrested TJ's aunt. She's in court today. On the day of her nephew's funeral. Can you believe that?"

"What? Why? What for?"

"The cops are saying it's because of what she did in the riot. They've been hassling his girlfriend too."

"That's appalling."

He thought back to his conversation with Morton the day before and remembered the cop's talk of mending fences. Whatever the police were doing, it wasn't in the spirit of reconciliation: Morton surely knew that?

When the rally finished, Thom had time to kill before his inter-view with Archie. He thought about calling on Lars and Cady but decided that would be cutting it fine. Instead, he went to a coffee shop to work on his interview questions, and he added one about TJ's aunt.

Just before 5pm, when he was expected, Thom wandered up Lawson Street to the Aspire office. A pair of police officers passed him on foot and a patrol car crawled by on the other side. The door was ajar when he got there so he went in without knocking.

Inside, he found Ellen standing at a table shuffling papers. There was no-one else around. She looked very different today. In her sharp pencil dress and heels, she could have passed for a senior partner in a corporate law firm.

"Oh, it's you, Bubbles," she said when she saw him. Her manner was mocking rather than hostile today. "Are you looking for Archie?"

"Yes, I am."

"Well you're out of luck. He's had to go to court. He asked me to tell you."

"Nothing serious, I hope."

Ellen stopped shuffling her papers and put her hand on her hip. "Nothing serious, I hope," she echoed, mimicking him. She reverted to her own voice. "No, nothing serious at all. He's going as character witness. The cops have framed another one of our people on drugs charges."

She turned her attention back to her papers. Thom wondered if the court case had anything to do with the riot. It occurred to him that there was a lot that Ellen could tell him. He just had to overcome her resistance.

"The police haven't made themselves popular around here, have they?" he suggested tentatively.

She ignored this and carried on.

Thom decided to try another tactic. He thought she might share more in anger. He'd be treading on thin ice, but he needed to provoke her.

At least I'm close to the door.

"Some people might think the police are justified," he added. "They *are* trying to fight a heroin problem after all."

Ellen stopped what she was doing and stared. Thom thought she might scream abuse or even charge at him. Instead, she let out a shrill squeal of laughter.

"You are priceless!" she shrieked, her shoulders shaking. She dabbed at her eyes.

After a moment, she stopped laughing and pointed into the distance. "The headquarters of the federal police are *over there!*" she hissed. "They're overlooking us! They know *all about* the heroin trade here."

Thom was nonplussed by this. It was a very loaded statement. He wondered if there was any truth in it.

"Let me tell you something, Bubbles," Ellen continued. "Because you clearly didn't get the memo. The cops in this town are as crooked as a witch's nose."

She watched him for his reaction. He tried to keep his face neutral. He didn't want her to think she had shocked him.

Ellen shook her head with an air of weariness. "You've got no idea what you've walked into, have you? No idea at all."

Chapter Eight

A COUPLE OF WEEKS ON, THOM WAS STILL HAUNTED BY Ellen's words. He wondered about her motives. Almost certainly she had her own agenda. Then again, she wasn't the only one. In the case of TJ, everyone he'd spoken to seemed to want to influence him, one way or another. It was as if he needed to look behind them to find the real story.

But this story was proving elusive. He was sat at the kitchen worktop with Craig's laptop open in front of him. Outside the window, evening was descending on Sydney. He looked despondently at his work on the screen. For something that was supposed to be career-making, there was a dreary flatness.

It's just bloody boring.

He'd written plenty about policy and politics. He'd even interviewed a couple of public figures which Holly, true to her word, had arranged. What he'd produced so far would have looked good in an academic journal. But it just wasn't journalism.

Feeling stale, he decided to take a break out on the balcony, thinking that some fresh air might help. He passed through the lounge where Craig was ensconced in his chair reading business documents. His briefcase was open on the floor in front of him. The TV was on, but he wasn't watching.

"How's it going, Tommo?" Craig asked without looking up.

"Oh, alright." Thom slid open the door onto the balcony.

He stepped outside and gazed at the view down below. He appreciated living so high up at moments like this. His eyes settled on the enormous Coca-Cola sign flashing above William Street which was busy with night-time traffic. Despite all the movement, what Thom could see had an odd sort of calmness.

I wonder if I'll ever get to understand this place properly. Or am I just too much of an outsider?

His mind turned back to the media debate about the Redfern riot. It was still raging like a bush fire. Some insisted, in their loud clarion voices, that the police had been too soft. Earlier that day, Thom had interviewed a criminologist on campus. This wasn't arranged by Holly and he was hoping that she wouldn't find out just yet, since she might not approve. The criminologist, a calm, measured man, blamed the police for the riot. He said they were deeply prejudiced against Aborigines.

"I thought you'd given up on the police angle," Craig said later that evening when they were in bed.

"It's a bit difficult to ignore," retorted Thom. "Especially when the media keep banging on about *softly softly* policing."

"I think they've got a point." Craig put his book down. "The cops have known for years what goes on in Redfern and they've ignored it."

"You are not the first person to say that to me."

"I'm sure I'm not, Tommo. There's more than one side to this."

"Yeah, I know." Thom was exasperated. "It feels like there're too many bloody sides. Makes it hard to get to the truth."

Craig rolled onto his side and put his hand on Thom's shoulder. "There are ways of changing the world," he said gently. "But kicking out against it doesn't work. The world has a nasty habit of kicking back."

Thom supposed Craig was right. He thought about the hours he'd spent protesting against capitalism. What had he achieved? What had he changed? Nothing. And, he remembered, the world had certainly kicked back.

"I know," he murmured, feeling a need to surrender. He was tired of fighting, tired of feeling frustrated.

He ran his finger along Craig's chest, tracing his tattoos. Craig kissed him slowly but firmly on the lips and they rolled under the covers.

The next morning, Thom met Archie on campus for coffee. They were finally going to finish the interview. Archie had e-mailed, the day after the burial, apologising and offering to meet somewhere convenient.

Once they'd installed themselves with their coffees, Thom looked across the table at Archie. "Thank you for coming. I know you've had a busy few weeks."

"No worries, Young Thom. You're right, a lot *has* happened, but I didn't want to let you down again."

"It's fine." Thom unpacked his things onto the table. "Hopefully, we won't be disrupted by any other *events*."

"Oh, I don't know, mate." Archie looked around in mock trepidation. "I'm always expecting you students to be revolting."

Thom laughed. "I was always revolting when I was at university in London. I think I've grown out of it now, though."

He looked down at his list of questions, which were mainly about policing in Redfern. As he was about to switch on the recorder, he remembered there was something else he wanted to talk about.

"Rob Morton gave me a lift home the other week. The day before TJ's burial."

"Oh yes?" Archie sounded mildly curious.

"I gather you've known him a long time."

Archie sighed. "Yeah, since he was about fourteen or fifteen. Rob's a funny one. He sort of got lost somewhere along the way."

"What do you mean by that?"

He didn't get to hear an answer. At that moment, they were interrupted by Holly, who came over carrying takeaway coffee. Thom was surprised when Archie turned to acknowledge her.

"G'day, Holly. How are you?"

"Do you two know each other?" Thom asked.

"We go way back." Holly smiled and patted Archie on the shoulder. "I've interviewed Archie heaps over the years. He's always been very generous with his time."

"And now Young Thom is following in your footsteps."

"Well, I'm trying," said Thom with another attempt at a modest laugh.

"How did you go with those interviews?" Holly asked, turning to him.

"Really well. They were very insightful. Thank you for arranging them for me."

"No worries. Look, guys. I'm running late for a meeting, but I just wanted to say hi. I'm sure we'll catch up very soon."

After Holly went, Thom decided not to follow-up with Archie about Morton. Something about her appearance in the coffee shop discouraged him. He thought he'd ask another day, but less directly. Pressing on with their interview, he found Archie gave him plenty to work with.

"It's been a pleasure, Young Thom," Archie insisted at the end. "Give me a bell if you need anything else."

Thom spent most of the day on campus, collecting books from the library and attending a class in the afternoon, but he was distracted by his thoughts. It was interesting that Holly and Archie knew each other. He remembered what she'd told him about TJ Hickey, and he wondered if she'd repeated it to Archie. Somehow, he doubted it.

Throughout the day, Rob Morton also played on his mind. He was still very intrigued by the detective's motives. Archie had called him "lost" which, though unexplained, made sense to him.

I knew a lost cop once.

He revisited the subject later that evening when he went over to Lars and Cady's for dinner – on his own, as Craig was at some networking event in the city. When he arrived at their house, which Craig called "the rat hole", Cady answered the door.

"Lars is in the shower," she told him, as he stepped in clutching the wine he'd brought.

The front door led straight into their lounge room. It was sparsely furnished but felt untidy and chaotic, like the rest of the house. A damp smell pervaded. Neither Lars nor Cady worried about cleaning. An adjoining hallway was cluttered with artwork.

"Have you recovered from Saturday?" Thom asked, handing her the bottle.

It had been the annual Mardi Gras parade and they'd gone on a bar crawl with Lars and Craig. Cady had got blotto on vodka and was bundled into a taxi by Lars just after midnight.

"Man, that was the worst hangover *ever*. I had to work on Sunday, so I've called in sick tonight."

"Well you were necking back the Smirnoff. Why didn't you call in sick *last* night?"

"Do you remember my friend, Lisa? Who I work with at the club? We were down to do a lesbian double act together, and I just couldn't let her down. There was only one other girl working and Lisa like totally hates her."

"That sounds like an occupational hazard," Thom murmured.

Cady was twenty, more than a decade younger than Lars. There was something childlike about her appearance. She was extremely small and slight with dyed black hair cut into a bob. Her face, when not made-up, was pale and freckly. She spoke with a sort of American accent although she'd never been out of Australia.

"Would you like a Mojito?" she asked, gesturing at the coffee table, where he saw a large glass jug and three glasses.

"That would be lovely, thank you."

He heard the bathroom door open at the back of the house, and then Lars padded through, wearing only a towel. This was something of a relief. One time when Thom visited, Lars had walked in from the bathroom wearing absolutely nothing at all. He hadn't known where to look. But Lars and Cady had been entirely nonchalant about it, in the way that only they could be.

"Hey, Thom," Lars said acknowledging him. "I'm just going upstairs to put some clothes on.

He came back a few minutes later, wearing jeans, socks and a t-shirt, and sank down onto a beanbag. Thom and Cady sat on the couch drinking their Mojitos. They were chatting about Cady's borderline personality disorder, with which she claimed to be diagnosed.

"I feel guilt *a lot*," she told Thom. "That's how I know I'm not a psychopath."

Lars looked like he wanted to comment about this but was biting his tongue.

"What are we having for dinner?" he asked.

"Pasta." Cady put her glass down. "Didn't you notice me cooking it?"

He doesn't notice stuff like that, Thom thought.

"Awesome." Lars poured himself a Mojito. "I knew you were cooking something."

Cady got up. "I need to check the sauce. Dinner will be ready in five. Hope you guys are hungry."

She disappeared into the kitchen.

Lars held up his glass to the light and swirled its contents. "How's the story coming along?" he asked Thom.

"Well, I've written *a* story. But I just don't feel like it's *the* story."

"Cryptic. What do you mean?"

Thom took a sip of his Mojito and felt the sugar fizz on his tongue. "I think the real story here is what happened to TJ Hickey. But nobody wants to talk about it. It's weird, but I feel like everyone is trying to deflect me."

"Well, either he was being followed by the cops or he wasn't."

"I think it's more complicated than that. There's this Aboriginal woman I know at Aspire, Ellen. She doesn't like me very much, but I had a conversation with her the other day. She claims the local police are corrupt."

Lars spluttered, spraying his drink everywhere. "No shit!" he cried, as if floored by Thom's naivety. "*Everybody* knows how corrupt they are."

"I know there's *a history* of it," Thom said defensively. "I just wasn't sure if it was still a thing."

"There was a royal commission a few years ago," Lars explained. "They investigated the cops at King's Cross. You name it, they found it – drug-trafficking, money-laundering...bribery. There wasn't much they *hadn't* done."

"Bloody hell. What happened?"

"Not much. Some of them were fired or went to jail. And some retired early. The government promised a shit ton of reforms, as you'd expect."

"Do you think anything changed?"

"Not at all. I think it was just the tip of the iceberg. In my experience, all cops are dirty."

"Hmm." Thom drank more of his Mojito. "Maybe *that's* what is at the root of all this."

Lars sucked in his breath. "How would you prove it?"

"I'm not sure I can. But I know one of the local cops, and he seems a bit troubled by something. And *I think* he might be willing to talk to me, off-the-record."

Lars looked sceptical. "Why do you think that?"

"Just a couple of things he's said to me. But he reminds me of Jake in London, who I told you about. Do you remember?"

Lars was one of the few people that Thom had talked to about Jake. He rarely spoke about his life before in London. Still, Jake was one of the reasons he'd left and ended up in Sydney. Even if Thom had wanted to talk about him, he wouldn't have. Not everyone would believe him.

Chapter 9

London, United Kingdom – May 2000

It was Richard who introduced him to Jake. They were at a demo against the World Bank in the City of London. Thom already knew Jake by reputation. His activism in far-flung places was legendary. He'd been shot at, tear-gassed and arrested countless times. People were often struck, even intimidated, by his self-confidence, which oozed from every pore.

Richard had spotted him in the crowd and greeted him effusively. He pulled aside Thom, who was standing nearby. "Jake, this is Thom, my housemate."

Jake took Thom's hand and shook it firmly. "Alright."

He didn't smile, but there was a gleam in his pale green eyes. Thom felt he was being regarded with a wry amusement. Jake was in his early thirties with a goatee beard and piercings. Thom looked at his lived-in but youthful face and was captivated instantly.

Why are men like him always straight?

He wanted, in that moment, to hold onto Jake's attention. And he tried to start a conversation.

"I heard what happened to you in Seattle," he ventured.

But Jake was looking distractedly over his shoulder. He'd clearly seen someone he wanted to talk to. "Yeah, mate," he muttered brusquely. "Sorry, I've just got to..."

He gestured vaguely in front of him and then he was gone. Thom was left feeling mildly stung.

Richard seemed embarrassed. He tried to laugh it off. "Popular bloke is Jake."

"Hmm," Thom murmured.

He didn't think they'd cross paths again.

Richard ambushed Thom in the kitchen on a Friday evening, just as he got home from work.

"Are you coming tonight?"

He meant the weekly gathering he held up in his room. And Thom didn't have an excuse not to go.

Barely hiding his irritation, he dropped his shopping on the cluttered worktop. "What? Oh. Erm yes. I am."

"Cool," Richard replied with a studied nonchalance and turned on his heel.

Thom groaned inwardly. He was tired and grumpy after a long, dreary week. His job consisted entirely of endless data-entry. All he wanted to do was cook himself dinner and read, alone in his room. Instead, he would have to make the effort to be sociable. He'd be obliged to listen to Richard droning on, in his privately educated drawl, about the working class.

Richard's Friday night gatherings were like a political salon for the crème-de-la-crème of London's anti-capitalists. At least that's what he thought anyway. They would spend long nights, lubricated by cider and hash, talking about socialism. Richard held forth expertly on what Karl Marx might make of anything, from the Cold War to *the Simpsons*.

Thom had got involved in anti-capitalism when he was at university. He'd been dragged along to protests and marches by friends. That was how he'd met Richard, a bearded mature student, who'd fortuitously had a vacancy in his shared house.

Upon the hour, Thom trudged up to Richard's room, before everyone arrived. He was installed on a cushion when the doorbell rang. Richard went down to answer it. There was then the murmur of voices as a dozen visitors traipsed up the stairs. Watching them file into the room, Thom was taken aback to see Jake with them. But he managed not to show it.

After some shuffling around by the newcomers, Jake sat himself down next to Thom. He gave him a half-nod of acknowledgement and then proceeded to ignore him.

A joint was soon lit and passed around the room. For most of the evening, Thom was bored and silent. He focussed on slowly drinking his can of cider, acutely conscious of Jake beside him. Jake, himself, contributed little to the discussions around them

But later, Thom noticed he seemed amused by an argument that started in front of them. It was between Richard and Flora, one of the other guests. She was an articulate seventeen-year-old who liked to talk about Marxism. Thom observed her as she rhetorically skewered Richard.

She'll have a book out before she's twenty.

Jake lost interest in them as soon as the joint came his way. When he'd finished with it, he handed it to Thom, leaning in close to murmur to him.

"So, are you going to this Carnival Against Capital?"

Thom was surprised he'd initiated conversation. And he was flattered. "Yes," he replied, eager to impress. "There are loads of us going, so we might get some media coverage."

Jake smirked at this. "You just want to get on the telly, so you can shock your middle-class parents, don't you?"

Thom bristled. This wasn't the response he'd wanted. "I think you're just making assumptions about me," he said defensively. He took another puff on the joint, inhaling deeply.

"Bet I'm right though," Jake snorted. "You look like a classic of the genre."

Thom was irritated by Jake's self-satisfaction. He wanted to puncture it with some snark of his own.

"You're right," he shot back. "I do. But shocking the parents is just the icing on the cake. I actually have a vital purpose. Which is to make the *real* heroes...*like you,* feel authentic."

Jake's lips parted in surprise. And then he chuckled. "Ouch."

He seemed delighted by Thom's combativeness. Laughing to himself again, he turned away to listen in elsewhere.

After the joint circulated one more time, Thom started to get distinctly woozy. His body was leaden, and he had to stop himself leaning against Jake, inviting though that was.

Jake, getting bored again, yawned and turned back to him. "Tell me, what's *your* story, Thom?"

Thom noted he'd remembered his name. "What do you mean?"

"Well, what do you do when you're not going on demos?"

"I'm just temping at the moment," Thom said apologetically.

"And what is it you *want* to do?" Jake asked.

Thom sighed. "I don't know. I only graduated last year. I thought I'd get a job in politics, as an MP's researcher or *something*."

"You did a politics degree?"

"Yes, I did."

"Where?"

"Queen Mary," Thom replied. "In East London. Do you know it?"

Jake nodded. "Yeah, I do. It's a good university."

"That's what I thought. But it hasn't done me much good." Thom suddenly felt very sorry for himself.

Jake looked at him probingly. "Why do you say that?"

Thom shrugged. "I don't know. There just isn't anything out there. It's all call centre jobs and temping. You don't need a politics degree for that."

Jake smiled, half mockingly, half sympathetically. "You've been robbed by globalisation, haven't you?"

"Something like that," Thom murmured, slumberous and feeling defeated.

His eyelids had become heavy, so he sat back and let his eyes close. He realised he was feeling the effect of the hash having smoked more than he normally would. When he opened his eyes again, the room was spinning. He could hear Richard, in the background, still talking ponderously. But the others had clearly zoned out and a couple of them were even asleep. Thom heard himself mutter something to Jake. And then, he blacked out.

He woke up to find himself lying in Jake's arms and wondered how he'd got there. Jake was asleep, his chest steadily rising and falling. Thom inhaled the scent of his t-shirt, which smelt of fabric conditioner and deodorant. He felt snug and comfortable.

He lifted his head briefly to see they were surrounded by other comatose bodies. The room was dark as someone had switched the light out. Feeling he was in no state to move, he let his head fall back onto Jake's shoulder. Jake stirred briefly and stroked his hair before they both went back to sleep.

Hours later, when Thom opened his eyes again, grey daylight peeked through the sash window. He saw from Richard's alarm clock that it was after 7am. Everyone else was still in some state of slumber.

The morning after the night before.

He propelled himself up pushing his hands into the carpet. There was a pervasive stale smell because of the abandoned cider cans and the overflowing ashtray. He turned around to look at Jake. As if conscious of Thom's gaze, Jake's eyes flicked open. He stared for a moment, his mouth a neutral straight line.

"Morning," Thom said to him warily.

Jake sat up without replying. He rubbed the sleep out of his eye, stretched out his arms, and looked back at Thom.

"Morning."

Thom felt awkward and strangely mortified, even though he had no reason to be. He wondered how much Jake remembered, and how much of it he intended.

It's like we've had a one-night stand. But we haven't.

"I must have crashed out last night" he told Jake, as if getting his excuse in early. "It's very embarrassing."

Jake regarded him with an inscrutable expression. "There's nothing to be embarrassed about, mate."

Thom realised they were being listened to. One of Richard's friends, a guy with a lank ponytail, had woken, and was now sat up staring at them with unabashed interest. Thom found the attention unwelcome and intrusive. He didn't want to be the subject of gossip. Mumbling an excuse to Jake, he went to make himself a coffee and have a shower. He didn't see him again that day.

Chapter 10

London, United Kingdom – June 2000

It was a bright summer's day in the City of London. Around two thousand people had gathered for the Carnival against Capital. The atmosphere was suitably carnivalesque, at least in the beginning. Many of the protestors wore fluorescent wigs and made noise with their whistles and their drums.

Thom and Richard were assembled with their comrades in a side street. Nearby, the Bank of England loomed imperiously. In front of its giant columns stood a line of black-clad riot police. Thom thought they looked like they were out of a dystopia movie.

"They're not here for the carnival, are they?" he muttered to Richard.

Richard responded with a knowing chortle.

The march was about to set off. But when they tried to move, they found their path blocked by the police. One of the cops even held a video-camera. Thom had seen them use divide-and-rule tactics before.

He felt apprehensive. "What are they playing at?" he wondered aloud.

"The usual," Richard told him. "We're just going to ignore them."

"What?" Thom was taken aback.

Richard cast a pointed glance behind him. "Look. There are five hundred of *us*. And six of *them*. They can just fuck off."

"You mean we're going to charge them?" Thom's incredulity was growing

He heard another voice, close by, answer him. "Exactly that."

Thom turned to find Jake standing next to them.

"Hi there," he said, mildly startled. Still, he'd been hoping to run into Jake here.

Jake gave him a brief meaningful look. "Alright," he nodded.

It was the first time they'd seen each other since that night, a couple of weeks earlier.

Before he could say more, Thom was distracted by a ripple among the crowd as they prepared to push off. Looking ahead at the police, he could feel them tensing up with anticipation. Jake tapped him on the shoulder.

"Pull your hood up," he whispered.

Behind them, the crowd had swelled, and expectation was mounting. Thom pulled up his hood like Jake said.

He then heard Richard screech "GO!"

The protestors surged forward, taking his cue. Thom, propelled by the mass of people behind him, barged past two burly policemen.

"Oi!" he heard one of them yell.

He felt a rush of exhilaration he'd never had before. The din made by the protestors got louder reaching a crescendo. They were almost drowned out by wailing sirens as police reinforcements arrived. Vans pulled up and cops with riot shields leapt out, enclosing the crowd in a pincer movement.

Suddenly, Jake grabbed Thom's arm and pulled him off the street, into an alleyway.

"Quick! Behind the bins," Jake barked. He dragged Thom down into a crouching position.

"What's going on?" Thom demanded, disoriented. The stench of rubbish and urine pervaded his nostrils.

Before Jake could answer, they heard the clumping of horses' hooves from the street. The whistles and drums stopped abruptly. Then, there was a thunderous fizzing sound. The protestors started screeching and yelling in anguish. Thom realised they were being teargassed.

Jake pointed in their direction. "*That's* what's going on. Believe me, you don't want to get gassed and arrested on the same day."

"What about the others?" Thom murmured.

Jake ignored this. "Listen. We need to get out of here." He stared intently into Thom's eyes. "Just follow me. If anyone stops us, let me do the talking. Okay?"

Thom nodded obediently.

Taking Jake's lead, he hauled himself back up. They were stood next to an open door to a busy kitchen. Jake put his hand on Thom's shoulder and steered him inside. As he propelled Thom through the kitchen, he took no notice of the suspicious stares they got from the staff.

They soon found themselves at the front of a steel-and-glass type establishment. Thom thought they must look conspicuous among the shiny-suited clientele, but no-one gave them a second glance. The melee outside was too much of a distraction.

The entrance had been locked and a security guard was stationed behind it. Some of the patrons stood at the windows, laughing or snarling disparagements. Lurking unseen behind them, Thom felt like an enemy infiltrator.

He glanced at Jake. "How did you know the police were going to do that?"

Jake sighed wearily. "I know how they operate."

"There you are!" cried Richard. "Did you get arrested too?"

Thom shut the front door behind him.

"No," he replied, wondering how to explain himself. "Were you?"

Richard's eyes darkened with barely suppressed rage. "I have spent the last six fucking hours locked in a stinking cell!"

"Did they charge you?" Thom asked, concerned.

"No! Of course they fucking didn't." Richard's voice was quivering now, as if he was about to cry. "They had fuck all to charge me with."

Seeing him so upset made Thom uncomfortable. "Oh god, that's awful, Richard. Were you on your own?"

"No," Richard replied, exhaling to release the tension. "There were a few of us." He then peered curiously at Thom. "Are *you* alright? Did you get teargassed?"

"No! Thankfully." Thom had to think quickly. "It was just total carnage. I didn't know where I was."

Richard nodded sympathetically. "Yeah, you were probably disoriented. I can see why."

Thom was relieved not to be probed any further. The deception caused him a little guilt. But he wasn't overwhelmed by it.

He didn't entirely escape the attention of the police. A few days later, they sought out the protestors who'd evaded arrest. They were quite innovative about it, publishing their photos on a website. Thom featured in one of the blurry images. To his amusement, one of his parents' golf club friends saw it and recognised him. He found out from Charlotte.

"It's *so* obviously you," Charlotte said reproachfully. "Mum and Dad are mortified."

Thom had met her for lunch at a cafe in Covent Garden.

"Well, they *are* easily mortified," he retorted. "And so is their stupid golf club. Anyway, that photo could be of anyone. If the police come knocking, I'll just deny it."

Charlotte raised her eyebrows. "Hmm. Are you sure it's worth all the hassle? This activist life of yours."

An image of Jake floated into Thom's mind. "It has its moments," he told her, smiling coyly.

Chapter 11

London, United Kingdom – May 2001

Thom and Richard were sat next to each other on the tube, lost in their own thoughts.

"A luta continua," said Richard breaking the silence.

"What?"

"A luta continua," Richard repeated. "The struggle goes on."

Thom frowned. "What made you say that?"

He wondered if this was an overture for a deep and meaningful. Perhaps Richard knew what he was feeling.

"No reason," Richard replied evasively. "It's just important to keep your spirits up."

Thom pondered this. "Can I ask you something, Richard?"

"Sure," Richard shrugged.

"Do you ever wonder..." Thom began. He stopped to choose his words carefully. "Do you ever have moments when you think that all this protesting we do – all these demonstrations are just a waste of time?"

Richard contemplated the banner rolled up between his knees. "Of course I do." He looked back at Thom. "But that's what they want you to feel. Don't you see? They want you to get so pissed off, so disillusioned, that you just give up."

"I suppose," Thom sighed.

"Well, you know what they say. Don't let the bastards grind you down."

Thom wanted to tell Richard that it wasn't *the bastards* who were grinding him down. It was the anti-capitalists themselves. He still went to their gatherings and spoke their language. But now, he felt like a churchgoer who'd ceased to believe in God.

Then there were the endless, dreary protests. They weren't just tedious; they were downright frightening. The police, who'd always been heavy-handed, had become proficient in psychological warfare.

"This is us," Richard announced, standing up, as they pulled into Oxford Circus. "Time for May Day!"

The tube station was heaving with hundreds of people carrying placards and wearing badges, all heading in the same direction. On the escalator up, Thom stood in front of Richard, staring ahead.

"I saw Jake the other day," Richard casually mentioned.

Thom turned around, startled by this news. "But I thought he was in India."

"Yeah, he was," Richard confirmed. "But he's back now. And he was asking after you."

"Was he now?" Thom was intrigued. But he wanted to appear indifferent. He hadn't seen Jake for nearly a year.

"Yeah." Richard's eyes narrowed. "What exactly was it that happened between you and him?"

"Well, nothing," Thom grimaced.

This wasn't entirely untrue. After their escapade at the Carnival against Capital, Thom thought that he and Jake had formed an intimate, clandestine bond. He'd imagined it would lead to some intense, passionate love affair. Instead, Jake left the country very soon after. Thom only found out about it second-hand. At the time, he felt cheated, disgruntled. But eventually he learnt to live with his disappointment. Until now.

The slight woman, agitated and dishevelled, marched up to the impervious policeman.

"How much longer are you going to keep us here?" she demanded.

Thom could hear the desperation in her voice. And he felt it too. They'd been confined at Oxford Circus with the other protestors for nearly seven hours. He'd lost Richard ages ago.

The police enclosed them early on. This was met with incredulity by the assembled mass, followed by frustration and eventually boredom as the hours wore on. Now, panic had set in, especially among those who had children with them. Thom was faint with hunger and acutely conscious of the pressure on his bladder.

Then, things got much, much worse as the police tightened their corral. The crush was unbearable. Thom felt his chest tighten. He pushed his way through and tapped on a riot shield to get attention.

"I need to get out of here!" he cried. "Can you please just let me go?"

There was no response. Instead, the police closed in again causing shrieks of horror. Thom began to hyperventilate.

"LET ME OUT!" he screamed. "FOR FUCKS SAKE!"

The riot shield was pushed harder against him. He beat his fists against it.

"Let me out! Let me out! Let me out! Just fucking let me out!"

He was convinced he was going to be crushed to death. And tears cascaded down his face as he kept pummelling. He used up all his strength and fainted, collapsing to the ground.

When he came around, he heard a voice say: "You're under arrest."

He was taken to Charing Cross Police Station and bundled unceremoniously into a cell. He expected to be there for hours but, in the end, it was only twenty minutes. After being charged with a public order offence, he was dismissed.

It was dark by the time he stepped out, dazed, into the street. Never in his life had he felt so utterly drained and defeated.

He barely noticed the figure standing beneath the streetlamp he walked past. But he heard the man call his name. He stopped and turned around.

To his astonishment, Jake stepped out into the gloom in front of him. At first, Thom thought he was hallucinating.

"What are you doing here?" he spluttered.

He assumed Jake must have been arrested at the same protest. Why else?

Jake came up to him and clasped his arms. "I'm looking for you." He peered at Thom in concern. "Are you okay?"

"Not really." Thom wanted to sink his head into Jake's shoulder and cry. "They've charged me. But I didn't do anything. I just wanted to get out of there."

"You'll be okay," Jake assured him. "The charge won't stick."

"How do you know?" snapped Thom. He instantly regretted his abrasiveness. "Sorry. It's been a long day. I should probably just be glad I wasn't in that cell for too long."

"That's because I got you out of there," Jake said quietly.

Thom stared at him in bewilderment. "What? How?"

Jake tightened his grip. "There's something I need to tell you. This is very hard, but *please* try to understand."

Thom felt his blood run cold. He didn't know what Jake was about to say but he dreaded hearing it.

"What?" he murmured apprehensively.

"We won't be seeing each other again," Jake told him. "I've got to get away from here."

Thom shook his head, confused. "What do you mean? You're not making any sense."

Jake, without taking his eyes off him, pulled a thin leather wallet from his back pocket and handed it over.

Thom opened it up. He saw it was a warrant card for a PC Jake Callaghan, with an old photo of Jake without his goatee beard and piercings.

"I don't understand. What is this?" Thom was even more dumbfounded.

Jake swallowed before looking him in the eye. "I'm an undercover police officer. And I work for a unit specialising in domestic extremists."

Thom looked at the warrant card again, and then back at Jake. "Is this some sort of joke?" he demanded. "Because it's really not fucking funny. Not today."

Jake shook his head. "It's no joke."

Thom felt like he was having an out-of-body experience.

He heard himself shriek: "So, all this time, you've been spying on us? Spying on *me*?"

"Yes, I have," replied Jake evenly.

"Oh my god!" Thom cried, looking up at the sky. "You think I'm a fucking extremist." He laughed mirthlessly. "And why the fuck would you tell me this now?"

Jake put his hands on Thom's shoulders. "Because I think you're right. Because I've come to believe the same things you do. The police are just an instrument of the capitalist state. I can see that now."

Thom bit his lip and glared. “How long have you been doing this?”

Jake took a sharp intake of breath. “Five years,” he sighed. “Five fucking years. That’s five years of being someone else. It fucks you up in the end.”

“Yeah,” Thom snarled. “It’s certainly fucked up!”

He pushed Jake’s hands away and flung the wallet back at him. Jake flinched as it struck the side of his face.

“Look, Thom. I don’t know if I’ve done the right thing by telling you and I understand you’re angry...”

“Understand?” hissed Thom. He was shaking now. “No, you really don’t fucking understand. You don’t understand what I feel, and you sure as fuck don’t understand what is and what isn’t right. So don’t stand there bullshitting me.”

“Okay!” Jake held up his palms in surrender. “I don’t want to argue with you anymore.” He leant down to pick up the wallet. “I just hope that one day this all makes sense to you and then maybe, just maybe, you can forgive me.” He started to back away. “I’m really sorry. Please, just take care of yourself.”

He turned around and walked away, quickly picking up speed. Thom stood and watched as he disappeared around the corner. When he’d gone, Thom looked at the street around him. Everything looked the same but the whole world was different: unknown and unknowable, without certainty or solidity.

Chapter 12

London – July 2001

Thom got into the office early, before any of the other secretaries arrived. He'd been temping at the hospital a few weeks. And he quite enjoyed the company of the middle-aged women he worked with. But this morning, he didn't want to be observed. He wanted to use the internet, which was frowned upon.

He switched on his computer and went online. For a couple of minutes, he just stared at the screen. When he finally felt ready, he typed 'PC Jake Callaghan' into the search engine.

This produced a list of weblinks. He clicked on the first one, and it took him to a local story about stolen traffic cones. He was confronted by a grainy photo of Jake in his police uniform.

So it's true.

He saw the article was nearly ten years old.

It's amazing nobody ever saw this. But then, why would they even look?

He'd since been told by Richard that Jake was back in India. This had to be a cover story of some sort. Still, it suited Thom fine. After the revelation outside the police station, he'd wanted to tell everyone about Jake, shout it from the rooftops, and let the whole world know. But he didn't. He felt like too much of a fool, a dupe, a victim.

More to the point, he didn't know who to trust anymore. Who else was spying on him? Perhaps someone at Richard's Friday night gatherings? What about Richard? Could he be involved?

Thom checked himself and shook his head.

That's just ludicrous.

He gazed at the Jake he'd never known on the screen. He resented him for the paranoia he now felt, this sense that he was always being watched.

At that moment, he heard a girlish voice behind him.

"Thom, what are you looking at?"

Thom quickly clicked out of the browser. He looked round to see his colleague, Babsy peering curiously.

"Oh, erm...just checking the internet works," he smirked.

Babsy chuckled knowingly. "So I see." She dropped her bag on her chair. "I thought it was strange you're in so early."

"Nothing wrong with my work ethic," Thom retorted.

He was glad that it was only her. Unlike the other matrons who worked here, she wouldn't be too disapproving.

. . .

The carriage wasn't particularly full, not for rush hour on the tube. Thom sat down, placing his backpack on his lap.

He cast a cursory glance at the other passengers. They all looked dead-eyed and sullen.

London does that – it sucks the life out of you.

Thom vividly remembered arriving here to start university. Escaped from his hometown, he'd rejoiced at being anonymous in this metropolis. Now, he found it exhausting and threatening.

As he ruminated, the train juddered to a halt in the middle of the tunnel. Then the lights started flickering on and off, plunging the carriage into darkness.

This wasn't unusual on the tube. Still, Thom loathed the claustrophobia. It brought back memories of Oxford Circus. He sighed inwardly and hoped they wouldn't be stuck there too long.

But the train stayed resolutely stationary. For Thom, it felt like an eternity. And he quickly became agitated. He noticed a suited, bespectacled man opposite. Thom had this notion the man was watching him.

He then glanced sideways. A young woman, in a denim jumpsuit sat a few seats away, chewing gum. She seemed to be surreptitiously observing him too.

Thom looked frantically around at the rest of the carriage. They were all in on it; they were all staring. He sprung up and leapt towards the door.

With a grinding sound, the tube started moving again. And the lights came back on. Thom stared at his reflection in the doors, willing the train to move faster. When it finally arrived at the next stop, he practically fell out of it.

He dragged himself to the back of the platform. And he held his breath as he waited for the train to go again. When the doors slid shut and it roared off, he gasped in relief. His forehead was damp with cold sweat. He knew full well it had all been in his head.

I can't go on like this.

Something had to give, and he came to a decision that day.

"You're going to Australia?" Babsy raised her eyebrows in surprise.

"Yep," Thom nodded. "I've now got my working holiday visa."

He and Babsy were eating their lunch on the hospital roof terrace. The Thames glistened in the distance.

Babsy took a sip of her Diet Coke. "What's brought all this on?"

"Oh, lots of things," Thom sighed. "I just feel like I could do with a fresh start...get away from everything."

"Is it because of the politics thing?" Babsy probed. "You sound like you've got a bit disillusioned. It's not surprising after all the trouble you've been in."

Thom had confided in her about the public order charge.

"Sort of," he murmured, distractedly chewing his sandwich.

He didn't want to elaborate. How could he even begin to explain about Jake? It was too much to share with anyone. But maybe one day, when he'd put it behind him. He imagined Babsy would be the first person he'd want to tell. They'd become close friends despite the thirty-year age gap between them.

Their lunch hour was nearly over when Thom's new phone rang. He had it out on the table. Fumblingly, he picked it up and answered.

"Hello?"

"Thom, it's Simon Chopra," said a well-modulated voice. "Is this a good time to speak?"

It was Thom's barrister, who'd been enlisted to defend him.

"Hi Simon. Yes, it is."

"Splendid," Simon drawled. "This won't take long. Just to let you know, the charge against you has been dropped."

"The charge has been dropped?" Thom echoed, staring across the table at Babsy.

Her mouth dropped open.

"Indeed," Simon confirmed. "And as you know, I had my own reasons for taking on your case, so I won't be billing you."

Thom felt a rush of elated relief. "Well, that's fantastic," he gushed. "I don't know what to say. Except thank you so much!"

"All in a good cause, comrade," Simon breezed. "Anyhow, must dash. Try to stay out of trouble."

He rang off.

"Did you hear that?" Thom asked Babsy.

"Yes, Thom. Yes, I did." Babsy smiled gladly. "And I'm so pleased for you. It must be such a weight off your mind."

"Oh god, yeah." Thom blew out his cheeks. "I'm just glad it's all over. I wish we had some champagne or something."

"We can still have a toast though," Babsy insisted. She held up her Diet Coke. "Cheers."

"Cheers," Thom said raising his water bottle.

They clinked their drinks.

Babsy put her can down and started to gather up her food wrappers. "Are you still going to go to Australia then?"

"I absolutely am. It's all happening."

"When?"

"Early January. *But*, before I go, I'm moving back to my parents for a few months..."

"But they live in Lymington, don't they?"

"That's right. I've got a job lined up there as a hotel receptionist. I need to save some money."

"Won't that be difficult? Living with your parents again."

Thom grimaced. "Well, they said they'll be glad to have me out of harm's way."

"Parents never stop worrying, Thom," Babsy said with feeling.

"Mine might have to," Thom replied. "I'm going to be a bloody long way away."

"That's true,“ Babsy conceded. She looked thoughtfully over at the Thames. "Well, I hope you find what you're looking for out there."

A few months later, Thom, newly arrived in Sydney, found himself drinking beer in a dimly lit bar. He was stood at the back, next to the jukebox. The place was starting to get busy with a crowd of mostly older, rather rugged looking men.

He didn't mind that he was here on his own. He found it liberating to be unknown in a new city, in a new country where he had no history. And where no-one was watching him.

He was living nearby in a youth hostel, and he'd just got a job in a call centre. Slowly, he was starting to make friends. He'd felt no urge to get politically active again, which was just as well; 9/11 in New York had killed the anti-globalisation movement.

His train of thought was interrupted when someone tried to squeeze past to get to the jukebox.

"Excuse me, mate," they demanded.

"Sorry." Thom shifted to make way for a guy with a Mohican.

His gaze then fell upon the bar, where his attention was caught by a man standing by it. Thom thought he looked like a handsome villain. The man didn't seem to notice him at first, but before long he turned his head in Thom's direction. And their eyes locked. Thom felt a shiver of recognition as if he could see into this man's past; he saw mischief, travel, adventure, danger. The man gave him a half-smile before turning his attention back to his drink.

For the next few minutes, they played this game of exchanging glances and then looking away. Eventually Thom, feeling bold, beamed at him. The man abandoned his spot at the bar and came over.

"Hello, mate. I saw you looking at me, so I thought I'd come and introduce myself."

“Looking at you?” Thom responded with a challenging stare. “But we were looking at *each other*, weren’t we?”

The man laughed. “You’re a caustic one, aren’t you? What’s your name?”

Thom extended his hand. “I’m Thom.”

The man gripped it firmly.

“Nice to meet you, Tommo. I’m Craig. Now, what’s a nice boy like you doing in a place like this?”

Chapter 13

Sydney, Australia – March 2004

"Your move, Tommo," said Craig leaning back contentedly.

He watched Thom contemplate the chessboard. He was almost certain to beat him for the third time that night.

Thom knew he was cornered. The only thing to do was go kamikaze. He moved his bishop diagonally across the board and assassinated Craig's queen.

"You cunt!" Craig spluttered. "What d'ya do that for?"

Thom smirked. "Bwahaha".

Craig turned his attention back to the board. "Hmmm."

He chuckled and then took brutal revenge using his knight.

"And *that* is what is known as checkmate, Tommo," he said triumphantly. "Ha! Take that, ya prick."

"Bollocks!" hissed Thom, frustrated.

Craig looked pleased with himself. "Another game, Tommo?"

"No!"

Thom lifted up the board, upending the pieces, and snapped it shut. He packed the chess set away and put it back under the coffee table where it belonged. It was the first game of chess that he and Craig had had for a while. When they first met, they'd played a lot. But Thom had soon tired of the constant defeat.

Craig stretched out his arms and yawned. "Righto, I should probably hit the sack. I've got a tricky meeting in the morning."

"What's tricky about it?"

"I've got to give a client some bad news. I've crunched the numbers and they're not going to get the loan they want."

"That must be an occupational hazard."

"Yes. Indeed," sighed Craig, picking up his mug of hot chocolate.

He drank the rest of it and took the mug into the kitchen to rinse. Thom thought he seemed down.

He's really not looking forward to that meeting

Thom knew that Craig's business wasn't going well. He often came home looking morose and deflated. His self-help books and seminars didn't seem to be working. Thom suspected he was more focussed on their move to New Zealand. He'd asked him what he planned to do when they got there. Craig just said he'd figure it out.

This wasn't hugely satisfactory. Still, Thom decided it was a question for another day which, right now, was way off in the future.

Feeling tired, he decided to go to bed himself. In the kitchen, the dishes from dinner had dried and Craig was putting them away.

"Do you want me to light the oil burner?" Thom asked.

"Yes please."

"Where's the lighter?"

"Top cupboard above the sink where it always is."

"It's not *always* there," snipped Thom. "You move it around."

"I do it to confuse you, Tommo," Craig retorted.

"You probably do," muttered Thom. He found the lighter.

"How's your story going?" asked Craig, changing the subject. "Have you finished it?"

"Very nearly," Thom replied. "I'm hoping to send it out next week. Holly, one of my lecturers, has given me some e-mail addresses."

He still had one more interview he wanted to do. It was with Detective Sergeant Rob Morton. Thom was sure that he wanted to unburden himself about something. But he wasn't going to tell Craig about this. He had this strong sense he wouldn't approve.

Thom wasn't entirely comfortable keeping it from him. It felt like some sort of illicit deception. Still, it was necessary. Craig would understand once the story was published, and his career was made.

He's the sort of man who likes success Thom told himself.

After class, the next day, he took a bus from the campus down to Coogee Beach where he'd arranged to meet Morton. Apparently, he lived nearby and had the afternoon off work. On the way, Thom thought about how he would get the detective to talk.

I need to be empathetic and non-judgemental.

After all, hadn't Jake, in the end, been afraid of being judged? Morton was probably burdened with secrets too. Who knew what he might have done himself? He'd have been under pressure that most people couldn't imagine.

Thom arrived a few minutes early at the café, which was Scandinavian in style with blond wood furniture. He took a seat facing the window and ordered a long black. It was a grey, overcast afternoon. Outside, passers-by languidly made their way to and from the beach.

Morton was running late. He sent Thom a text to let him know.

'*Be there in 5. xx*'.

"Familiar as ever," Thom muttered to himself

While he waited, he picked his backpack off the floor and opened it on his lap. Inside were his Dictaphone, notepad, and pen. He thought about whether to put all of these out on the table. He didn't want to scare Morton off with a recording device. But he did want to establish a bit of professional distance, and so he settled on just the notepad and pen.

As it turned out, Morton was more like ten minutes late, not five. Thom was looking at his phone when he heard the cafe door open. He made a point of not looking up. As he pretended to read a text, he saw a long shadow spread across the table. He then felt a big heavy hand ruffle his hair. He looked up to see Morton standing over him.

The detective grinned. "How're you going, mate?"

It was the first time Thom had seen him dressed so casually. He was wearing a long-sleeved hoodie, cargo shorts and flip-flops. He hadn't shaved that day, and the stubble around his throat was all mossy.

"Hi Rob. Thanks for coming."

"The pleasure's all mine." Morton sank into the chair opposite. His hazel eyes gleamed at Thom. "I can think of worse ways to spend a Friday afternoon."

Thom laughed awkwardly. He wondered how he was going to deal with the flirtatiousness. He was prepared to indulge it, but only to a point.

Morton raised his hand to get the attention of the waitress. When she came over, he didn't bother looking at the menu.

"G'day love. I'll just have a chocolate milkshake and a strawberry gelato, thanks."

Bit old for that, aren't you? Thom said inwardly. *It's the sort of thing a kid would order.*

"I'm on holiday, mate," Morton told him defensively as if overhearing Thom's thoughts.

Thom was slightly disconcerted. Surely the detective wasn't telepathic? "That's good," he said uncertainly. "How *is* work?"

"Oh, you know. Busy...stressful...long hours...and everyone hates us. But that comes with the territory."

"I can imagine." Thom briefly glanced down at his empty pad. "I appreciate you taking the time to talk to me today. I just want to get some background information from you. I know you went to school in Redfern and then joined the police, so I think you have some useful insights."

As he said this, he felt Morton press his knee against his under the table. He didn't find the sensation as disagreeable as he thought he should.

"Just ask away, mate." Morton gazed into Thom's eyes. He pushed harder with his knee. "I'm here to help."

Thom sat up and pulled his legs away from him. "And I appreciate it, *Detective Sergeant*."

There was a pause.

Morton guffawed. "It's so cute the way you get all stern and formal. Very English."

"Rob, *please!*" Thom tried not to laugh. "This is serious."

He knew that he was enjoying the attention a little too much.

"Okay!" Morton raised his palms into the air, as if surrendering. "I'll be serious for you."

The waitress brought his order to the table. Morton took a slurp of the milkshake through a straw and attacked the gelato with a spoon.

"Mmmm. This is good. Do you want to share it with me? We can get another spoon for you."

"I'm fine, really."

"Are you sure?"

"Yes, honestly."

"You're too healthy." Morton put his spoon down. He slid his hand under the table and squeezed Thom's thigh, digging his fingers in.

"Rob!" shrieked Thom in protest. Morton's grip made him wince and he tried to prise his fingers off. "Look, *this* is *really* inappropriate."

The attention had now become a problem, and he was visibly annoyed.

Morton pulled his hand away. "I'm sorry, mate." He looked stung by Thom's sharpness. "Just having a bit of a joke with you."

"That hurt," Thom chided.

"I said I'm sorry."

Thom looked steadily at him across the table. "Just so you know, I live with somebody, and I'm really not interested in getting involved in *anything*."

"I totally respect that, mate," Morton assured him. "If you don't mind me saying, *this somebody* is a very lucky guy."

"Okay," said Thom forgivingly. "Can we get back on topic?"

"Absolutely." Morton took another couple of slurps from his milkshake.

"What I really want to talk to you about is TJ Hickey."

"Yes, TJ," the detective murmured. "I knew him"

He looked away and bit his lip. There was a faraway look in his eye. "I feel so bad about that kid" he said with a tremor in his voice. "He was a beautiful boy in his own way."

Thom saw his opportunity.

Now this is interesting. I need to play it carefully.

"Rob," he said gently. "I understand you must have divided loyalties, and I'm not here to judge you. I just want to understand. Anything you tell me is off-the-record and it won't go any further."

Morton stared downwards and nodded. He looked troubled.

Thom carried on: "TJ was being followed that night, wasn't he?"

Silence. Morton's eyes were dark with misery. His head still lowered, he reached over the table and took Thom's hand in his.

Thom squeezed back. "What happened, Rob?"

Morton slowly lifted his head and looked Thom in the eye. "Do you really want to hear it?"

This is it! Thom thought excitedly. *He's going to tell me.*

"Yes," he replied. "Yes, I do."

"The truth is..." began Morton. He stopped and looked away, and then back at Thom. "The truth is" he said again, his voice harder this time. "It was just a freak accident."

The detective's eyes had turned steely.

"There's no conspiracy. No cover-up. The kid was just unlucky. But maybe that's not what you want to hear."

Thom realised he'd been well and truly stonewalled. The detective had played him, and he was certainly a half-decent actor. He tried to withdraw his hand, but Morton wouldn't let go.

"It's easy to overthink things." The detective locked eyes with Tom. "And dangerous too."

He released Thom's hand and smiled benevolently at him.

"I see," said Thom coolly.

Morton turned his attention back to his gelato. Thom watched as he finished eating. Wanting to salvage something, he tried another line of attack.

"You can see why Aboriginal people feel harassed, can't you? Especially after TJ's aunt was arrested."

"It's a horrible, horrible situation." Morton shook his head regretfully. "We can only do our best."

Thom persisted. "Well, the conduct of the police has been an issue, hasn't it? There was that Royal Commission a few years ago."

"That's old news, mate," Morton said dismissively. "Things have changed. We get sent on courses these days. Like conflict management. I did one at *your* uni. I learnt *so* much."

Thom realised he'd been defeated by his glib deflection. The detective had clearly intended to waste his time. But why had he bothered? Surely this was a waste of his afternoon off.

Morton had finished his milkshake now. He pointed at Thom's empty cup. "Do you want another one?"

"No, I'm fine." Thom looked around for the waitress. "We should get the bill."

"It's on me, mate."

"No, I shouldn't..."

"I insist." Morton pushed his chair back and stood up. "My shout."

He went and paid at the counter while Thom packed away his notepad and pen.

"Thanks for that," he said when Morton came back.

"You're welcome, babe. Are you ready?"

"Erm, yes." Thom gathered up his bag.

On the way out, Morton held the door open for him, and briefly touched the small of his back. Outside, the sun had reappeared from behind the cloud.

They stood facing each other on the street. Thom assumed they'd be saying their farewells.

He was about to thank the detective for his time, but Morton spoke first.

"If you've got a minute, mate, I'd like to show you something."

"I really need to get back..."

"It won't take long," Morton insisted. "Go on. Indulge me."

"Okay," Thom said reluctantly. He felt obliged to humour him.

"This way." Morton pointed in the direction of the beach.

Chapter Fourteen

The detective led Thom down the street onto the beachfront, strolling a couple of paces ahead. His hands were buried deep in the pockets of his hoody. They walked across a carpark and onto the beach. It was quiet, apart from a few surfers and swimmers out on the ocean.

"Where are we going?" Thom asked as they traipsed across the sand.

"Just over there," the detective replied. He pointed, in the distance, to a rockpool underneath granite cliffs.

What the hell is he playing at? Thom wondered to himself.

He regretted letting the detective overcome his resistance.

They carried on walking for a couple of minutes.

"Nearly there, mate," Morton insisted as they approached the rock pool.

Once again, it was as if he'd heard Thom's thoughts.

They didn't stop at the rockpool. Instead, they crossed through it onto rocky terrain on the other side. Their path was darkened by the cliff face looming over them.

Morton's flip-flops squelched on the wet sand. He climbed up onto a rock in front of them and turned around.

"Come on!" He waved his arm at Thom.

Thom hauled himself up. Looking around, he saw they were some way from the beach now, and there was no-one else around.

Morton grinned, looking pleased with himself. "This is the famous Coogee-to-Bondi Walk."

"I take it we're not walking all the way over to Bondi," said Thom warily.

"No, mate," Morton replied. "I just want to show you something." He reached out to Thom. "Hold my hand," he demanded.

Thom hesitated. He could feel his boundaries being trampled over again. He tried to remonstrate. "I don't think ..." he began.

"What's your problem, mate?" snapped Morton. "No-one can see us, if that's what you're worried about."

It's not that! Thom said inwardly.

Feeling he wasn't in a position to argue, he gave Morton his hand. The inside of detective's palm felt warm and rough. Once ensnared by his powerful grip, Thom found himself pulled up onto a boulder.

"And here we are," Morton announced.

He put his hands on the back of Thom's shoulders and manoeuvred him to the edge. There wasn't really enough room for the two of them. Thom could see there was quite a drop to the craggy, shingly surface below. He guessed it was about two metres. Not enough to be fatal but even so. He felt Morton's chin on the back of his head and realised the detective had him pinned down.

"What are we looking at?" he asked, keeping his voice steady. He didn't want to give off any hint of panic.

Morton squeezed Thom's shoulders. "This place has special memories for me. It was the scene of my first homicide case."

He raised his arm and pointed towards the cliff.

"We found the body of a boy...about your age over there. Some bastards chucked him off that cliff, and he was *so* badly mashed up. *I* had to tell his mother."

"It sounds very traumatic," Thom said after a pause.

He wondered if his tone was a bit dry.

"Oh, it was, babe," Morton sighed. "I can't tell you."

"Well, thank you for sharing that with me." Thom tried to step back.

But the detective was immovable. He dug his fingers deeper between Thom's shoulder blades.

"It's sad story," he went on. "The problem with this boy was that he was a bit of a smart-arse. He upset the wrong people by asking too many questions. Eventually, they wanted him out the way."

"Did you catch them?" Thom asked, although he'd already guessed the answer.

Morton shook his head.

"A lot of horrible, horrible shit happens in this town. But you don't want to worry your pretty little head about that, babe. You should just focus on having a nice life with Craig."

Thom felt his blood cool when he said this. How did Morton know Craig's name? He hadn't told it to him.

Morton stepped back and pulled Thom away from the edge.

"Let's go."

He turned around and scrambled back over the rocks. Thom followed, but less surefootedly. They retraced their steps through the rock pool and back onto the beach. Again, Morton sauntered a couple of paces ahead, his hands in his pockets.

When they got to the carpark, the detective stopped and pulled his phone out. He'd had a text message. He read it and smirked to himself before turning to Thom.

"Sorry, babe. I've gotta run. I was gonna give you a ride home, but something's come up."

"Please, don't worry," Thom said magnanimously. "I'm more than happy to get the bus."

This was true enough.

Morton put his phone back in his pocket. "Well, I'll see you around, babe. Take care of yourself."

Thom watched as he hurried towards the carpark. He realised the detective's shiny, black car was parked there. He saw him unlock it and get in.

Well, that was enlightening. In its own way.

On the bus back into the city, he replayed the afternoon in his own head. He was in no doubt that the detective had intended to give him a stern warning. It was obvious why. The police had something to hide.

Sunlight is the best disinfectant.

It occurred to him he should be more wary of Morton. Still, Thom couldn't *really* imagine the detective harming him. He'd obviously been lent on to give him the hard word. Besides, once his story was published, he'd be safe from any reprisals by the police. It would be too risky for them.

Chapter Fifteen

Craig dropped Thom off on campus so he could go to the library. They'd driven back from Manley Beach where they'd had brunch as they often did on a Saturday.

Thom had told Craig he was meeting Lars who was, in fact, working all day. The truth was that he wanted to finish his article in peace, without any awkward questions.

Sat at a computer, he put the final touches to his work. The death of TJ Hickey was weaved through it like a thread, from the first paragraph to the last. He covered the Royal Commission and included his own vivid first-hand account of the riot. He ended with an acerbic remark about the police.

Now this is a story.

Feeling pleased with himself, he e-mailed the article to Holly's contacts. He was sure they'd all be quick to respond. Then it wouldn't be long before he was interviewed on TV. This was going to be life-changing stuff. He just had to stay calm in the meantime.

"How was your afternoon, Tommo?" Craig asked when he got home.

"It was...productive," Thom replied

As soon as he got back to campus on Monday morning, for a seminar, he checked his e-mails. It was nearly 10am. Somebody would have read his article by now. Finding nothing in his inbox, he refused to feel too disappointed. He reminded himself that he'd given his mobile number. It might be worth keeping his phone switched on.

He arrived late to his seminar and took a seat opposite Lars who was already there. Holly conveyed her disapproval with a half-glance. The class were talking about the concept of truth in journalism. Thom realised he was woefully underprepared as he hadn't done any of the reading.

The seminar was only for an hour but felt longer. Thom spent it waiting for his phone to vibrate. When it did, he'd have to decide whether to leave the room or let it go to voicemail. Half-listening, he heard Lars, who *had* done the reading, talking expertly about *epistemology*. He couldn't remember what that was.

"Anything to add, Thom?" Holly asked in front of everybody when Lars finished.

Thom had been caught off guard. "Erm..." he mumbled.

His classmates stared on expectantly. He was mortified to be caught out like this and felt himself going red in the face.

"Well..." he began, hoping desperately that something would spring to mind.

He then rambled about something he remembered reading weeks ago. Holly regarded him coolly as he stuttered and faltered.

"Thanks, Thom," she said when he'd run out of steam. The hour was now up.

She turned her attention to the whole room. "Okay, great stuff, guys. This has been a good session. Just a reminder about our drinks next Thursday. From 7pm at the Bank Hotel in Newtown. I'll see you there."

The room was pervaded by the scraping of chairs as it was vacated. Lars waited for Thom by the door.

"How did your meeting with the cop go?" he murmured discreetly.

"Really interesting," Thom told him. "There's definitely something going on..."

They were interrupted by Holly who'd been hovering. "Sorry, guys. Thom, do you have a moment?"

"Sure."

Lars made to leave. "We'll catch up later," he told Thom.

Holly waited for Lars to close the door behind him. She peered at Thom. "Is everything alright?"

"Fine" he replied. "I'm sorry I was late."

"It's not that. You seem very distracted this morning. And you obviously haven't done the reading. It's not like you."

"I've just been a bit caught up with my article." Thom tried to reassure her. "But it's done now, and I've sent it off. Thanks for all your help by the way."

"No worries." Holly seemed mollified. "Let me know how you go with it. But just a word from the wise, Thom. Stay focussed and keep your expectations realistic. It takes time to build a career."

Thom nodded in agreement. "I know."

For the next week, he checked his e-mails several times a day. Nothing. His frustration made him increasingly agitated.

"You've got to give them time to read it" Craig said, mildly exasperated, one evening.

Thom had logged onto his laptop for the third time.

"I guess you're right," he sighed wearily.

By now, he'd told Craig that he'd sent it off but said nothing about the content.

Eventually, he received a couple of politely worded rejections. They thanked him for his submission, but the article was 'not quite right for us'. They wished good luck with his future endeavours.

Fuck you! He screamed inwardly.

It was the day of Holly's drinks. Thom went into the library yet again to check his emails. But he no longer expected to find anything. To his surprise, there was an e-mail waiting for him from Geoff Crozier, of *the Australian* newspaper. It was titled 'Your article'. Excited, he opened it.

'Tom,

'You sent me this article about the TJ Hickey case. Firstly it's too long and not that interesting. There's heaps of waffle about government policy. Who cares? The big revelation is that there's strife between the police and the Aboriginals. AND that Redfern has a drug problem. You reckon?! Not sure what they're teaching you at UNSW these days. But in my opinion, these graduate programs aren't a substitute for talent.

Geoff'

Thom stared at the screen for several minutes. He reread the e-mail again and again, the words stinging more each time. His work had been judged, by a professional, and it had been found terminally lacking. Clearly, he had no future in journalism.

He logged out and went for a walk through the campus, contemplating its grey rectangular buildings. He was wasting his time here, he decided. He'd been deceived by his own vanity. The only reason he'd got onto this graduate programme was because his parents had paid for it. But what else was he going to do with his life? He felt heavy with gloom.

Chapter Sixteen

"You seem a bit down," Lars observed to Thom.

They were on their way to Holly's drinks in Newtown. Thom had called by Lars' house beforehand. It was early evening, and the sun was setting, turning the sky orange pink.

"I've had a shitty day," Thom replied.

"Why? What happened?"

"My writing is boring and I'm talentless, apparently."

"What!" shrieked Lars. "Who said that?"

"Geoff Crozier of *the Australian.* I sent my article to him. It's not the first rejection I've had but at least the others were polite about it."

"You shouldn't let them get to you." Lars shook his head wearily. "Because you know what's really going on here, don't you?"

"Nope."

"It's the old media having their last gasp. They're dinosaurs! The newspaper industry is dying on its arse. If you want to know where the future is, look at the *new* media. It's all online with websites and blogs. Now *there's* a possibility for you."

"What do you mean?"

"Well, why not start a blog?" Lars suggested. "It's the easiest thing. You could publish your story online. I think it would get a lot of interest."

Thom found himself intrigued by the idea. Lars was probably right about the old media feeling threatened, and it seemed a shame to let his work go to waste. He felt there'd be something quite empowering about generating his own coverage.

They had a long walk to the bar down King Street, with its indie bookshops and vegetarian restaurants. Every subculture was represented here, and they passed dreadlocked hippies, goths and even the odd punk along the way.

When they got to the Bank Hotel, Thom remembered how confused he'd been, arriving in Australia, to hear pubs called "hotels". He and Lars made their way through the sports bar at the front to the beer garden where Holly had reserved a couple of tables. Outside, it was busy. The outdoor heaters were switched on because the evenings had begun to cool. But the retractable roof was pulled firmly back.

Glancing around, Thom saw there were about twenty people squashed around both tables. They were mostly classmates but there were a few people he didn't recognise. Holly was chatting to a couple of her faculty colleagues at the far table. She waved at him when they made eye contact.

Someone yelled "Last Chance!" at Lars.

It was Chris, a particularly garrulous, extroverted classmate of theirs. He was sat at the other table with a couple of girls who looked familiar. Chris was an aspiring sports journalist with whom Lars had a sort of friendly rivalry. Lars jokingly called him his "arch nemesis".

Lars raised his hand in greeting. "Hey!"

He and Thom went over and sat down next to Chris and the two girls. Chris introduced them as Amy and Kylie. Thom then got up to buy drinks for him and Lars from the bar. When he came back, he drank his quickly. He hoped it would help him overcome this odd detachment he was feeling.

Lars and Chris competed, like stags, to impress the two girls. Lars often called Chris "a jock", sometimes to his face, because of his love of football and he liked to think that he was his antithesis. But it struck Thom, as he watched them try to upstage each other with their jokes and their banter, that they were actually very similar.

Before long, it was Lars' turn to buy a round of drinks. Thom gratefully accepted the second bottle of Corona he was given. It seemed to go to his head quickly as he drank it, and he found it difficult to focus on the conversation. Looking across at the other table, he saw that Holly was now talking to Archie who he hadn't seen arrive nor expected to see this evening. Sliding out of his seat, he went over to say hello.

"Young Thom!" Archie greeted him as he approached. "How are you?"

Holly smiled and shifted aside encouraging Thom to take the space between them.

"I'm alright," Thom replied, sitting down on the bench.

"Thom's finished his story," Holly told Archie. "And he's sent it off to the press."

"Yes," said Thom tightly. "And I've heard back..."

Holly looked at him in anticipation. "And?"

"They said that I've written a non-story and I'm completely talentless."

"Oh mate," gasped Archie. "That's rough."

"Who said that?" Holly sounded outraged. "It's very unprofessional."

"Geoff Crozier of *the Australian*."

"Geoff Crozier!" cried Holly. "Oh, you don't want to take any notice of him. He's just a glorified sub. He's not exactly a great talent himself."

Thom shrugged despondently. "Well, it's hard to believe that someone like him doesn't know what he's talking about."

By now, he was feeling extremely sorry for himself. He wanted sympathy, and he'd drunk too much to be embarrassed about it.

Holly put her hand on his shoulder. "You need a thick skin in this industry. Don't take it to heart."

Archie chipped in with some counsel of his own. "Holly's right, young fella. You've just got to keep on going and rise above it."

"I will." Thom tried to sound more positive. "I'll regroup in the morning."

"You've just had a bad day," Archie assured him. "Things will look better tomorrow."

Thom nodded. He felt uplifted by their display of support.

He then heard Lars calling from the other table.

"Thom! Chris is getting shots. Do you want one?"

Lars didn't wait for his response and called out to Chris. "Yeah, Thom will have one."

Thom muttered "I shouldn't really mix drinks."

"I think you deserve to bend your own rules a bit, today," Holly told him. "Go on."

When he went back, Lars handed him a tequila shot. Chris and the girls also had one each.

Lars held up his shot glass. "On your marks!" he boomed. "Get set. Go!"

They downed their shots in tandem. Thom felt the effect of the tequila straightaway. The beer garden seemed to be swimming around him. The sounds of laughter and chatter blended into a single cacophony, and his vision became blurry.

"God, that's strong stuff" he heard himself say, slumping against the edge of the table.

Chris nudged him. "Do you want another Corona, mate?"

"Yes, please."

After Chris came back from the bar, Thom's phone rang. It was Craig. He was driving back from Newcastle where he'd met a client that afternoon.

"Where are you, Tommo?" he asked. "Are you still in Newtown?"

"Yep. You?" Thom was deliberately monosyllabic. He didn't want Craig to think he was drunk.

"I'm just driving down the Parramatta Road. Do you want me to pick you up?"

"That would be great. By the way, you shouldn't be talking...on your phone...while you're driving."

"Yes, Tommo. You can tell me that again tomorrow when you're nursing your hangover."

When he hung up, Thom saw Lars was now sharing a bottle of red wine with Amy and Kylie. His arm was wrapped around Amy's shoulders as if he were using her to prop himself up. He was talking animatedly, jabbing his finger against the table.

He's even more shit-faced than I am Thom thought.

In his inebriated state, he felt like he was drifting in and out of sleep. Around him, people and conversations seemed to swirl as though he were dreaming. Eventually, Craig appeared in the beer garden, dressed in a suit, carrying a beer.

Lars looked up. "Hey, Craig."

"Lars," said Craig in acknowledgement and sat down next to Thom.

"Craig is Thom's partner," Lars told Amy. He still had his arm around her.

"Oh," she nodded.

"You look a bit worse for wear, Tommo," Craig said to Thom.

"I've had...a...long...day," Thom slurred, taking a sip of his Corona.

Sometime later, Thom found himself standing around a barrel with Craig, Lars, and Chris. He remembered Holly briefly coming over to say goodnight before she left. Most of the others, including Amy and Kylie, had gone by now.

Chris was, by now, at his most rumbunctious. "So, *Last Chance,*" he said to Lars. "What is your real name?"

"Lars Chance *is* my real name," Lars insisted. "I changed it by deed poll."

Thom became more alert when he heard this. He and Craig knew the story of how Lars became Lars. But not many other people did.

"What did you do that for?" Chris asked.

"It was after a court case," Lars told him. "I was cleared."

Thom anxiously tried to catch Lars' eye, sensing danger. He wouldn't be telling Chris any of this if he were sober.

"What did you do?" probed Chris, clearly enthralled.

"I didn't. That was the whole point."

"What happened then?"

"I was charged with manslaughter. I found my friend, Ben, dead from a heroin overdose. The cops thought I was responsible because we used together."

"Fuck me, Last Chance!" exclaimed Chris, "I never had you down as a junkie!"

"I'm not," said Lars evenly. "Not anymore. I kicked that shit after the court case when my parents sent me to rehab."

"Wow." Chris shook his head in wonderment. He took another swig of beer. "So, what is your real name then, Last Chance?"

Lars tapped his nose. "I never tell anyone that."

"Okay," said Chris giving up. But his curiosity wasn't yet sated. "How did you prove you didn't do it?"

"I didn't have a motive," Lars shrugged. "I had no reason to give him that hot-shot."

This didn't quite ring true with Thom.

Wait a minute.

Something was bothering him, but he didn't know what.

The conversation was halted by Craig yawning ostentatiously. "Righto," he said looking at his watch. "I think it's time we were going. It *is* a school night."

"Can I have a ride home?" Lars asked him.

"Sure, mate."

They said their goodbyes to Chris outside the bar. Craig's jeep was parked in a side street nearby. As they made their way, Craig supported a wobbly Thom by holding his right elbow. Lars stumbled and staggered alongside them.

"*Look* at the state of you two," Craig said chidingly. "I feel like a suburban dad picking up teenagers from a party."

"I'm not sure you're quite old enough to be *Lars'* father," Thom muttered.

Lars snorted. "It's funny you should say that. Because I've often wondered if you're with Craig because you have daddy issues."

He was instantly punished by the gods for this when he walked straight into a wheelie bin and landed on top of it.

Thom let out a howl of laughter. "Oh my god!" he cried, convulsed by hysterical giggles. He stood pointing at Lars semi-prostrate form.

Craig released Thom's elbow and hauled Lars up by the scruff of his neck. "Up you get. Honestly, you are a disgrace, Last Chance."

They bundled Lars into the back of the jeep and drove off. He dozed, resting his head on the window, talking to himself every so often. He stirred when Craig turned onto his street.

"Is Cady in?" Thom asked him.

"Who knows where that mad bitch is?" Lars murmured sleepily. "She's a crazy, crazy girl."

Thom suddenly realised what had bothered him back at the bar.

"Lars, do you remember when we were talking about your friend, Ben?

"Yeah."

"You said that that someone gave him *a hotshot.* But I've always thought it was an *accidenta*l overdose."

"Accidental?" Lars sat up. "No, no. Ben was involved in some serious shit. He didn't just use heroin. He sold it. He had some deal going with this dirty cop, and that's who I think gave him the hot-shot. But I couldn't prove it."

Before Thom could ask anything else, Craig interjected.

"Will you be okay getting in, mate?"

"Yeah, I'll be fine," Lars replied.

Thom got out the passenger door and pushed the seat forward to let him out.

"Thanks, guys," Lars raised his hand in farewell. "See you soon."

He clambered up the steps to his front door as Thom and Craig watched from the car.

"He's going to have a worse hangover than you, Tommo," Craig chortled. "And he'll be nursing it in that rat-hole too."

Thom woke the next morning with a mild headache himself. But it didn't stop him going to the gym for his daily workout. As he pedalled away on the stationary bike, he thought more about Lars' idea for a blog.

Craig had gone to work by the time he got back. After taking a shower, he opened his laptop on the kitchen counter. Once he was online, he went about creating a blog which was easy enough to do, as Lars said. He called it 'Thom in Oz' and wrote in the bio that he was a journalism student.

He decided his story needed a bit more editing. Taking Geoff Crozier's advice, he watered down the detail about policy. He now had to decide on the title. Reading it back, it came to him straight away. He called it 'Death and Denial in Sydney'. This was it - the finished article, his first blog post. He took a breath and pressed 'Publish'.

Chapter Seventeen

"Woah!" Lars cried, transfixed by the screen. "You've had ten thousand hits in five days. That's pretty impressive for a new blog."

"Hmm," Thom murmured. He was subdued rather than elated.

They were sat on stools, looking at Thom's blog, in the dusty hallway of Lars' house, which he used as a study. His laptop was open in front of them on the tiny writing desk. Next to it was an unfinished nude painting of Cady. The adjoining galley kitchen looked like a bomb had hit it; it smelt even worse as no washing up had been done for days.

"You've had seven hundred comments," Lars observed

"I read a few of them," said Thom tightly. "That was enough."

The vitriol of these responses had shocked him, and the overt racism was even worse. He'd been lambasted him for his naivety and accused of bad faith. These comments weren't always expressed with any great eloquence.

'*Its the abos who are crims mate not the police stop ur bullshit*'

'Fuck off back to England if you don't like it here. There are plenty of darkies there to take you up the arse'.

"They're not all bad," Lars insisted.

This was true enough. Some had come to praise Thom and been thoughtful and scholarly. He felt bad about not responding, but there were just too many.

"Anyhow," Lars continued. "This all shows that you're having an impact. I reckon you could even get some advertising revenue"

"Really?" Thom was sceptical.

"Well why not? Advertisers pay for coverage. You just need to keep posting and getting the hits."

"That could be a bit of a mission. It takes dedication to piss off hundreds of people on a daily basis."

"You don't have to be controversial every day. It's all about building up a following."

They heard the door open at the front of the house. Cady had come home from work early. She slammed it shut and stormed through, her face blotchy and tearstained.

Lars was surprised to see her. "Hey, what are you doing back? Is everything okay?"

Cady tore her bag off her shoulder and angrily threw into a corner, upsetting some pottery.

"I quit!" she hissed. "I'm sick of working in that whorehouse. *And I'm sick* of being a whore."

With that, she stamped up the stairs. Lars and Thom exchanged glances.

"Is she alright?" Thom asked.

Lars sighed wearily. "I'll give her a moment to calm down. If I go and talk to her now, she'll just get angry and blame me for everything. Women! You're lucky you don't have these problems."

"No," Thom replied. "I just have different problems."

"True," Lars agreed. "Have you spoken to Craig?"

"Nope."

"How long is this going to go on for?"

"Up to him."

"You're just waiting for him to blink first, aren't you? Like you always do when you have one of your little spats."

"Maybe," Thom conceded.

Lars yawned. "Oh well, I suppose I better go up and talk to her." He clearly wasn't enthused by the prospect. "Are you okay to shut all this down?" he asked gesturing at the laptop.

"Sure. I'm probably going to bed soon myself."

"Cool." Lars got up. "See you in the morning."

When he disappeared up the stairs, Thom sat and stared at the laptop screen for a moment. His eyes fixed on the title of his blog post; 'Death and Denial in Sydney'.

Has it been worth it?

He then shut down the laptop and trudged cheerlessly up to the room he'd been sleeping in since the night before. It was a dreary, bare cell with one tiny window and a mattress on the floor. Lars and Cady had intended it for a lodger but never got around to getting one. His phone was on charge in a corner, next to his discarded backpack.

He checked for messages or missed calls from Craig but there weren't any. Feeling deflated, he lay back on the mattress. He wondered what Craig was doing back at home.

The night before, they had had an almighty great row about the blog. For the first few days, Craig had known nothing about it. As it began to attract more and more attention, Thom decided to tell him. He casually mentioned it as Craig was leaving for work after breakfast.

"Oh," Craig said clearly taken aback. "I didn't know you were going to do that. Couldn't you get any media interest?"

"No," Thom replied. "Probably a bit too marginal for them. Lars thought it would work as a blog."

"Did he now?" Craig raised an eyebrow. "Have you had much reaction?"

"A bit."

"What's it called?"

"What?"

"Your blog. What have you called it?"

"Oh. It's called *Thom In Oz*."

"Hmm. Interesting title, Tommo." Craig leaned down to pick up his briefcase. "Righto. See you later."

He pecked Thom on the lips, as was his habit, and closed the door behind him.

That evening, when Thom came back from the supermarket, he saw the kitchen light was on. Craig's briefcase was in its usual spot next to the door. He took his shopping into the kitchen where he found him sat on the stool in front of the window, with his laptop open.

"Evening" Thom said cheerily.

Craig didn't respond. His back stayed turned.

Thom dropped his bags on the counter and peered over his shoulder. He saw that he was reading the blog. His upper body seemed to be clenched.

"What do you think?" Thom asked nervously. He would have liked effusive praise, but he knew he wouldn't be getting any.

Craig slammed the laptop shut and swung around. His mouth downturned, he fixed Thom with a dark stare.

"You don't give a flying fuck what I think," he growled. "Otherwise, you wouldn't have written this trash."

Thom waited a moment before replying. "So you don't like my writing then?" he said, drily.

"DON'T FUCKING GET SMART WITH ME!" Craig roared.

Thom stepped back, shaken by his virulence.

Craig carried on. "You're just a spoilt, entitled, little white boy with no fucking clue about anything!"

"What? Why...what have I done" Thom stuttered.

"You said you were dropping the police angle. That's what you told me."

"No, *you* said that." Thom was beginning to recover himself. "Why are you so angry about it anyway?" His shock was now giving way to bubbling resentment. "Oh, I get it!" he cried, laughing sardonically. "I know what this is *really* about."

"What?"

"It's about you wanting to control me," said Thom looking him in the eye

"No. I'm trying to protect you."

"I don't need fucking protecting!" Thom heard himself shriek.

Craig folded his arms. "Do you have any idea how much trouble this is going to cause?"

Thom shook his head. "Why do you say that?"

"Just *look* at what you wrote. You said the cops are corrupt, and that Aboriginal kid was mixed up in it. You also say there's been some sort of cover-up."

"I haven't exactly *said* that."

"No, of course you haven't. You've just *implied* it."

"I've invited the readers to draw their own conclusions."

"Fuck!" exclaimed Craig, exasperated. "You just can't go around doing this sort of shit. This is the problem with you."

"*What* is the problem with me?"

"Like I said, you're spoilt. You've lived your whole life in this bubble. And you don't really think anything bad is going to happen to you. Because there's always been someone to bail you out."

"Is that what you think?"

"It's what I *know!*"

"Well, let's talk about what's wrong with *you.*" Thom was determined to turn the tables now. "You'll accept any sort of corruption and any sort of injustice as long as *you're alright.* You once told me how you bribed that Malaysian cop to get out of paying a fine. *That* fucking stinks. These people get away with it because people like you give them a free pass."

Craig sprung up from his stool. "You might look down your snooty, judgmental little nose at me," he snarled. "But your lifestyle, and all of this, is paid for by me!"

"Oh, so you think I've been bought and paid for, do you?"

"PRETTY MUCH!"

Silence.

Thom bit his lip and inhaled deeply through his nose. "Well, get this, Craig" he said, his voice trembling. "You *don't* own me, you *don't* control me *and* you *don't* get to tell me what to write!"

He turned on his heel and walked out of the kitchen. Grabbing his backpack, he opened the front door.

"Where are you going?" Craig called after him.

Thom ignored him. He slammed the door as he left and stomped towards the lift. His whole body felt possessed by a righteous fury.

How fucking dare he treat me like some fucking rent-boy he raged inwardly. *Arrogant fucking arsehole! Nobody treats me like that.*

Down in the foyer, he responded curtly to the concierge's friendly greeting. He went outside, into the walled grounds, walking past the swimming pool and the tennis court, and left by a side gate. He steamed through King's Cross furiously ignoring attempts to lure him into dens of iniquity.

Before long, he found himself sat in the tiny all-night café where he'd met Lars, drinking coffee. He found the framed photographs on its walls pleasantly distracting. The elderly Italian owner darted around delivering food, drink, and waspish remarks.

His phone rang in his pocket. Seeing it was Craig, he didn't answer. He wasn't going back tonight. There was a fundamental principle at stake here. But he'd need somewhere to go in the meantime, so he called Lars.

When he got to Newtown, Lars and Cady listened sympathetically enough. Thom launched into a highly dramatic tirade in their lounge room about Craig. He suspected afterwards, once he'd calmed down, that they thought he was overreacting. But they lent him their spare room anyway and made him welcome.

Chapter Eighteen

THOM WAS ON CAMPUS HEADING TOWARDS THE LIBRARY when he saw Holly Mailman striding towards him. She didn't return his smile.

She didn't bother with a greeting either. "I read your blog. It's certainly causing quite a stir."

This clearly wasn't something she considered to be a good thing.

"Yes," Thom replied. "I gather."

Holly's lips were pursed. "I'm very disappointed in you actually."

"Really?" Thom was taken aback. "Can I ask why?"

It wasn't like he'd expected Holly to be entirely pleased. But he didn't think she'd feel strongly enough to be confrontational about it.

"I don't know where to start." Holly shook her head disbelievingly. "None of it is what we agreed. Then there are all the baseless insinuations. But do you know what really gets me? You used *my* name and my contacts to try and sell it. There's just no way I'd risk my professional reputation like that."

"Let me put your mind at rest," Thom pleaded. "I completely rewrote it for the blog. What you read is not what I tried to sell."

"Well, that's something I guess," Holly said huffily. "But here's another thing. You seem to have this idea that Aboriginal people are powerless victims. Do you really think we need you as our white saviour?"

"That is *not* what I think!" Thom felt himself going red with mortification.

"Really? Because it sure sounds like it."

"Well, it isn't."

Holly looked at him intently. "You know, Thom, if you're going to make it as a journalist, you're going to have to learn the value of professionalism. That's what makes or breaks you. You really haven't done yourself any favours with this publicity stunt. See you in class."

She walked off abruptly, leaving him feeling chastened. He realised he should have known this would happen. Still, he was desperately sorry to be so diminished in her opinion. Holly was someone he respected. Once again, he found himself wondering if the blog had been such a wise move.

Inside the library, he checked his e-mails again. He'd set up a separate address for the blog, which Lars suggested, thinking it would be good for advertisers. He'd had a surprising number of messages already.

Most were spam but there were a couple that weren't. He was struck by one sent by a Jerome Thomson from within the university. It was titled 'In strictest confidence'. Curious, he opened it.

'Hi Tom,

I'm a graduate law student here at UNSW. But that's not why I'm contacting you.

Until recently, I was the Aboriginal Liaison Officer for the police in Redfern. I've read your blog and would like to talk you in the strictest of confidence. Can we meet in person? I'd prefer not to discuss this by email.

Thanks,

Jerome'

Thom was intrigued. He wondered what this Jerome could have to tell him. It wouldn't do any harm to find out, he decided. He replied to say he was happy to meet and gave his mobile number. He had this feeling Jerome would be calling soon. His misgivings about the blog quickly receded to the back of his mind.

On his way home, early evening, he had shopping to do and so he stopped by the Broadway shopping centre. He went first to the Target store to buy clean underwear and socks. He'd run out, and he didn't know how much longer he'd be staying in Newtown. Then, he went to the supermarket as he'd offered to cook dinner for Lars and Cady.

He walked home, laden with carrier bags, along City Road. It was a cool, dusky evening. The roar of the rush hour traffic blared in his ears. He felt a prickling sensation on the back of his neck as he sensed he was being watched.

Glancing around, it was impossible to know where from. There were thousands of cars passing in both directions. The semi-darkened Victoria Park, on the other side, was surely too far away.

His phone vibrated in his pocket. He assumed it would be Jerome, so he stopped to answer, dropping his bags on the pavement

"Hello." His gaze settled on the door grille of a nearby house.

"Thom Allerton?" inquired an unfamiliar male voice.

"Yes."

"I have a message for you, Thom." The voice sounded pleasant enough to begin with.

There was a pause. Then the tone and pitch changed.

The voice snarled: "Back off you little poof or you'll end up like TJ Hickey."

Thom was uncomprehending at first. "Who is this?"

"Don't ask any more of your fucking questions," the caller hissed and hung up.

Thom stood frozen in shock on the pavement, clasping his phone. Looking wildly around him, he saw threat everywhere. He had to get back to the safety of Lars' and Cady's house. But what route? He felt dangerously exposed out here on the road, but he was equally keen to avoid the poorly lit side streets. As he started to run, he felt like he was in a jungle being stalked by an unknown predator.

"What the hell happened to you?" demanded Lars

Thom had rushed in through the front door, visibly shaken and out of breath.

Cady stopped the DVD she and Lars had been watching, and they looked at him expectantly.

Thom left his bags by the door and sank onto the couch, taking a moment to compose himself.

"I've just had a threatening phone call," he told them.

Lars frowned. "Who from?"

"I don't know!"

"Well, what did they say?"

"They said that if I don't stop asking questions, I'll end up like TJ Hickey."

"Whoa!" exclaimed Cady. "That's scary."

"Do you think this is about the blog?" Lars asked.

"Yes. Yes, I do. You know, I've just had this feeling like I'm being watched."

"You haven't mentioned it."

Thom shrugged. "I thought I was being paranoid."

His phone suddenly rang in his pocket, startling the three of them, and they exchanged anxious glances. Thom pulled it out and looked at the screen with trepidation.

"Is it them?" Cady asked nervously.

"No, it's Craig," Thom replied. He let the phone carry on ringing.

Lars looked exasperated. "Well, aren't you going to talk to him?"

"I can't right now," Thom said irritably

He hoped Craig would leave a voicemail.

"Well, it sounds like someone's trying to scare you," Lars told him. "It's the price of fame. I honestly don't think you should worry too much about it."

"But I *am* worried about it," Thom fretted. "I feel like a sitting target, and I'm now scared to go outside. I just don't think the blog is worth all this hassle."

"That's what they want you to think," Lars insisted. "Look, if they were serious, you wouldn't be sitting here now. Dangerous people don't tend to give warnings. Trust me."

"That's reassuring"

But Thom didn't sound the least bit reassured.

"You know what, Thom," said Lars trying to rally him. "I think you're feeling a bit vulnerable because of this thing with Craig. Call him back! He obviously wants to work things out, and I know you want the same. Trust me, you'll feel better."

"Yeah, I guess you're right," Thom conceded. At that moment, he wanted nothing more than to be back at home with Craig.

He called Craig back later that evening before he went to bed, as he was sat cross-legged on the mattress upstairs.

"Tommo," said Craig when he answered.

"I'm just returning your call." Thom tried to sound unruffled.

"Yes, Tommo. Have you made your point now?"

"I hope so."

"Good. Are you going to come home?"

Thom waited a moment before answering. "Yes, I am."

There was another pause on the line. He knew Craig was smiling to himself on the other end.

"Excellent," Craig said, his tone neutral. "Do you want me to come and get you from the rat-hole?"

"It's a bit late." Thom stifled a guilty giggle about "the rat-hole". "How did you know I was here?"

"I just knew, Tommo. How about I pick you up in the morning?"

"That would be great" Thom said gratefully.

"Is 9am too early?" Craig asked. "I know that no-one over there gets up before midday."

"That's *not quite* true. But yes, I'll see you then."

"Righto, Tommo. See you tomorrow."

He hung up. Thom lay back on the mattress feeling happy, relieved and a little elated to be going home. He felt like a dark, heavy cloud was lifting. He decided that in the morning, he'd have a shower back at the apartment. It would be good not to have to endure Lars' and Cady's dank, sticky bathroom again.

At least he had some clean socks and underwear. He sat up and reached into his Target carrier bag. Inside, he noticed a folded piece of paper that was too big to be a receipt. Opening it up, he saw a handwritten message.

'BACK OFF PRETTY BOY'

Chapter Nineteen

THE NEXT MORNING, CRAIG ARRIVED ON THE DOT. HE insisted on carrying Thom's backpack to the jeep. Apart from that, his manner didn't give much away. Lars and Cady, who *were* up, saw them off at the front door. Thom was still feeling groggy after a very uneasy night's sleep.

"Did you enjoy your stay at the rat-hole, Tommo?" Craig asked as they drove off.

"It had its moments" Thom replied, permitting himself a slight smile.

They didn't say much on the way home. As Thom gazed out at the streets which were lit by morning sunshine, he realised that Sydney had become sinister and menacing to him, like London had before he left.

There's been one consistent factor in all of this. Me.

Perhaps he was in a situation of his own making. Ignoring all advice, he'd gone wading into something that had nothing to do with him. He'd fought with Craig and antagonised Holly. His career prospects hadn't exactly been helped either. And now, he was under threat from mysterious persons unknown. Why had he done it?

Am I addicted to self-sabotage?

When they got in, Craig made coffee and they sat down together on the couch, looking out at the balcony. Thom was glad to be back in this fortress-like building with its concierges and security guards, and he felt much safer. In the meantime, he and Craig needed to talk.

They had a quiet moment sipping coffee before Craig spoke up.

"I'm sorry I lost my temper with you, Tommo. I shouldn't have yelled like that."

"It's okay," Thom said quietly.

"But there is just something I really don't understand."

"And what's that?"

"Your motives," Craig replied. "I just don't get why you're always on some lefty crusade. It's not like you've been disadvantaged, or underprivileged, is it? You grew up in a nice home, with loving parents, and all the trimmings in your leafy English country town. And your life here is pretty good."

"I've never pretended otherwise. It doesn't mean I shouldn't care about things outside my own life.

"That's not what I'm saying, Tommo. It's just you have *this need* for controversy, and it doesn't make sense to me. Is it because you want attention?"

Thom raised his eyebrows. "That's a pretty confronting sort of question."

"I'm sorry to be so blunt," Craig told him. "But I just want to understand."

Thom put his mug down on the table and sighed. "I don't know why," he said wearily. "I just know that I have this talent for getting into trouble. And I've certainly landed myself in it this time."

"What do you mean? What's happened?"

Thom turned to face him. "I've been getting these threats. About the blog. Someone actually called my phone to warn me off. And they dropped a note in my shopping bag while I was out.

"What did they say?"

"That I'll end up like TJ Hickey. When I told Lars, he said it was nothing to worry about, but that was before I found the note."

"How long's all this been going on for?"

"The phone call and the note - yesterday. But I've had this feeling for days now."

Craig cleared his throat. "It sounds to me like they're just telling you to fuck off, Tommo. What are you going to do?"

"I don't know what I can do," Thom shrugged. "I don't really want to go to the police. Maybe I should just delete the blog post."

"Yeah, I think that would be for the best," agreed Craig. "I'm pretty sure they'll just leave you alone after that."

"Will they? How do you know?"

"Because I know the criminal mind," Craig replied. "I'd feel happier too. You're safe here at home but I don't want you to be a prisoner here and never go out."

"Neither do I."

Craig put his mug down and pulled Thom towards him.

"You just have to pick your battles carefully. That's how you win them."

"I know," murmured Thom, nuzzling into his shoulder.

Craig kissed the top of his head. "Welcome home, Tommo."

Thom was in the Queen Victoria Arcade in the CBD. He wanted to buy himself a pair of Adidas trainers he'd coveted for ages. He had some time to himself as Craig was at a motivational workshop for most of the weekend.

The arcade was busy with Saturday shoppers. They were treating themselves to food, drink and luxuries under its steel and glass roof. As Thom crossed the tiled floor towards the escalator, he felt glad to be among them. There was something reassuring about their leisureliness. For the first time in a long time, he felt carefree. There was a reason for this. That morning, he'd deleted the blog post.

He found the store he wanted, a couple of floors down, where he tried on the trainers. They were black with white stripes, and he loved them, so it wasn't a difficult decision. As he left the store with his new purchase, his phone rang. He thought twice about answering when he saw a number he didn't recognise. But something in him felt emboldened today.

"Hello,"

"Is that Thom?" Another unfamiliar male voice

"Yes, it is," Thom replied tensing up.

"Hi Thom. It's Jerome. We spoke by e-mail."

Thom relaxed. "Hi there."

He'd forgotten about Jerome.

"I know this is really short notice," Jerome said apologetically. "But are you free today for coffee? I'd really like to talk."

Thom hesitated. He thought he should tell him he was finished with the blog. But there was this compelling note of urgency in Jerome's voice. Despite everything, Thom really wanted to hear what he had to say.

"Sure. Where would be good for you?"

They arranged to meet an hour later in the Surry Hills. After Thom hung up, he exited the arcade onto George Street, which always reminded him of Manhattan. He was relieved, after the last few days, not to be constantly looking over his shoulder. But glancing at his reflection in a store window, he saw a shiny black car, like Rob Morton's, cruising past him on the street. When he turned around, it had gone.

The coffee shop Jerome suggested was near a small park. For somewhere so close to Oxford Street, it felt surprisingly secluded, and there weren't many people around. As Thom approached, he saw a young Aboriginal man about his own age sitting at a stool in the window. He walked in and went over to him.

"Jerome," he said extending his hand. "I'm Thom."

"How're you going, Thom." Jerome motioned at him to sit down. "Thanks for coming."

"No problem. Can I get you a coffee or something?"

"Let me get you something." Jerome sprung up. "What do you want?"

"Okay, thanks. I'll have a long black"

When Jerome came back from the counter, they settled in the window.

Thom took a sip of his coffee. "So you're a law student?"

"I'm doing a graduate diploma," Jerome replied. "That's so I can *practice* law. But I did a law degree before I got side-tracked."

"Side-tracked? By joining the police? How did that happen?"

"Well, I graduated. But I wasn't ready to be a corporate lawyer like my parents wanted. My goal is to go into politics. So I thought I'd do something in the community. I wanted to prove that not all conservatives are uncaring arseholes."

"Conservative?" queried Thom, raising his eyebrows.

"Yeah, mate. I'm a John Howard supporter."

Thom snorted involuntarily. "Isn't that a bit unusual for Aboriginal people?"

He instantly wanted to push the words back into his mouth, mortified by his own crassness.

Jerome just laughed. "Not as much as people think. A lot of Aboriginal families *are* conservative, with a small 'c'. They believe in hard work and looking after your family."

"I hope you don't think I was making assumptions," said Thom trying to row back.

"Well, you sort of were. But it's fine. Anyway, I didn't come here to talk about politics. I read your blog and thought it was awesome..."

"Thank you."

"A lot of the stuff you said about the police in Redfern is pretty accurate."

"Well, I guess you'd be in a good position to know," Thom suggested. "Being a police officer there yourself."

"I wasn't," Jerome told him. "I just worked for them as their Aboriginal Liaison Officer. I was like their link to the community."

"I see. What made you leave?"

"Because of what happened with TJ Hickey and the riot," Jerome said quietly. "I saw it coming a mile off. I warned them months ago and they just ignored me."

"And that's why you resigned?"

"It wasn't *that*." Jerome shifted uncomfortably. "It was after they threatened me."

"Threatened you?" Thom looked at him open mouthed. "Why?"

"To stop me giving evidence to the inquest into TJ Hickey. They said if I didn't shut up, I'd end up like him."

"Oh my God!" Thom sputtered. "That's happened to me too!"

"What?"

"It's true. I've had these mysterious messages with exactly the same warning."

"Fuck," gasped Jerome. "This is why I wanted to talk to you."

"Sorry, what?"

"I want to go public," Jerome insisted. "I want to blow the whole thing wide open. I thought I could give you a story for your blog."

Thom looked out the window and contemplated the enormity of this. He was scared of getting involved again. But then, this was how these people got away with it, he thought. They threatened and intimidated to enforce their own little *omerta*. If Jerome was prepared to take a risk to expose them, why shouldn't he?

"So would you be prepared to be go on record and be interviewed?" he asked.

Jerome nodded.

"Okay," Thom nodded. "Just so you know, I deleted the post this morning, but not the blog itself. I'm willing to help with this. But we'll have to arrange to meet at another time. I need my Dictaphone and a list of questions. Are you okay with that?"

"Totally." Jerome gulped down the rest of his coffee.

They were about to leave when something occurred to Thom.

"Tell me, is Detective Sergeant Morton involved in any of this?"

Jerome didn't reply but the look on his face answered Thom's question.

They said goodbye outside, shaking hands again, and headed off in different directions. Thom cut up a lane that was lined with garage doors. As he walked, his sixth sense warned of another pair of eyes upon him. Looking around, he couldn't see anyone. The children's playground in the park opposite was deserted, the swings swaying gently in the breeze.

Still, he quickened his pace. He then heard footsteps behind him, but he didn't get to see who it was. Before he could turn around, he was coshed over the back of the head, and he fell to the ground. As he lay, knocked out, on the pavement, a hooded figure bent down over him and scooped him up

Chapter Twenty

His head hurt, and he'd dreamt of being submerged in a black void. When he half-opened his eyes, he lifted his head to see that the room was in darkness. Closing them again, he sunk back into the pillow, wanting to sleep some more.

Thom had no memory of going to bed. He didn't even know what time of day it was. He thought it was probably morning and he'd overslept. Rolling onto his side, he pulled the sheets up over his shoulders and decided to make sense of it later.

He became aware of Craig's body lying in the bed next to him. Like him, he was also completely undressed. Perhaps it was the middle of the night. There was something strange though. They weren't on their usual sides of the bed. Craig was always very insistent about this.

We must have come home very drunk last night.

He felt Craig stir and wrap his arm around him. Enveloped in his sinewy embrace, Thom sleepily ran the tips of his fingers across Craig's forearm. He had this dreamlike notion that he felt different in some way. He didn't smell the same.

"Craig, what time is it?" he mumbled.

"It's after 6pm, babe."

That wasn't Craig's voice. Thom's eye's snapped open. He sat up and turned around, his eyes adjusting to the dark. Then, he saw that he was in bed with Rob Morton.

"What the fuck!" he gasped.

Morton sat up and switched on his bedside lamp, revealing them to be in a motel room. He smiled knowingly.

"Where am I?" Thom barked at him.

"Chill, babe," Morton implored him. "You're *here*. With *me*."

"How did I get here?" Thom demanded.

"Oh, it was terrible, babe." Morton shook his head as if reliving a trauma. "I found you lying face down on the street. It looked like you'd been mugged or something. And I couldn't just leave you there."

Thom remembered having coffee with Jerome and talking about an interview. After that, there had been the footsteps behind him on the street...

"Did you see what happened?" he asked. But he already knew it was pointless to ask.

"No, mate," the detective replied.

Thom looked at him in askance. "A normal person would have taken me to hospital. Or called the police."

"But I am the police, mate," Morton spoke in a tone of utter reasonableness, as if to a mad person.

"So why are you in bed with me?"

"I just felt like a little snooze," Morton said breezily. He then laughed nastily. "Why? Are you worried what Craig would think? Imagine if he saw us now. In bed together!"

"We are *not* in bed *together!*" cried Thom indignantly. "I've had enough of this." He swung his legs onto the floor and looked around the room.

"Where are my clothes?"

"In the boot of my car."

"Well, can you go and get them?"

"Yeah, in a minute, mate," the detective yawned. He lay back down on the bed, crossing his arms behind his head.

"No, now," Thom insisted.

Morton turned his face towards him, his eyebrows raised.

"You're an imperious little thing, aren't you?" he said looking down his nose. "Well, you're just gonna have to wait."

"That's it!" snapped Thom, throwing off the sheets and springing up. "I'm getting out of here."

He stood by the bed, looking around for something, *anything*, to cover himself with. Morton, meanwhile, looked him up and down, appraising his body.

"Yeah, mate," he sniggered. "If you want to walk out there, butt-naked, be my guest. It would be fucking hilarious."

Thom stormed into the bathroom to look for a towel, but there weren't any. Feeling ridiculous and defeated, he climbed back into bed, pulling the sheets up over his shoulders. Morton glanced at him out of the corner of his eye. He smiled to himself and closed his eyes.

For a few moments, Thom sat up in bed, thinking. Eventually, he sighed defeatedly. "Why did you bring me here, Rob?"

"I was worried about you, babe" Morton replied, his eyes still closed. "I found you on the street, looking like a little abandoned rag doll, and I thought to myself, that's a boy in trouble. I've got a bit of a thing about boys in trouble."

"I bet," muttered Thom.

The detective ignored this.

"Well, I suppose I have been in trouble," Thom conceded. "I've been followed around and threatened and hit over the head. But you'd know all about that, wouldn't you?"

Morton opened his eyes. "I'm not sure we're on the same page, babe."

"Really?"

"Yeah. It's the strangest thing because I thought – last time we saw each other - we'd come to an understanding. But you're *still* running around town asking more of your questions."

Thom looked at him probingly. "Have you got something to hide, Rob?"

"No, mate," Morton said exasperatedly. "I'm just mystified. I get that you're too gung-ho to worry about your own safety. But maybe you should think about your boyfriend's. He likes to ride around on his Harley, doesn't he? I hear terrible things from the traffic division boys about motorbike accidents."

Thom snapped when he heard this barely veiled threat. Without thinking, he launched himself at Morton, grabbing his jaw.

"If you ever do anything to Craig, I'LL FUCKING KILL YOU!" he yelled. "I swear to God."

Morton swung up, with a hiss, like an enraged predator, swatting away Thom's arm. He pushed him down onto the mattress, clasping his throat with one hand and pinned his wrists back with the other.

"FUCKING WHAT!" he roared, his eyes turning black. "YOU'LL FUCKING WHAT?"

Thom tried to free himself, but he was completely immobilised. The detective was at least twice his weight.

"Go on. Fucking say it again," growled Morton.

A bead of sweat trickled down his hairless torso.

"I said that if you do anything to Craig, I'll fucking kill you," Thom said calmly this time.

Morton tightened his grip on his throat.

"Don't think so, mate. I could snuff you out right now. Fuck! Maybe I will. Nobody would ever know."

His rage had given away to a sort of animalistic excitement. There was a bloodlust in the smile playing at the corners of his lips. He pinched Thom's windpipe, making him cough and splutter.

"Boys like you disappear all the time," he murmured.

Thom, not even able to scream, began to thrash about in desperation, but it was hopeless. His eyes were wet with tears of fear and frustration.

At the very moment he thought he was going to black out, Morton suddenly let go. He gasped with relief.

"Just don't threaten me again," the detective said glaring. "I don't like it."

Thom just stared back at him without replying. Morton's expression softened and he leaned in closer so that their faces were almost touching.

"Kiss me," he whispered. "Go on. I know you want to."

"No," Thom said obstinately.

"Why not?"

"Because you're a dangerous psychopath."

"No, I'm not," said Morton evenly.

"What? Do you think this is how normal people behave?"

Morton rolled back onto the other side of the bed. "The problem with you, babe, is that you see everything in black and white. And people aren't black and white. They have many different shades."

"Yours are pretty dark," Thom retorted.

"We're all dark in different ways, mate," said Morton leaning back. He stared up into the air as if in contemplation.

"Is that what you think?" Thom asked.

The detective didn't respond. They lay together in a thoughtful silence before Thom decided it was time to strike a bargain.

"If I agree not to write any more about TJ Hickey," he ventured, "will you let me go?"

"Mate, you're not a hostage." Morton sounded irritable. "If you want, I'll go and get your clothes and run you home."

"Yes. Please." Thom was almost grateful. "That would be good."

It was almost too easy.

Morton lifted off the sheets and slowly got up. He made a point of parading his naked body in front of Thom, smiling, as if encouraging him to admire it. He reached under the bed and pulled out some clothes and a pair of trainers.

"You didn't leave *your* clothes in the car then?" Thom observed.

The detective hoisted up his underpants. "I'm not an idiot, babe."

Once he was dressed, Thom noticed he was wearing the same hoodie he'd worn down at Coogee Beach. After fishing his car keys out of his pocket, Morton made for the door.

"Be right back. Don't go anywhere."

He guffawed at his own joke as the door shut behind him. Once he'd gone, Thom got out of bed and looked around the room. He saw that there was no phone, TV or even a clock.

Peering through the blind, he made out the room was on the third floor, overlooking a carpark, just off a busy highway. Apart from a garage in the distance, there were few other signs of civilisation. He had no idea where he was, or even if he was still in Sydney.

Thom had assumed Morton would only be gone a few minutes. He'd got back into bed and waited, and then waited some more. After what seemed like an age, he went back to the window to see if the detective was in the carpark. But there was no sign of him. Outside, it was now dark.

Increasingly agitated, he was pacing up and down the room. He realised it must have been hours since he'd eaten. He had no way of telling the time in here. By his reckoning, Morton had been gone at least two hours. Thom wondered what he'd do if he just *didn't* come back.

Eventually, the door opened, and the detective reappeared, with Thom's backpack slung over his shoulder. He was also carrying a takeaway food bag which smelt of warm spices. They assailed Thom's nose, reminding him how famished he was.

Still, he was in no mood to be polite. "Where the hell have you been?"

The detective looked taken aback by his tone. "I went to get some food, mate. I figured you might be hungry".

He wasn't wrong. Thom was positively faint by now.

Morton tossed the backpack across the bed. "Your clothes are in the bag."

"Thanks."

Thom opened it and quickly put his clothes back on. It felt good to be dressed again, like being back on dry land. Rummaging inside the bag, he found his phone, wallet, and keys. Meanwhile, Morton sat down on the couch, and unpacked the takeaway onto the coffee table.

"I got Indian. Is that alright for you?"

Thom thought he should refuse, on principle, to eat any of it, but he had no energy left for resistance.

"Fine," he replied.

He sat down next to him and helped himself. In the end, neither of them ate much. When they'd finished, Morton gathered up the leftovers.

As they were about to leave, Thom remembered something.

"I bought a new pair of trainers today," he told the detective. "They were in a bag. Did you see them?"

"Don't think so, mate. You just had your backpack when I found you. What brand were they?"

"Adidas."

"Oh, okay," said Morton as if something had clicked. "*That's* what happened. You were mugged for your trainers."

Thom was almost impressed by his commitment to this fiction.

Despite everything, Thom was glad to be driven home. He realised the motel was out in the Western suburbs. Before long, they were heading down the Parramatta Road towards the city. They spoke little along the way, but Morton would periodically deliver these peculiar soliloquys.

"You know, life is *so* easy," he insisted to Thom at one point. "I don't understand why people make it so difficult for themselves."

Thom was silently disbelieving when he heard this.

You are completely unhinged as well as corrupt.

It then occurred to him that Morton might not be corrupt at all. He could just be utterly, utterly mad, which would certainly explain a lot. But it would have to be a dangerous sort of madness.

The detective ploughed through the dense Saturday night traffic around Oxford Street and dropped him outside his apartment building.

"Great to see you, mate," he said casually when Thom got out.

Thom wasn't sure of the form for addressing former captors. "See you," he muttered distantly and slammed the car door behind him. He heard the detective drive off as he marched towards the building.

Inside, he stopped in the foyer to check his phone. It was after 10pm, and he'd had a couple of missed calls from Craig who'd be wondering where the hell he was. But Thom could hardly tell him. In the lift, he decided to say he'd been at Lars' house. As an explanation, it was suitably vague and believable.

Chapter Twenty-One

"At last!" Craig switched off the TV and got up from his chair. "I thought you'd been kidnapped!"

Before Thom could answer, he picked up an envelope off the coffee table and waved it at him.

"Here. This came for you today."

Thom took it from him and saw the governmental postmark. He realised it would be about his residency application. Craig watched him intently as he opened it and read the letter inside.

"Well, what does it say?"

Thom's eyes were fixed downwards as he carefully read each line: "It says... I've been granted permanent residency in Australia". He looked back up at Craig, the news sinking in. "Oh my god!" he whooped.

He dropped the letter and leapt into Craig's arms.

"Oh, Tommo," breathed Craig. "That's fucking amazing!"

They jumped up and down on the spot together, hugging.

Thom was beyond elated. "I can't believe it's finally happened."

"There's a bottle of Champagne in the fridge," Craig told him. "You get the glasses."

They found what they needed in the kitchen and took the Champagne out onto the balcony, where they popped the cork in front of the indigo sky. Beneath them, the city lights flickered and shimmered.

Craig poured Thom a glass and handed it to him. "This is the beginning of the next chapter, Tommo."

Thom took a sip of his Champagne. "I'm certainly ready for that."

All his recent trials and tribulations now seemed insignificant.

"Cheers." Craig clinked their glasses. "Here's to our future."

"To our future."

"You know, Tommo, this means we can move to NZ anytime we like."

Thom hadn't thought of this. Still, it was exciting to have so many options.

Craig raised the subject again, the next day, while they were doing the laundry. He was emptying the tumble dryer as Thom loaded the washing machine with their bedsheets.

"I've been thinking, Tommo. You're finishing your course at the end of the year, aren't you?"

"That's right."

Thom emptied a cup of powder into the machine and put the lid down.

Craig shut the tumble dryer. "Well, there's nothing to stop us going to New Zealand in January."

"In January? Really?" Thom was surprised. "What about your franchise?"

"I can sell it."

This felt a little sudden. Thom had imagined their move *much* further in the future. But then again, a new start might be the best thing for them, especially after the last few weeks. No more ominous shadows and lurking threats.

No more self-sabotage.

"On one condition," he told Craig. "I want to live in Auckland or Wellington, not out in the country."

"Of course, Tommo. I know you're a city boy through and through."

Later, Craig went out for an afternoon ride on his Harley. Thom had reluctantly volunteered to put the dried sheets back on the bed, a task he disliked and always took him ages. He took a break at one point to gaze out the bedroom window.

Down far below, he could see the gothic spire of St John's Church. In the churchyard, there was a gathering of people dressed in their finery for a wedding or a christening. Watching them, Thom felt this strange yearning. He realised he hadn't been invited to anything like that since he was a teenager.

It would be nice to belong somewhere.

A couple of days later, he was on campus for one of Holly's seminars. He hadn't seen her since she'd confronted him about the blog. She gave nothing away during the seminar and seemed pleasant enough. Thom thought about staying behind afterwards to make amends. He could apologise and he'd be able to tell her the blog post had been deleted.

But he decided against because there was something still unresolved. He needed to speak to Jerome. After the seminar finished, Thom paced up and down outside the library, steeling himself to call him. He had to let him know that he wasn't going to help. Trying to find the words, he felt like a terrible coward. No doubt Jerome would think so too. But he'd made his mind up.

Eventually, he decided what to say and called Jerome's number, but the line was dead. He frowned and tried again but to no avail. The number seemed to have been disconnected. There was something odd going on.

Next, he went into the library to check his e-mails. He reread his exchange with Jerome, but it didn't reveal anything. Then he looked more carefully at his e-mail address and realised the domain name was wrong. It wasn't a university one at all.

"What the fuck?" he hissed aloud

Jerome had used a fake e-mail address. He'd clearly set out to mislead from the start. But why? Was he even who he said he was?

Thom knew it was pointless for him to try and guess. But there was someone he could ask.

When Thom arrived at the Aspire office, Ellen was coming out the front door. Today, she wore a Malcolm X t-shirt, looking every inch the professional activist.

"You again, Bubbles," she said with a mocking smirk. "Haven't seen ya for ages."

"Is Archie in?" Thom asked.

"Sure he is." She opened the door and called into the office. "Archie! His Royal Highness is back."

Thom stepped past inside as she closed the door behind her. After a moment, Archie emerged from the back of the building.

"Hello, mate." His greeting was distinctly offhand. "What can I do for you?"

Thom guessed the reason for his coolness. But he decided not to say anything.

"Hi Archie. I've come to ask you something."

Archie puffed out his cheeks. "Well, that depends, mate. I wouldn't want anything I say to be taken out of context."

"You're talking about the blog, aren't you?" Thom said warily.

"Yes, I am. I know Holly's pretty dirty with you about it and I can't say I blame her."

"I really didn't expect it to cause offence," Thom insisted. "I should have thought more carefully."

Archie visibly relented when he heard this. "Well, we all make mistakes," he said understandingly. "Don't take this the wrong way, Young Thom. I know you mean well. It's just that every time you open your mouth, the white privilege is very audible."

"I know I've made some missteps," Thom conceded.

"Yes, you have," nodded Archie. "And I get it. You're in a country where you sort of speak the language, but you don't really understand the culture and the history and all the sensibilities."

"That's true enough. But I am learning. It's a work in progress."

Archie smiled at this. "Look, I can see you're keen to educate yourself. And I've got something that might help you. Give me a second."

He disappeared into the back, for a couple of minutes, and came back with a book; a dusty smelling hardback, which he handed over.

"This is a collection of essays. If you read them, you'll get to see an Aboriginal perspective of this country."

Thom looked at the cover. It was called *White Man Got No Dreaming*.

"Thank you very much." He felt touched, as if he'd been taken into a confidence. "When do you want this back?"

"Whenever," Archie replied. "What was it you came here to ask me?"

"Oh yes." Thom had almost forgotten why he'd come. "Do you know someone called Jerome Thomson? He used to work here for the police, as an Aboriginal Liaison Officer."

Archie shook his head. "No. There's never been anybody of that name."

"Are you sure?"

"Totally. I have known every single one of those police liaisons for the last twenty years. Not one of them has been called Jerome Thomson."

"But..." Thom began before trailing off. He looked searchingly at Archie for an answer he couldn't give.

"I think somebody's been having you on, mate," Archie sighed.

When Thom thought about it later, he decided that Jerome had to be an accomplice of Morton's. It was the only thing that made sense. He should have found this deeply unsettling. But instead, he felt oddly liberated; it meant that he was obliged to no-one. Whatever the truth was about the death of TJ Hickey, it wasn't up to him to find it. He was now entirely free to walk away.

Chapter Twenty-Two

Thom was sat at the kitchen counter working on an assignment. He'd got behind with his studies because of recent distractions.

Craig came in, in his leather jacket and biker boots, carrying his helmet.

"I'm just going out for a ride, Tommo. I'll be about an hour."

"Okay," Thom murmured distractedly as he carried on scribbling.

His phone vibrated when he had a text from Lars inviting them to have brunch with him and Cady at a nearby café.

"They're at that place on Stanley Street," he told Craig. "Do you want to come?"

"*You* go, Tommo. I want to get my ride in. I'll swing by later if you're still there."

Thom abandoned his work to go and meet Lars and Cady, after Craig went out. The café was on a long, sloping street which curved downwards before stretching up towards the CBD. It was lined with cafes, restaurants, and hostelries, which were heaving with the studiedly casual Sunday morning crowd.

He found them sat at a table outside and they had brunch, al fresco, beneath the awning. When they'd finished eating, they drank coffee and talked about the election in America.

"John Kerry has got to win," Cady insisted. "Especially after Iraq. I can't believe Bush got elected in the first place."

"I'm not sure Kerry is going to cut it," mused Lars.

"I don't see why not," Thom countered. "Being a Vietnam vet must be a huge advantage."

"Yeah, but the Republicans even seem to be turning *that* against him."

They were distracted from this conversation by the roar of Craig's Harley Davidson as he drew up on the pavement in front of them. His arrival attracted glances from neighbouring tables. As he dismounted, Thom noticed he was wearing a backpack.

Pulling off his helmet, he came over and sat down with them. "Good brunch?"

"Hey Craig," Lars said greeting him.

Thom squinted at Craig with mild suspicion. "I didn't notice you take the backpack out with you. You don't usually."

"No, Tommo." Craig opened the bag. "I went back home for the spare helmet. I thought maybe you'd like to go for a ride afterwards."

Thom raised his eyebrows. "You know I'm terrified of that thing."

"But *I'm* not!" Cady interjected. "I'd *love* to go for a ride."

"Would you?" Craig looked surprised.

"Really I would. Can we go now?"

"Craig might want to have a coffee first," Lars suggested.

"No, it's fine." Craig pushed his chair back. "Let's do it. Come on."

He and Cady got up and Craig handed the spare helmet to her. Thom and Lars watched from the table as they navigated getting on the bike together. Cady patted her hair down before putting on her helmet. It looked incongruous with her polka dot dress.

"Be careful!" Lars called over to her.

She wrapped her arms around Craig's waist, as the engine began throbbing, and shrieked when they roared off. At tables along the street, heads turned to watch them as they sped up the hill towards the CBD.

Lars chortled. "I don't know how I feel about them riding off into the sunset."

"They'll get sick of each other soon enough," said Thom drily.

"Ha!" Lars took a sip of his coffee. "It's great news about your residency, by the way. Glad you're sticking around."

"Except we're not, exactly."

"What?"

"We're moving to New Zealand next year."

"Seriously?"

"Yep."

Lars inhaled deeply as he processed this. "Well, I'm pretty surprised. You've always said that you wanted to stay here."

"Well, I *did,*" Thom sighed. "But I've really messed things up by pursuing this TJ Hickey story, and it's spoilt everything. I want a new start."

At that moment, Craig and Cady whizzed back past on the other side of the street. Cady squealed and hollered as she waved at them. She and Craig were gone in an instant as the Harley zipped up the hill.

"Are you going to do anything else with the blog?" Lars asked, resuming their conversation. "Seems a shame to just drop it."

Thom nodded pensively. "Yeah, it sort of does. But it's really not worth all the hassle. I just..."

Before he could finish, Craig and Cady came back on the bike, stopping on the kerb, the engine still running. Cady lifted her visor.

"That was amazing!" she called over to them. "I think I'm going to get my own bike."

Lars looked alarmed. "Oh God. Please don't."

"Can we go again?" she asked Craig pleadingly.

"Maybe just another couple of circuits around the block." Craig looked across to Thom. "Is that alright with you, Tommo? You're not in any hurry?"

"No, you go," Thom replied. He was just glad to be able to carry on talking to Lars.

He and Lars watched as Craig and Cady took off again. Once they'd gone, he turned back to Lars.

"I feel like I've just repeated history. Until all of this happened, I think I was happy living here. But now, I'm paranoid and always looking over my shoulder, like I was in London."

"I can understand that," Lars told him. "I went through exactly the same thing when Ben died. But I had a reason to be paranoid; I'd been set up to take the fall for a dirty cop."

Thom shook his head uncomprehendingly. "How do you move on from something like that?"

"Changing my name helped," Lars replied with a laugh. "But seriously, you have to accept what's happened and let go of it. Eventually, you learn to live again."

"But don't you want some sort of justice for Ben?"

"I wanted full-on vengeance and retribution. But it's all gone now. You can't change the past."

Thom looked at Lars intently. "If you could prove what happened to Ben, would you?"

"How would I?" Lars shrugged. "I was acquitted because I convinced the jury it was an accidental overdose. I can't now turn around and say someone gave him a hotshot."

"I see your point," Thom conceded.

He found himself with a renewed appreciation of Lars' resilience. The more he thought about it, the more he thought it was about time he found some of his own.

A few days later, Thom and Lars were on campus, after a seminar, trying to decide what to do about lunch.

"I need to go to the toilet," Lars announced when they were outside the library. "Back in a minute."

He disappeared inside and Thom waited at the bottom of the steps. Glancing around him, he noticed how busy the campus was this afternoon. The library lawn was fully occupied by groups of students eating, chatting, and lolling around in the sun. Dozens more people darted past in all directions.

Behind him, Thom heard someone whistle for his attention. Assuming it was Lars, he turned around. He was shocked to find a grinning Rob Morton standing in front of him. The detective was wearing his work suit and carrying the bag with Thom's new trainers.

Thom stared at him in askance. "What are you doing here?"

"Looking for you, babe," Morton replied. "I thought you'd want your flashy new trainers back."

He handed the bag over.

"Erm...thanks," said Thom dubiously. "Where did you find them?"

He'd almost come to believe that he *had* been mugged for the trainers.

"Let's just say that I managed to *recover* them," Morton told him. "Anything to make you happy."

Thom decided not to probe this any further. "Well, thank you for that.".

He was pleased to have his trainers back. But the detective's sudden appearance on campus was disconcerting. How had he even known where to find him?

"You're so welcome, babe." Morton winked at Thom. "I have to say I almost didn't recognise you with your clothes on.

He said this very loudly and chortled, earning them an inquisitive look from a girl passing by. Thom felt himself going slightly red.

"Thank you, Detective Sergeant," he said stiffly.

Surely, he'd take the hint and go.

"Well, it's been nice, babe." The detective gave one of his exaggeratedly benevolent smiles. "But I gotta run. Stay lucky.'

He turned and swaggered away as Thom watched his departing back, hoping he wouldn't be seeing him again. He seemed to have powers that were almost supernatural. By now, Thom had plenty of reason to be wary.

He wondered where Lars had got to and turned back towards the library only to see him standing a few steps above looking on. His face was ashen white.

Thom sensed something was wrong.

"Is everything alright, Lars?", he called as he walked up the steps towards him.

Lars stared, as if he'd been visited by a ghostly apparition. "That man you were talking to..." he murmured.

"That's Detective Sergeant Rob Morton," Thom said uneasily. "He's the cop I've been talking to."

"Fucking hell, Thom. He's fucking dangerous."

Thom's eyes widened. "You know him?"

"Yeah, I know him alright." Lars was shaking now. "It was him who killed Ben."

Chapter Twenty-Three

"WHAT HAPPENED?" THOM'S EYES WERE FIXED ON LARS.

They were now sat in a coffee shop on campus. After Lars' revelation outside the library, he'd decided they should go somewhere more private.

Lars spooned sugar into his coffee. "I've never really talked much about Ben to you, have I?"

"Not *really,*" Thom replied.

When he thought about it, he realised Lars almost never talked about his life before he was Lars.

"Ben and I were at uni together," Lars told him. "Studying English. He wanted to be an actor. He was like the good looking, charismatic one everyone was drawn to, and I was just the sidekick. It was a bit like you and me, but in reverse."

"Fuck off!" spluttered Thom outraged.

Lars giggled at his reaction. "Anyhow," he continued. "We moved into a flat together, in Newtown, when we graduated. Life was pretty tough to begin with, because there wasn't much work for aspiring actors and writers. When I say *not much,* I mean there was absolutely *zilch.*"

"I bet."

"We saw ourselves as poor bohemians, and we were certainly *poor.* We hung out with, I guess, a fairly sort of *counter-cultural* crowd. That's when we started using the brown stuff."

Thom gave a pointed look. "You mean heroin."

"Yes, heroin," Lars confirmed. "I don't think Ben really had a problem. He could take it or leave it. But I got hooked soon enough. I'll tell you what heroin's like. It's like being wrapped in a great big warm blanket on a cold night."

"Was that really what you wanted?"

"Yeah, I guess it was at the time. It took the edge off things. I was feeling depressed because I was stuck in this cycle of shit jobs and no money. Even now, I can't express how much the drudgery got to me. And I was anxious all the time. I didn't know how we were going to pay the bills."

"I can relate to that," Thom nodded. "I definitely went through a similar phase in London."

Lars sighed. "Yeah, your early twenties are supposed to be like this amazing time. But real life doesn't always live up to the hype."

"So how did you meet Morton?"

"Ben met him first. But I'll tell you more in a minute. I need more caffeine. Do you want anything?"

"I'm fine, thanks."

Lars got up and went over to the counter. He came back with a can of Coca-Cola and sat down again.

"I don't know exactly *how* Ben met him," he said opening the can. "It would have been when he started dealing."

"How did that happen?"

"Well, Ben used to get bits of paid TV work here and there. It might be as an extra on *Home and Away*, or as a runner on some other show. Through that, he got roped into running these little drug errands. Then he met someone who gave him some heroin to sell around town. And he was good at it. He was soon supplying the whole of Newtown and part of Redfern."

"How did you feel about that?" Thom probed.

Lars took a swig of his coke. "Don't judge me," he said sheepishly. "But I was pretty happy with it. At least for a while. Because Ben always had shit loads of money and he was fucking generous with it. He paid all the rent and the bills and bought all the food. He didn't ask me for *a cent*. It meant I could focus on my writing, and I wrote some of my best stuff in that period."

"I can understand," Thom said awkwardly. "But I guess you were living in a bit of a fools' paradise."

He hoped he didn't sound judgemental.

"Yeah," Lars concurred. "It was a total fools' paradise. I realised that when Rob Morton walked into my life."

He briefly looked over Thom's shoulder, out of the window, and swallowed. His focus returned to the table, and he carried on.

"Ben told me he was working with this cop. I soon realised that he wasn't *working with* him, he was *working for* him. The cop ran the whole operation. He started coming over the flat to see Ben.

That's when *I* met him. Seemed friendly enough. They'd go into his room to talk and shut the door."

Thom's eyes widened at this. "Do you think that they were involved?"

"Involved?"

"Sleeping together."

"No." Lars shook his head. "Ben didn't swing that way. But he once told me that Morton was into skinny blond boys. Now *you'd* fit the bill! No wonder he's so keen to talk to you!"

He cackled. Thom shifted uncomfortably in his seat.

Lars gulped more of his drink. "You know what? I was quite amused by the whole dirty cop thing. That was until Ben got scared of him."

His shoulders tensed at this point. Thom knew he was steeling himself to relive something he'd tried to forget.

Lars exhaled before going on. "Morton came over one night. He didn't say much to me, but I could tell he was fucking angry. Livid. He went into Ben's room to talk to him. I couldn't hear what he said but he meant business. When he left, Ben was shaking."

"Did Ben tell you what it was about?"

"Yes, he did. He'd fucked up very, very badly. He'd somehow managed to lose this consignment of heroin that was worth serious money. I'm talking six figures."

"Christ!" gasped Thom.

"I know," Lars groaned. "He was in serious shit. Some big, bad, fuckers were convinced he'd ripped them off. It wasn't surprising they thought that. Morton came over to tell him that he had to find it, or else."

"What did he do?"

"What *could* he do?" retorted Lars sounding exasperated. "He really had no idea where he'd lost this fucking haul. I mean he was a dickhead for losing it, but still. He didn't have half a million bucks in his piggy bank either. He was well and truly out of road."

"He should probably have just disappeared," Thom suggested.

"Well, *that's* what he was going to do," Lars insisted. "I was going to go with him. The plan was to get a train out of town, buy a car and drive to Perth. And we were all set to go."

"But that's not what happened, is it?"

Lars took a moment to answer. "No" he said quietly. "It wasn't. On the day we were supposed to skip town, I went out to get some groceries for the journey. Ben was really paranoid and didn't want to leave the flat. He told me to be careful. Anyhow, I was walking home, and I saw Morton driving away from our street."

"Are you sure it was him?"

"Yeah! It was definitely him. When I got in, I found Ben lying in bed with a needle in his arm. He was stone cold dead."

Lars looked away and bit his lip. He and Thom sat in silence.

After a few moments, Thom spoke up. "Lars, I know this is difficult. But are you absolutely sure it was Morton who did that to him?"

"Yes, I am." Lars looked him in the eye. "I know he did it because he told me."

"What! When?"

"It was in the cop shop afterwards. They took me in for questioning because Ben's death was suspicious. I was there for fucking hours, and they asked me the same questions, over and over again."

"Was Morton there in the interview with you?"

"No, he wasn't. They let me have a break to go to the toilet. Morton was already in there waiting for me. He pushed me up against the wall and grabbed me by the throat. He said I was a pathetic little junkie and told me I had to keep my mouth shut or I'd end up like Ben."

Thom found he wasn't even slightly surprised.

"Did you mention any of this in court?" he asked.

"I *thought* about it," Lars replied. "But I didn't for a couple of reasons. One, I was shit scared. Two, the lawyer my parents hired told me not to. And he was right. In the end I got off. After that, I went to rehab, came out and carried on living my life."

"And Morton's just left you alone, has he?"

"Yes. It's funny because I've always known he's still around, but I've just never seen him again. Not until today. That's like seven or eight years. Honestly, I've been completely happy to forget about him, like he was just some creature from a nightmare."

"He has been pretty close by all this time."

"Yeah." Lars sucked in his lips and nodded. "I know. Maybe I've just chosen not to see him. Because I'm a coward."

"You really shouldn't talk like that. What you went through was pretty traumatic. But you survived and moved on."

"I think I've just been in denial," Lars mused. "Seeing him strutting around like that today brought it all back. It's made me realise how much I want justice for Ben."

Thom peered at him. "You're not going to try anything stupid are you, Lars? He is, like you say, very dangerous."

Lars emitted a hollow laugh. "*Me* try anything? I don't think so. I should have, but it's too late now."

Thom wanted to be able to tell him that justice would prevail, and that Morton would pay in the end. But he knew he couldn't say it convincingly.

Lars looked up into the air and shook his head. "Fucking hell, Thom! If I'd known it was *him* you've been talking to... You really don't want someone like that in your life. You should steer clear of him."

"That shouldn't be a problem," Thom assured him. "He was only interested in me because of the story I was writing. And I've dropped that now."

"Well, that's good," Lars murmured.

He'd finished his drink now. As he slowly crushed the empty can, his eyes had a haunted look that Thom hadn't seen before.

Chapter Twenty-Four

Craig and Thom were in bed reading with their lamps on, as was their habit before going to sleep.

"I forgot to mention, Tommo," Craig said breaking the companionable silence. "We've got visitors on Saturday."

Thom looked up from the book Archie lent him. "Oh, really. Who?"

"Mike and Barbara," Craig replied. "They're coming over from New Zealand to visit her cousin, Melanie. She lives over here. I used to know *her* too."

"I don't think you've mentioned them before. How do you know them?"

"Well, Mike was a *prospect* in the Mongrel Mob, when I was running the local chapter in Lower Hutt. As for Barbara, he got together with her while she was married to someone else. Someone I knew, in fact. But that's a whole *other* story."

"Prospect?" Thom was intrigued. "Did he become a full gang member?"

"No, he didn't," Craig said reflectively. "To tell you the truth, he just wasn't cut out for the Mongrel Mob. He doesn't have that brutal edge, and it didn't help that he was white either. He's a very nice, sweet, guy at heart."

"Did he leave of his own volition?"

"I'm not totally sure. He was supposed to have his patching ceremony while I was in jail, but it didn't happen. I suppose he must have just drifted away after he married Barbara and had kids. Would have been for the best."

Thom pondered this for a moment. "This is all a bit of a surprise. You don't tend to keep up with people from your Mongrel Mob days."

"No, I don't as a rule," Craig agreed. "But Mike got in touch with Mum, and I thought why not? They're coming over for coffee in the afternoon and I said we'd have dinner with them and Melanie. They're staying at a hotel at Kings' Cross."

"I'm looking forward to meeting them. I guess you haven't seen them for ages."

"It's been *years*. I haven't set eyes on them since before I went to jail."

"That was over twenty years ago," Thom observed. "Before I started primary school."

"Yes, Tommo," Craig said through gritted teeth. "You don't need to labour *that* particular point. You'll come as enough of a shock to them. Back in those days, I was still rooting women."

"Well, I don't think you're obliged to explain anything on that score."

Thom closed his book and put it on the bedside table. As he was about to switch off his lamp, something occurred to him.

"Has anybody else from the Mongrel Mob ever tried to get in touch?" he asked.

"Ah yeah. Some dodgy fuck turned up here a few years ago and came looking for me. He wanted me to get in on some fucking drug deal. I shook him off, told him I wasn't interested."

"It's funny how the past always catches up with you," Thom said thoughtfully.

Craig yawned. "I supposed it is, Tommo."

The next afternoon, Thom was in the university library. He was supposed to be looking for reading material. But instead, he found himself thinking about Lars and Morton. He wondered if the detective's activities had attracted any media attention. To satisfy his curiosity, he went online.

He typed 'Rob Morton' and 'police' into the search engine. Some news articles popped up. He clicked on the top one from the *Sydney Morning Herald* a couple of years earlier. The headline was 'Cop cleared of assault'. The story was about a suspected drug dealer who'd had his nose broken in police custody. Detective Sergeant Morton had been found, by the magistrate, to have been acting in 'reasonable self-defence'.

"Of course he was," Thom muttered to himself.

He clicked on another article. This one was a bit older. It was about a police officer, a superior of Morton's, tried for corruption in the wake of the Royal Commission. Morton himself had appeared in court as a witness. He professed to have been "deeply shocked" when asked by the defendant to intimidate a suspect.

"I bet you were," Thom said aloud.

His eye was caught by another headline from 1999: 'I was framed says Mongrel Mob boss'.

'Mongrel Mob boss Sonny Tauroa claimed in court yesterday that the drugs found in his hire car were planted. Mr Tauroa, 40, from Lower Hutt in New Zealand, had been in Sydney for a week "on business". He was arrested by Detective Constable Rob Morton after his vehicle was pulled over on Glebe Point Road. Police found a consignment of heroin in the boot with a street value of $50,000.'

Thom was struck by the coincidence, and he made a mental note to ask Craig about it. He'd surely know something. There wasn't much else he could find about Morton. He always seemed to be on the periphery of things, a bit part player in other people's dramas.

His curiosity still unsated, Thom recalled the few details he knew about Lars' manslaughter trial. He entered them into the search engine, producing three different newspaper reports. Clicking on the top one, he saw a picture of Lars outside the court. He looked pale and spindly in his grey flannel suit. He was carrying a briefcase. The article gave his original name which Thom hadn't known before.

Lars before he was Lars.

He read the article which described, with some relish, how a diplomat's son had sunk into a spiral of drug-addiction and debauchery. Much was made of Lars' expensive schooling. Thom began to feel uncomfortable, like he was invading his friend's privacy by snooping, and so he clicked out of the screen.

Mike and Barbara arrived after lunch. Craig buzzed them in, and they found their way up to the apartment in the elevator. When he opened the door to them, Barbara shrieked and threw her arms around him. After she released him, Mike shook his hand repeatedly and vigorously. He began telling him, excitedly, how they'd managed to find the building. As he watched, Thom could see the joyousness and the awkwardness of this reunion.

"Hi, I'm Thom," he said introducing himself to Barbara, while her husband carried on with his story.

"Nice to meet you," she replied. She had a raspy, smoker's voice. "You're English, aren't you?"

"Yes, I am."

"So was my mother. I went over to London once, about fifteen years ago, for a couple of weeks."

"Did you like it?"

"Loved it!" She looked around at the apartment. "I've got to say that this is quite some place you've got here. What a view!"

Thom guessed that she was in her early fifties, which would make her a bit older than her husband. Like him, she was clad in blue denim albeit a lighter shade. Slim with high cheekbones but a weathered complexion, she wore her straight greyish-blonde hair in a tight ponytail.

Craig then introduced him to Mike.

"Good to meet you, Thom," Mike said shaking his hand firmly.

He was a short, stout man with a ruddy, reddish complexion and small eyes. He wore a check shirt underneath his denim jacket.

"I'll make some coffee," Thom told Craig. He asked Mike and Barbara whether they took milk or sugar and went into the kitchen to switch on the percolator.

Craig gestured at them to sit down on the couch while he settled into his chair. They took a moment to appreciate the vista beyond the balcony. While he was making the coffee, Thom could hear them talking about the people they'd known.

"Is Sly still around?" Craig asked them.

"Yeah," Mike nodded. "He's with this young chick now. She's always giving him grief because she reckons he doesn't love her enough."

"There was only ever one woman for him," Barbara opined. "And that was Tracie and she's been gone twenty years. When she died in jail, I just knew he'd never love anyone like that again. I've always said it haven't I, Mike?"

Craig smiled ruefully. "To be honest, I never could see Tracie getting old. It just wasn't her style."

Thom came back with a tray and put it down on the coffee table. He handed them each a mug and sat down next to Barbara.

"We still visit Sam's grave every year," Mike told Craig. "On the anniversary. A whole load of us ride up there."

"Sam was a friend of ours," Barbara said for Thom's benefit. "He was killed on his motorbike. He was only nineteen. Craig gave the eulogy at the funeral."

Thom looked towards Craig. "Did you?"

"Yeah." Craig took a gulp of his coffee. "I did."

Mike leaned forward. "I don't know how often you get back to New Zealand, Craig, but it would be great if you came with us one year. If you were around."

Craig wore a guarded expression.

"I will one day," he said quietly.

Thom could feel the shared history that Craig had with Mike and Barbara. They'd been through all sorts of things together: laughter, joy, skirmishes and adventures, and grief. But somehow, these old friends had become virtual strangers. Why had Craig isolated himself from them to live his life in exile?

When he thought about it, Thom realised that Craig had told him very little about his life before in New Zealand. He had assumed it was just something he'd wanted to get away from. But he began to realise the truth might be more complicated.

Craig lightened the tone by changing the subject, and he and Mike were soon talking animatedly about motorcycles, a shared passion of theirs. Barbara rolled her eyes and turned to Thom for a separate conversation. He found they got on well. She described her job in a women's refuge, and he enjoyed her anecdotes about the seamier side of Lower Hutt.

"The local prostitutes have their own hierarchy of who's the biggest slut," she told him. "There's one hooker who looks down her nose at this other girl. And do you know why? It's because she takes payment in cigarettes. She thinks that's really low class."

Thom roared at this. "I really had no idea so much went on in small town New Zealand."

"Oh yes."

That afternoon, Mike and Barbara had their own tourist plans. But Thom and Craig met them for dinner at the Thai restaurant in Paddington, where they'd eaten a few weeks earlier. They were joined by Barbara's cousin, Melanie, an effervescent divorcee who worked in recruitment.

"Oh my god! she cried when she saw Craig. "Where did you find this old reprobate?"

"Hello, Melanie." Craig leaned down to kiss her on the cheek, looking like a shy, embarrassed teenager.

The meal was lively and chaotic with numerous bowls delivered to the table, and confusion about who'd ordered what. Thom enjoyed listening to the old anecdotes. He got to hear plenty about Craig, or a version of him he'd never known. While sat at the table, he drank a great deal of a flowery tasting wine. He noticed that Mike's appetite for food was enormous.

After they'd finished their main course, Melanie leaned towards him. "What's it like for you?" she asked. "Hearing all this ancient history about Craig?"

"It's really quite fascinating," Thom smirked. "I always like to hear what he was up to before I was born."

This produced splutters of laughter from Mike and Barbara. Craig smiled tightly.

After dinner, Melanie took a taxi home to her house in the western suburbs. Mike and Barbara invited Craig and Thom for a drink back at their hotel. They walked up the Darlinghurst Road towards King's Cross. Along the way, they passed the towering wall of the old gaol.

Craig and Mike sauntered on ahead, deep in conversation. A couple of metres behind, Thom and Barbara followed at a slower pace. Barbara, tipsy from the flowery wine, had taken Thom's arm.

"We'll just let the boys talk about frigging bikes and frigging engines. *We* can do our mother-and-son thing."

Thom laughed awkwardly at this. But it then occurred to him how rarely he thought about his own mother. Suddenly, he found he missed her intensely.

Barbara looked on in front of her. "I'm so glad we've finally caught up with Craig. It means a lot to Mike, especially. He used to really look up to him and still does, I think."

"What was Craig like?" Thom asked. "When you knew him."

Barbara pondered this. "What was he like? He was sort of cheeky. A bit devil-may-care. I remember he always used to insist on calling me *Mrs* Murphy. I was married to someone called Murphy back then. He always said it with this glint in his eye. I thought he was a bit of a spunk to tell you the truth."

"He still is!" Thom cried in mock outrage.

"Yes," Barbara replied. "But not in the same way."

Chapter Twenty-Five

Thom left the apartment in a hurry. He was running late for Holly's weekly seminar, where Lars was meant to be giving a presentation.

As he cantered up the street towards Taylor Square to catch the bus, he passed a row of parked cars. Once again, he had this notion that he was being watched. But, in his rush, he quickly dismissed the thought.

He heard a car door open behind him, and someone get out. He didn't pay it any attention.

A man's voice then called out to him. "Hey Thom!"

Thom stopped and turned around to see Jerome Thomson, standing inside the car door, wearing a dark suit.

"You!" he hissed under his breath.

He was astounded. He hadn't expected to see Jerome again. The idea that he was Morton's sinister, shadowy, accomplice had taken firm hold in his mind.

Jerome shut the car door.

"What do you want?" Thom demanded as he approached.

"I need to talk to you. About Rob Morton."

"Really. I'm pretty sure you can talk to him yourself. Didn't he send you here?"

"Things aren't what they seem, mate," Jerome insisted.

He pulled a thin wallet from inside his jacket and handed it over. Opening it, Thom had this sense of *déjà vu.* It was the police warrant card for a Detective Constable Jerome Taylor.

"I'm with Special Crimes and Internal Affairs," Jerome revealed. "We're a unit that investigates police corruption."

Thom carefully scrutinised the card before giving it back. "You should ask Detective Sergeant Morton about *that,*" he said acidly. "I don't know why you want to speak to me."

"You're not *obliged* to talk to me, mate..." Jerome began.

"You're right," snapped Thom cutting him off. "I'm not. In fact, I'm in a bit of a hurry..."

"*But,*" Jerome persisted. "If you're prepared to hear me out, I can explain."

Thom looked hard at him.

"The thing is, *Jerome,* nothing around here is ever what it seems. Especially where the police are concerned. You've already lied to me once about who you are. Why should I believe you now?"

"I thought you might say that." Jerome reached into his trouser pocket. He pulled out a business card. "Look. I'm based at the

Police Integrity Commission. Why don't you come by the office today?"

He pressed the card into Thom's hand. "The address is on here," he added.

Thom stared down at it. "I really don't want to get involved in all this again."

"You don't have to. But you've got nothing to lose by talking to us. It's up to you."

Despite everything, Thom was intrigued. He was still determined to avoid Morton at all costs. But the prospect of revelation was tantalising. They might tell him what the detective was hiding. Then, he'd know whether his instincts had been right.

"Alright." He handed Jerome's card back. "What sort of time?"

"4pm would be good if you can make it. Just ask for me at reception."

"Fine. See you then." Thom turned to make a run for his bus.

He only just made it to the seminar on time. He noticed straightaway that Lars wasn't there. This made him uneasy. Lars wasn't known for his punctuality. But he made the effort for Holly's seminars, especially when he was the one presenting. The class sat waiting for him for a few quiet, awkward minutes.

Eventually, Holly ended the impasse. "Okay, I think we'll make a start. It doesn't look like Lars is going to be joining us. Thom, you haven't heard he's sick or anything?"

"Erm, no," Thom replied shaking his head.

"Oh." Holly frowned. "I thought you'd know."

His classmates were now looking at him as if he were somehow responsible for Lars' absence. It felt a little unreasonable. He made a mental note to call him later to find out where he'd got to.

He spent most of the day thinking over his encounter with Jerome. He decided he had to tell Lars about it when he knew more. If Jerome was for real, it raised the possibility of justice for Ben. Lars had a right to know about that.

That afternoon, he arrived slightly early at the Police Integrity Commission, opposite Hyde Park. He waited for a few minutes in reception before Jerome appeared, proffering his hand.

"Thom, thanks so much for coming." Jerome sounded slightly formal, as if they were meeting for the first time.

"That's okay," Thom murmured as they shook hands awkwardly.

"If you'd just like to come this way."

Jerome led him into the elevator and pressed the button. On the way up, they neither spoke nor looked at each other. Jerome's eyes seemed to be fixed resolutely upwards. But Thom desperately wanted to ask him about the time they'd met for coffee. Was anything he'd said about himself true? And why such an elaborate ruse anyway?

When they arrived on the tenth floor, Jerome ushered him along the corridor and into a meeting room and closed the door behind them. The room was bare apart from a small conference table with chairs and a flipchart. Thom walked over to the big window to look out at the view over Hyde Park. In the distance, he could see the Opera House and his own apartment building.

Jerome was still stood by the door. "We're just waiting for my colleague, Sinead," he told Thom.

Thom turned back around. "Oh, okay."

They didn't have to wait much longer as the door then opened, and a slim woman walked in.

"Here she is," Jerome announced.

She was in her mid-thirties, with an equine face and long dark hair tied back in a ponytail. She wore a white shirt and a charcoal pencil skirt and looked tall in her heels.

"Hey Jerome," she said acknowledging her colleague. She quickly turned her attention to Thom, smiling broadly at him. "Thom, how *are* you? I'm Sinead Morris."

"Nice to meet you." Thom went over to shake hands.

"Thanks so much for coming." Sinead motioned at the table. "If you'd like to take a seat, we'll talk about why we've asked you here."

The three of them sat down, Sinead and Jerome next to each other with Thom facing them. A certain deference in Jerome's body language conveyed her superior rank. She opened the bottle of water that was on the table.

"Would you like a glass?" she asked Thom.

"I'm fine, thank you."

She poured water for her and Jerome. Taking a sip, she then looked pointedly at Thom signalling it was time to start.

"Well, I've read your blog," she smiled. "So I guess you know all about the Police Integrity Commission."

"I know that you were set up after the public inquiry."

"That's right. My role here is as a senior investigator. We work in partnership with the New South Wales Police. And that's why we have Jerome with us."

"You're not a police officer yourself then?"

"No, I'm not. But I *am* leading the investigation."

"You must have learnt a lot about the heroin trade in Redfern."

This made Sinead's mouth twitch, as if she were suppressing an urge to say more. She and Jerome exchanged glances.

"Sort of," she replied. "But there wasn't much we didn't already know."

"How can *I* help?" Thom said warily.

"We need to know everything. We have a duty to leave no stone unturned. Everything is relevant."

"And where do I come into this?"

"Well," began Sinead. "As I'm sure you're aware, Detective Sergeant Morton has taken a highly unusual interest in you. We know he's used police resources. And it really doesn't make any sense to us."

Thom wasn't especially surprised. "It's my blog. He didn't want me writing about police corruption, or about TJ Hickey either."

"No." Sinead shook her head. "We really don't think it's that."

"Really?" Thom was baffled. "Why not?"

Sinead hesitated before replying. "I thought your blog was great. It was beautifully written, well-researched and...compelling. But it wasn't..."

She paused and pulled a face before carrying on.

"It wasn't exactly ground-breaking. There was nothing in it that hasn't been said before. Nothing that would rattle Rob Morton's cage."

"Oh," said Thom somewhat miffed.

Jerome cut in. "We thought at first you were working for him, as some sort of mule."

Thom was appalled. "That's absolutely preposterous!" he spluttered. "I've never been involved in anything like that in my life."

"We ruled that out *very* quickly," Sinead assured him. "It just didn't stack up when we started looking into you."

Looking into me? Thom wondered how many people had been watching him all this time.

As for Morton, he had nothing to offer them by way of an explanation or a theory. But he then remembered what Lars had told him.

"I gather Detective Sergeant Morton likes skinny blond boys," he said to Sinead and Jerome. "I suppose I fit the profile."

"Yes, we know that," Sinead told him. "But Rob Morton tends to compartmentalise. He keeps his private life separate. His interest in you isn't consistent with his normal patterns of behaviour."

"You sound like a psychologist," Thom said jokingly.

"That's because I am. At least I used to be."

Jerome folded his arms impatiently. "What we want to know, mate, is if you'd be willing to help us."

"Help?" Thom echoed. "How exactly would I be able to *help*?"

"We'd have to work out the details," Sinead said cautiously. "But it would probably involve you talking to him while we're listening."

Thom bit his lip and inhaled deeply though his nose. "I have to say, *that* is a bit of an ask. I don't want to get involved in this. For a couple of very good reasons."

"And they are?" Jerome prompted.

"Well, I don't want to end up dead," Thom retorted. "I know he has form for that."

"Isn't that all the more reason to bring him to justice?"

"Probably," Thom shrugged. "But I've come to the conclusion that fighting other people's battles isn't wise."

Jerome and Sinead didn't say anything to this.

"And the other reason?" Jerome probed.

Thom gave him a pointed look. "I'm a bit sick of being a pawn in police games."

"What do you mean?"

Thom pushed his chair back and got up. As they watched, he walked over to the window and looked out of it, folding his arms.

"It sounds like you've done your homework." He gazed down at the view with his back turned to them. "So you'll know that, a few years ago. I was involved in the anti-globalisation movement. Back in London."

"Yes, we knew that," Jerome confirmed.

Thom turned back around to face them. "Well, I found out we were spied on by an undercover cop."

He watched their faces for their reaction. Sinead's mouth dropped open slightly. She and Jerome looked disbelieving.

"Are you sure about that, mate?" Jerome asked disdainfully.

"Yes, I'm sure," Thom replied meeting Jerome's sceptical gaze. "It doesn't even make any sense to me. It wasn't like we were doing anything illegal. And we weren't exactly a threat to national security either. I mean we probably liked to think we were. But we weren't really."

A heavy quietness descended on the room. Sinead and Jerome didn't seem quite equal to this revelation.

The silence was broken by Sinead. "I can't comment on what happened in London, Thom. But just to be clear, *we* don't spy on political activists..."

"Just corrupt cops," interjected Jerome with a laugh.

Sinead shot him a look and carried on. "I want to assure you that your safety is our first priority. We won't ask you to do anything that puts you in danger."

Thom didn't see how it could be anything other than dangerous.

"You'll have the inside scoop too," Jerome added. "For any blog or article you want to write. I'll even give you an interview."

Now this was far more persuasive to Thom. Jerome had a point. It would be a huge story if it came out, perhaps even bigger than the death of TJ Hickey. If so, it might be worth the risks.

"You don't have to make a decision right now," Sinead insisted. "We just want you to mull it over for a couple of days. And please, feel free to give me a call if you have any questions."

On the way out, she gave him her business card. Jerome offered to drive him home, but Thom had an overwhelming urge to walk. His mind racing, he strolled through Hyde Park which was busy with office workers and joggers enjoying the early evening sunshine.

Wanting a moment to collect his thoughts, he sat down on a bench and looked back at the Commission building. He knew he shouldn't let himself be enticed into Sinead and Jerome's scheme. But his curiosity had been stirred. The real reason for Morton's interest was now even more of a burning question. If it wasn't corruption and it wasn't lust, what was it?

There was one person Thom wanted to consult: Lars. And so, he pulled out his phone and called him. But it went straight to voice-mail, and he didn't leave a message. Then, he remembered that Lars had been AWOL from the seminar that morning.

What is going on with him?

The next day, he was home alone in the apartment. As he sat at the kitchen worktop making notes for an assignment, he was surprised by the entry-phone ringing. Getting up off his stool, he went to answer it.

"Hello?"

"Thom, it's Cady. Do you have a minute to talk?"

This was unusual. Cady was not in the habit of turning up unannounced, especially without Lars.

"Sure," he said keeping the surprise out of his voice, and buzzed her in.

When he opened the door to her, a couple of minutes later, she was visibly agitated.

Thom was slightly alarmed. "Is everything alright?"

"Not really," she replied stepping in. "I really didn't know who else to talk to".

Thom closed the door behind her. "Let's sit down. Can I get you something to drink?"

She sank onto the couch. "No, I'm good thanks."

"I'm guessing this is about Lars." Thom sat down beside her. "I thought something was up, because he didn't turn up to our seminar."

Cady looked like she was about to cry. "Oh Thom, I'm so worried about him. He just vanished on me for two whole days. No phone calls, no texts, nothing."

"Do you know where he is now?"

"Yes, he came home this morning. But he won't tell me where he's been. He won't communicate with me at all"

"This is about Rob Morton, isn't it?"

"The cop who killed his friend? Yeah. He said you guys saw him last week."

"Yes, we did. And I haven't seen or spoken to Lars since. I've been a bit worried about him myself."

"He's just got obsessed," said Cady despairingly. "He keeps going on and on about how guilty he feels, how he let Ben down. And he says he wants revenge. It's *just* not like him."

"No, it isn't. You don't think he's going to try anything, do you?"

Cady shrugged. "I don't know. He came up with this crazy idea for getting this cop to talk and recording him."

"That's illegal in Australia," Thom told her. "I know that because I saw it on *Neighbours* years ago."

They both laughed grateful for the moment of light relief.

"Oh man," Cady said incredulously. "I can't believe how popular that show is in England."

Thom had a brief nostalgic moment remembering afternoons in front of the TV with Charlotte.

His mind quickly snapped back. "Seriously," he stressed to Cady. "Lars has got to stay away from him. He *is* dangerous."

"Yeah, he knows that. It's just that it's brought it all up again. When he was in rehab, they said he had to let go of the past."

The mention of rehab set off a piercing klaxon in Thom's head. "Cady, do you think Lars is using again?"

Cady looked down at the coffee table and took her time to answer. "I don't know," she said resignedly. "But if he isn't, it's not going to be long before he is."

It slowly dawned on Thom, as they sat there, that there was something he could do. But he didn't mention it to Cady. It wasn't the time. When she went, he found Sinead's business card. He stared apprehensively at it for a moment before calling her.

"Hello, Sinead," he said when she answered. "I've given it some thought. And I'd like to help."

He was scared but his mind was clear. If Lars was to be saved, Rob Morton had to be brought to justice.

Chapter Twenty-Six

Thom visited Lars to tell him about the investigation into Morton. He'd imagined that Lars would be pleased, and perhaps even elated, as it offered up the possibility of justice for Ben, and closure for him.

Instead, Lars paced up and down his lounge room, agitated, with his hands in his pockets. He looked paler than normal and had lost weight.

"I don't get it," he said uncomprehendingly. "What is it they want *you* to do?"

"They want me to talk to Morton."

"Why? Where do you come into this?"

"Well, apparently, he's been using police resources to find out more about me. And they don't know why."

"I do. It's because he wants to get into your pants."

"That's not what *they* think. It's possible there's a connection to you. He almost certainly knows that we're friends."

Lars looked sceptical. "This all sounds a bit tenuous to me."

"I agree that it's not obvious, Lars. But they think it's worth exploring. Sinead, who's running the investigation, is a psychologist. And she thinks I might have a bit of an in with him. I've had an idea for getting him to talk about what he did to Ben."

"And how the fuck are you going to do that?"

Thom paused to choose his words carefully. He didn't know how Lars was going to react.

"I thought I could do another blog post. About Ben."

Lars stopped pacing and stared hard at him. "Are you fucking serious?" he hissed. "What's that going to achieve?"

"It might get him to talk to me while I'm recording him."

Lars snorted. "I think it will get you a needle in your arm. Anyway, recording people without their consent is illegal."

"It's not when there's a warrant from a Supreme Court judge," Thom shot back.

Lars took a moment to process this. He shook his head as if it were all just too much to contemplate and slid down onto the couch.

"Fuck," he murmured.

"Look," Thom asserted. "I'm not going to pursue this if you don't want me to. And I can understand why you might not."

They were interrupted by the front door opening. Cady had returned home laden with groceries. She stopped and looked at them, clearly sensing an atmosphere.

"Everything okay, guys?"

"All good," Lars told her.

Thom nodded and smiled.

"Okay," she said sounding unconvinced.

She made her way past them to the kitchen, pausing briefly as Lars squeezed her hand.

Thom had noticed a new dynamic between them. As Lars had become more withdrawn and vulnerable, he'd become more dependent on her. And she had developed a palpable air of protectiveness towards him.

Lars waited until Cady was out of earshot. "Okay. What do you need from me?"

"Just some background information about Ben. And some dates and times."

"Is that all?"

"Pretty much."

"Have you told Craig about this?"

"No. I don't want to worry him. Not after everything what happened last time."

Lars sighed. "I really hope your Police Integrity buddies know what they're doing."

"I like *that!*" Thom was entranced by an image on the screen.

The object of his fascination was an ultra-modern cube, seemingly made of glass and chrome.

Craig snorted. "It looks like a spaceship, Tommo. You might be desperate to return to your home planet but it's out of our budget."

His laptop was open in front of them on the coffee table. They were looking online at houses for sale in Wellington. Craig had been talking more and more about their move to New Zealand.

He leaned over and tapped on the keyboard, bringing up pictures of a Colonial weatherboard house.

"Now *that* is more me. I want somewhere with a crooked staircase and period features."

"Yuck! I'd feel like I'd died and gone back to England."

"We might have to buy houses next door to each other, Tommo." Craig shut down the laptop. "Are you ready?"

"I'll just get my shoes." Thom got up off the couch and disappeared down the hallway.

Today was a Saturday and they had plans to spend the morning at the Art Gallery of New South Wales. And, afterwards, they were going to have lunch on the Woolloomooloo wharf.

In the bedroom, Thom opened the wardrobe and pulled out the Adidas trainers he'd bought. They were still in their box.

"Very smart, Tommo" Craig said approvingly he came back. "I'm surprised you haven't worn them before."

"Oh well, I've had other priorities."

They walked to the Gallery, which was next to the Royal Botanical Gardens with its palm trees and spiky foliage. Thom thought this made the building, with its Gothic façade, look even more like an imperial monolith.

Inside, they went first to look at paintings from 19th-century Europe. They separated and worked their way around at their own pace. Craig was far quicker to look and move on.

For several minutes Thom stood and stared at 'the Banks of the Marne' by Cezanne, its vivid pastel colours evoking Mediterranean France.

"Wow," murmured Craig, appearing behind him. "That looks idyllic."

Thom turned around. "Can we go and see the Aboriginal art?"

Craig regarded him for a moment before nodding. "Okay."

Over in the modern extension, Thom was struck by a black and white photograph while Craig was looking elsewhere. It was of a youngish Aboriginal man frowning in suspicion.

Eventually, Craig came over to see what was arresting him. "Hmmm," he said uncertainly.

He stared back at the man in the photograph as if meeting a challenge from an adversary. Thom, glancing at his profile, even thought that they looked like each other.

Stepping sideways, Thom came to a painting called 'Gateway', in which the light-at-the-end-of-the-tunnel was rectangular, like a door. Perhaps it was a portal to another dimension.

"Very abstract," Craig observed when he came over.

"It's definitely meant to be symbolic of something."

They finished up in the photography exhibition. One photograph struck a chord with Thom especially. It was of a woman staring enigmatically out of a plane window. He'd often seen long-distance travellers wearing her expression.

When they left, Thom and Craig walked down the slope behind the gallery. The grass smelt like it had been freshly cut. In the distance, there were a couple of kids flying a kite.

Craig sighed with satisfaction. "I enjoyed that."

"It's a very extensive collection," Thom replied.

"Well, it's as good as anything they have in Europe. You might find Wellington a bit of a cultural desert, Tommo."

This made Thom contemplate the vista, before them, in which the nearby skyscrapers seemed to lean, almost benevolently over the park.

"Won't you miss all of this?" he asked Craig.

"Ah yeah, I guess. I *have* lived here for twenty years. But I'm not one for dwelling, Tommo. I'm more interested in the future. *Our* future."

Thom smiled as Craig put his hand on his shoulder and they walked on. At that moment, he felt carefree.

"When can you get this done by?" Jerome demanded.

"Erm, tomorrow evening, I guess." Thom was slightly taken aback by the urgency of his tone.

They were sat with Sinead in the same meeting room as before. Thom's idea for a blog post had, to his surprise, been leapt on.

"And your friend, Lars is onboard with this?" Sinead queried.

"I guess he is. At least, he's agreed to give me the details I need."

"Okay, that's all good," Jerome nodded. "When you've published, you need to call Morton ASAP and arrange to meet him."

"Wouldn't it be better to let him come and find me?"

Jerome looked pointedly at Sinead to defer to her on this. She hesitated before replying.

"In an ideal world, yes," she said reticently. "But we need to move fast on this. I'm worried about leaving you exposed, because we don't have the resources to give you round-the-clock protection."

Now she tells me.

Sinead continued. "I'm going to level with you, Thom. We're under huge political pressure to wrap this up and get a result."

"What sort of political pressure?"

"It comes from the top, the police and the state government. We tend to rock the boat with them, so they're always complaining about our methods and that we're secretive. But God knows how else they expect us to do our job."

Jerome chimed in. "There's a lot riding on this. We really have to prove this operation has been worth two years of work."

"I just thought you should be aware," Sinead added. "I want you to know you can change your mind if you're not comfortable."

When she said this, Thom noticed a flicker of irritation on Jerome's face. Still, he'd already decided, by now, that he was committed.

"Well, I'm an all or nothing person," he told them. "So, I'll publish and be damned."

Sinead chuckled awkwardly.

"Good on you," said Jerome.

Despite his display of bravado in front of Jerome and Sinead, Thom felt profoundly uneasy about publishing when the time came. He was sat in the library making final edits to the blog post he'd spent two days writing. Needing a title, he decided to call it 'the Darker Side of Sydney'. He reread the opening paragraph.

'In July 1997, aspiring actor Ben Dawson was found dead from a heroin overdose by his flatmate. He was portrayed in court, and by the media, as a hapless junkie. The truth was that he barely used heroin, but he made a living selling it...'

Thom had spiced up his piece with references to police corruption. For a couple of minutes, when he finished, he just stared at the screen, putting off the inevitable. Then, unable to prevaricate any longer, he pressed the 'publish' button and hurriedly logged off. This time, he didn't need to see how many hits he'd had. There was only one intended reader.

He'd expected to feel relieved to get it out the way, but he wasn't. That night, as he and Craig were reading in bed, he was consumed by worry. To distract himself, he tried to focus on his book. But his brain wouldn't lift the words off the page. All he could think about was Morton's reaction to the blog. He began to wish he'd backed out when Sinead gave him the chance.

On the other side of the bed, Craig yawned, put his book down and turned to look at him.

"You remember I'm going to Melbourne on Thursday? For that sales conference."

"What? Really?"

"Yeah! I mentioned it *weeks* ago."

He had, but Thom had completely forgotten. The upshot was that Craig would be staying overnight in Melbourne, leaving him alone in the apartment. He found the prospect alarming and he really didn't want him to go. But he couldn't say anything.

Chapter Twenty-Seven

Holly glanced down at her notes. "I thought you structured your argument quite well," she told Thom. "But you could have used some practical examples. To draw out the theory."

Thom nodded. "That makes sense. Well, thank you. That's been very helpful."

He was in her office getting feedback for his assignment. He'd been disappointed by the mark she'd given him.

"No worries," Holly said closing her folder.

It was the first time they'd spoken properly in a while, although they saw each other every week at their seminar. She was always breezily professional towards him, but impersonal.

Thom still felt mortified about offending her. He decided now would be a good time to try to clear the air. As he stashed his notepad into his bag, his mind scrambled for suitable words of apology. But Holly pre-empted him.

"There's just one more thing, Thom," she began. "I've reflected on what I said to you the other week. About your blog. I was way too harsh on you, and I'm sorry for that."

"Oh, please don't worry!" Thom raised his hand as if in protest. "*I* was just about to apologise to *you*."

"There's really no need."

"Well, I'm glad we've sorted that out. I felt awful about what happened. I just got a bit carried away."

"Happens to the best of us." Holly shifted in her chair and watched him as he zipped up his backpack. "*I have* read your new blog post," she added.

That was quick! I only put it up yesterday.

"Oh? What did you think?"

He didn't especially want to hear the answer. He began to think their rapprochement might be short-lived.

Holly glanced upwards, clearly thinking how to put it.

"I thought it was very...*intriguing*. The way you've written it, it's like a crime novel. But I'd like to give you some advice *if* you want to hear it."

"Of course."

"When I read it, I had this strong feeling that there is this whole *other* underlying story."

If only you knew.

He gave her a slight smile of affirmation.

"I'm not going to ask for the inside scoop," Holly continued. "But Thom, you really should be very careful. In my experience, people don't think twice about using you for their own agendas. If one is cynical, one might think it's human nature."

"Yes, I understand what you mean."

Holly clenched her teeth in mock frustration. "Just don't get caught up in it!" she implored him. "It's way more trouble than it's ever worth. Trust me."

Thom laughed in agreement. He had to fight off an overwhelming impulse to take her into his confidence and share his burden. It would have been good to have someone to talk to.

Outside on the library lawn, he paced up and down with his phone in his hand. He was steeling himself for a conversation he didn't want to have. Eventually, he stopped pacing and called Morton's number.

When he heard the ringtone, he hoped it would go straight to voicemail. But Morton picked up.

"Mr Allerton."

Thom couldn't discern his mood from his tone.

"Hi Rob. How are you?"

"I'm good, mate."

He left it for Thom to carry on the conversation. Thom realised he hadn't planned how to broach the subject.

"Erm. I'm just wondering if you've seen my latest blog post."

"I have, mate."

He didn't elaborate any further.

"And what did you think?" Thom asked.

To his surprise, the detective laughed.

"*I think* that you are just like *the most* intrepid little journo. You know, you remind me of that cartoon character. Belgian kid. What's he called? Tintin!"

Thom heard himself titter mirthlessly. He hadn't anticipated mockery from the detective.

"Well, I'm doing a follow-up piece," he said trying not to sound phased. "And I'm wondering if you'd like to contribute."

There was another pause.

Eventually, Morton replied. "I would *love* to, mate. I think we could have a real long natter."

Thom heard a chill in his words.

"Excellent," he said cheerfully. "How are you fixed for this week? Is tomorrow any good?"

"Tomorrow? Tomorrow's Thursday. Yeah, that's good. Do you know the Entertainment Quarter at Fox Studios?"

"Yes, I do," Thom confirmed.

He and Craig used to drive out there for dinner and a movie. They'd always forget where in the multistorey they'd parked.

"Okay, meet me in the Bavarian pub at 6pm," Morton instructed. "Looking forward to it, babe."

He rang off.

Jerome came over the next day to fit him with the wire. Craig had gone to Melbourne that morning, leaving Thom with the jeep at his disposal. He was meeting Morton in less than an hour.

When Jerome finished, Thom pulled down his T-shirt and looked at his reflection in the wardrobe mirror.

"Looks good." Jerome seemed pleased with his handiwork. "Nobody would know."

Thom scrutinised his upper body for tell-tale signs of the wire. "You don't think he might suspect something?"

"I dunno. But you're meeting in a public place. He's not going to undress you in there, is he?"

You don't know Morton.

Thom reached into the wardrobe and pulled out the denim shirt he was going to wear. He slipped it on.

"So, is this wire going to be recording me?" he asked, buttoning up his shirt.

"Yeah, it will transmit to the van tailing you. And I'll be on hand in my car as well."

"What happens if he just comes out with it and tells me he killed Ben?"

"Then we jump out and nab him."

Jerome's matter-of-fact tone made Thom shudder. He wasn't sure whether it was dread or excitement, or both.

"And what if he tells me nothing?"

"Don't worry," Jerome said with a hint of impatience. "We'll debrief you afterwards. Are you ready?"

On the way out, Thom grabbed his phone and the car keys. Opening the front door, he let Jerome out first. Before he closed it, he glanced back, remembering he'd be coming home to an empty apartment.

"Are you nervous?" Jerome asked in the elevator down to the ground floor.

"I'd be lying if I said I wasn't.," Thom replied apprehensively.

Chapter Twenty-Eight

THOM AND JEROME WENT THEIR SEPARATE WAYS IN THE foyer with Jerome leaving by the front entrance. Thom nodded to the concierge and made his way down to the carpark.

Unlocking the jeep, he realised he hadn't driven since the day of the riot, a couple of months earlier. He carefully reversed out and headed towards the exit. The cantilevered gate rolled up. Outside on the street, he glided past Jerome, who was sat in his parked car.

It was a grey, overcast evening. The neon signs of Oxford Street perforated the gloom. On Anzac Parade, he was slowed down by heavy rush hour traffic. The empty parkland, on both sides, felt ominous and filled him with foreboding. He looked in the rear-view mirror to see if he could see Jerome, or if there was a van following him. But he saw neither.

Noticing it was nearly 6pm, he started to worry about being late. When he made a left turn, he picked up speed. He soon became aware of the police patrol car which had appeared behind him. There were two figures in the front. They signalled for him to pull over, so he stopped on the side of the road, and they parked behind.

In his side mirror, he saw the driver's door of the patrol car swing open. A young, baby-faced cop got out and came over. He looked about nineteen or twenty. Thom wound down his window.

"Can I help?"

The cop frowned. "Can I see your license, mate?"

Thom was perplexed. He couldn't see why he'd been stopped. "Erm, okay."

He leaned back to pull his wallet out of his jeans pocket. Finding his licence, he handed it over. The young cop stared at it, looking unconvinced, and gave it back.

"I'd like you to step out the vehicle for me, thanks."

He pulled the door open and stepped aside. Thom reluctantly unfastened his seatbelt and got out.

"Can I ask what this is about?

"What speed were you doing, mate?"

"I believe I was under the limit," Thom said lamely.

"You believe?" The young cop's voice was acid. "You should know, mate."

Thom tried to think of an answer to this. He was *almost* certain he hadn't been speeding. But as he didn't know for sure, it was difficult to argue. He was now hoping Jerome would appear and intervene to spare him this unnecessariness.

At that moment, the passenger door of the patrol car opened, and the darkened figure in the front got out. It was Rob Morton.

He slammed the door shut and approached. "It's alright, mate. I've got this".

The young cop was hesitant. "Are you sure, boss?"

"Yeah, mate. You get off back to the station. And enjoy your evening."

The young cop glanced at Thom before retreating. As he passed, Morton playfully punched him on the shoulder. He got back into the patrol car and started up the engine. Morton gave him a friendly wave when he drove off.

Once he'd gone, Thom was surprised when the detective walked around to the other side of the jeep, got in, and buckled up.

Morton motioned at him to get in. "Come on, mate."

Thom stood looking at him open-mouthed for a few seconds. But he gingerly climbed back into the driver's seat and closed the door.

"Put your seatbelt on," the detective said sternly.

He then looked around at the inside of the jeep and chuckled to himself.

"You're hilarious, babe."

"Really? Why?"

"Well, you make out like you're this little eco-warrior. And here you are, driving around town in this gas-guzzler."

His remark made Thom so prickly with irritation, he forgot how disconcerted he was. "I've never made out any such thing. And this isn't even my car."

"No, that's right." Morton laughed again. "It's your boyfriend's. And so is the million-dollar apartment you live in. I've got to hand it to you, babe. You've done pretty well for yourself. For a backpacker."

Thom no longer had the patience to entertain this conversation. He wanted him to get to the point. "I was on my way to meet you, as we arranged."

"I know you were. I just thought I'd surprise you."

"You did."

'Hijacked' is probably a better word for it.

Morton's phone buzzed in his inside pocket with a text. He pulled open his jacket to look at it and Thom caught a glimpse of the gun holster underneath.

"Well, drive on," the detective told him.

"Where to?" Thom asked nervously.

It occurred to him that he'd been commandeered by an armed man. He wondered if Jerome and his team had any idea where he was.

Morton looked at him as if he were being exasperatingly dim. "Fox Studios. Like we said."

He put his phone back in his jacket.

Thom was relieved Morton wasn't taking him anywhere else. And so, he started up the engine.

As they drove off, the detective stared ahead. "You know, babe. I was just *so* glad when you called me up and asked to talk."

Thom looked ahead at the road. "Were you?"

"Yeah. We seem to have this real special connection. It's not like I've known you long, but I feel like I can tell you anything."

"That's good." Thom could hear the doubtfulness in his own voice.

He was also acutely aware of the wire for the first time since Jerome fitted it. It felt cold against his body.

When he indicated to turn, Morton asked him where he was going to park.

"The multistorey," he replied. "That's where we usually go. But we can never find the car."

"Ah," the detective murmured.

Driving into the multistorey, Thom took a ticket from the machine, and the barrier rose to let them through.

"Go up to the next level," Morton ordered.

"*Okay.*" Thom changed gear.

Once they were up on there, he waited, with the engine running, for further instruction.

The detective looked around at the parked cars. "Can you go up two more, mate?"

"Fine."

Pressing down on the accelerator, Thom swung the jeep up another couple of ramps.

"Just one more," insisted Morton.

This was becoming rather tiresome for Thom. But he did as he was asked, taking them up onto the next landing.

The detective scanned the scene. "This looks good."

Thom saw there were very few cars parked up here. In fact, there was nobody around at all. He glanced at Morton and had a disturbing thought.

Is he going to pull out his gun and blow my brains out?

"Park over there." Morton pointed to a space.

Thom manoeuvred the jeep in and stopped the engine. His palms were sweaty, but he tried to stay calm. He was about to spring out the car and run for his life. He watched Morton out of the corner of his eye. Any second now, the detective would reach into his jacket and whip out the gun..

Butinstead, Morton just stared at the wall in front. He put his hand on Thom's thigh and rubbed it.

His eyes stayed fixed ahead. "Babe, babe, babe," he murmured.

Thom didn't flinch. He allowed himself to relax just a little and turned to look at his passenger.

Morton inhaled deeply as if about to unburden himself. "I've got to say that your blog has got to me. I've had to take a really long, hard look at myself."

"Have you?"

"I'm not going to lie to you babe. I've done some pretty unpleasant things in my time. Necessary but unpleasant."

"I'm sure."

Thom hoped the wire was working up here. Jerome's crew would want to hear all of this.

The detective shook his head. "It's the guilt that gets to you. It doesn't matter how tough you think you are. Or how many lies you tell yourself."

"Guilt?" Thom probed, mindful of the wire.

Morton sighed. "That kid was just a liability. He *had to* go. But I wanted to do it humanely. I didn't want him to experience any pain. I..."

He broke off as if overcome and bit his lip.

Thom found himself imagining the terror of Ben's last moments, seeing Morton appear with a syringe. But would it have been painful though? He remembered Lars likening heroin to a warm blanket.

After swallowing, Morton regrouped. "I persuaded myself it was like taking an animal to be euthanised. At the vets. Sad but has to be done."

This made Thom recoil. "Ben wasn't a dying animal!" he hissed.

Morton turned and frowned at him. "Ben? Ben? Wait. Do you mean Ben Dawson?"

Thom just nodded, taken aback by his reaction.

"Well, I'm not talking about *him*," Morton said with disdain. "That guy dug *his own* grave."

Thom was now utterly bewildered. "Well, who *are* you talking about?"

Morton's frown deepened. He seemed irritated by Thom's incomprehension.

"I'm talking about TJ," he said coldly. "*I* killed TJ Hickey."

Chapter Twenty-Nine

"WHAT!" THOM GASPED. "HOW?"

"Like I said, the kid was a liability." Morton gave another regretful sigh. "I took a patrol car out that night. And I followed him, and then I rammed him. It was all over pretty quickly."

Thom clasped at the steering wheel. "How could you do it?"

The detective gave a half-shrug. "It's amazing what you can do when you have to."

Thom shook his head in disgust. "But you didn't have to do *that*."

Before Morton could respond, Thom was startled by the screech of tyres and flashing blue lights. A police convoy erupted onto the landing, surrounding them in seconds. Morton showed no reaction.

From the back of a van, four cops in navy overalls sprung out, carrying machine guns. Two stood back while the other pair staked their positions on either side of the jeep. They pointed their weapons, signalling readiness to fire.

Behind them, a uniformed officer stepped out of a patrol car carrying a megaphone.

"This is the police! Get out of the vehicle. Put your hands up. And lie face-down on the floor."

Thom looked at Morton for some sort of cue. He felt like *he* was the one about to be arrested.

Morton raised his hands. "Just do as they say," he told Thom.

The two cops stood aside, responding to Morton's signal, but with their machine guns still trained. Morton opened the passenger door and slowly let himself out, his hands still up. Thom hesitated before following his lead. Glancing sideways, he saw the detective shuffle down onto his front.

"GET ON THE FUCKING FLOOR!" screeched the cop by Thom's side.

Thom sank to his knees and wriggled onto his stomach. The ground was cold and dusty. On the other side of the car, he heard Morton being ordered to stand up and then the click of handcuffs. There was a pause.

"He's all good!" shouted the cop standing over Thom. "Get up, mate."

Thom hauled himself back up. He gingerly turned around to find he was being watched by Jerome and an older man - potbellied, suited and wearing a police cap.

Jerome gave him a nod of encouragement before turning his attention to Morton, now detained by the patrol car. He stepped towards him.

"Detective Sergeant Rob Morton, I am arresting you on suspicion of corruption in public office. You do not have to say anything. But anything you do say may be given in evidence."

Morton seemed unmoved. "Understood, mate."

He looked over at Thom and smirked. Then, he was manoeuvred into the back of the patrol car, with his head pressed down. Once the door had been slammed shut, he was speedily driven off.

It's like he was expecting it Thom thought.

Thom stayed standing where he was, waiting to be told what to do next. Jerome finished a confab with the others and came over.

"Well done, mate." He patted Thom on the shoulder. "We couldn't have done this without you."

Jerome's normally inscrutable face was now lit by quiet elation, and his brow glistened.

"What happens now?" asked Thom. "Is there anything else you need me to do?"

"Not tonight. We'll just take that wire off you and you can head off home. We'll be in touch for a debrief."

"That would be good." Thom suddenly felt overwhelmed by tiredness and adrenaline.

At that moment, the magnitude of it all hit him. He'd done what he'd set out to do. Facing down his fears, and overcoming serious danger, he'd helped bring Morton to justice. There was someone he really needed to tell.

Outside Lars' and Cady's house, Thom galloped up the steps to their front door and banged loudly. Impatient at the slow response, he pummelled again, with greater fervour. The door quickly swung open, and Lars appeared looking alarmed.

"What the..."

"They've got him!" Thom was shaking. "They've got him!"

Lars peered at him warily. "I've got no idea what you're talking about. But come in."

He stepped aside to let Thom past and closed the door behind him. Indoors, Cady was sat cross-legged on the couch. She waved at Thom in greeting and muted the TV. In front of her, the coffee table was strewn with discarded plates and cutlery.

Lars remained standing. "What *is* going on, Thom?"

Thom took a breath and tried to keep his voice steady. "Rob Morton has just been arrested. They've actually got him on tape admitting to murder."

Cady's mouth dropped open. Lars just stared.

"How do you know this?"

"Because I was there!" Thom cried. "They had me wearing a wire while he was talking to me."

Lars took a sharp intake of breath. "Fuck," he murmured. His eyes became watery, and he bit his lip to control himself.

Cady, without speaking, lifted herself up off the couch and wrapped her arms around him. They stood for a few moments, clinging to each other, in a silent embrace.

Eventually, Lars disentangled himself from her. "Well, I think this calls for a drink. Have we got any booze in the house?"

"Just that bottle of vodka in the kitchen" Cady told him.

"That will do." Lars grinned. "Thom, will you join us?"

"I can't. I'm driving."

"That's a bummer."

A few minutes later, Lars and Cady were sat back down on the couch, with a glass of vodka each, as Thom regaled them with the story of his evening. Thom was now ensconced on the beanbag, wishing he could have a drink too. He certainly felt he'd earnt one.

"So then what happened?" Lars demanded.

Thom had, by now, told them about being hijacked by Morton.

"Well, we drove to the multi-storey at Fox Studios, and he made me go up all these levels. When we finally parked, he started rambling about how guilty he feels. *And then*, he told me he killed... *TJ Hickey*."

"What" shrieked Cady, nearly dropping her glass. "TJ Hickey?"

Lars raised his eyebrows. "Are you serious?"

Thom nodded.

"Oh my god." Lars struggled to take it in. "Why?"

"He'd fucked something up, apparently. I don't know what though."

"But what about Ben?" asked Cady. "Did he admit to killing him too?"

"No." Thom suddenly felt uneasy. "He sort of denied it."

An awkward silence descended, and Lars frowned.

"Well, that's weird."

The atmosphere of celebration had drained from the room. Thom could tell Lars and Cady were disconcerted. He wanted to reassure them.

"The police have probably got other evidence about Ben. Whatever happens, Morton's going to jail for a bloody long time."

"That's true, I guess," Lars conceded.

Soon after, Cady left to go to work at the club, but Thom stayed on for a while.

"This story is going to be even more immense," Lars told him, pouring another vodka. He looked over at Thom. "Are you going to do anything with it?"

Thom was pleased to be able to sound him out. "I was thinking about another blog post. Jerome and Sinead said they'd help."

Lars nodded approvingly. "I think that would be a really smart move. But, if I were you, I'd do it as a teaser to get media interest. And not put all your goods in the shop window."

"That's pretty much what I was thinking."

Lars took a long, thoughtful swig from his glass. "You know, everybody is going to be totally thrown by this. It's going to turn everything they thought they knew – about TJ Hickey, about the cops - on its head."

Afterwards, Thom drove home to his silent apartment. He felt Craig's absence keenly. But tomorrow, Craig would be back. At some point, Thom would have to tell him about Morton. He wondered if Craig would be angry about being kept in the dark. Thom knew by now he didn't like surprises.

He found it difficult to sleep that night. The empty space on Craig's side of the bed was distracting enough. But his mind was whirling with ideas for his new story. As he lay awake, he decided that he wanted to dig a little deeper and find the humanity. He needed to talk to someone who knew both Morton *and* TJ Hickey.

"Young Thom," said Archie opening the door. "Good to see you. Come on through."

Thom had called first thing that morning asking to see him and was invited to drop by Aspire after lunch.

Archie took them into his office at the back. Installed behind his desk, he motioned at Thom to sit down.

"What is it you want to talk to me about?"

Thom realised this was going to be difficult. "There's something I thought you should know, Archie."

The Pastor looked at him expectantly.

Thom carried on. "Rob Morton was arrested for corruption in public office. And...he's confessed to the murder of TJ Hickey."

Archie jerked backwards in his chair and stared at Thom disbelievingly.

"No." He shook his head. "No. You must have got that wrong, mate. There's just no way."

"It's true," insisted Thom. "I heard him. I was wearing a police wire when he said it."

"How the hell are *you* mixed up in all of this?"

Thom sighed. "It's a very long story. But the Police Integrity Commission have been looking into him for months. Maybe longer."

"Look," Archie said testily. "I've known Rob for twenty odd years. I *know* he's not exactly the cleanest of cops..."

Understatement of the century Thom thought.

"But," Archie continued. "I don't believe he killed that kid. He just wouldn't."

Thom felt he had to disillusion him. "I don't think you know Rob Morton as well as you think you do, Archie."

For a moment, the Pastor regarded him with a cold resentfulness.

"When did all this happen?" he asked eventually

"Last night."

Archie shook his head again. "There's something not right about all this. I just don't know what's going on."

Thom decided that now was not the time to ask for an interview. Archie was so consumed by denial that he'd probably react with hostility. But Thom reasoned he would, in time, come around. He might even be grateful to have heard it from him first.

Getting ready to leave, Thom scraped back his chair. "I just thought you should know."

Archie looked at him wearily. "Listen, mate. I appreciate you coming over. But I think you should keep this to yourself for now. At least until we know all the facts."

"I will," Thom assured him.

Chapter Thirty

In the supermarket, beneath the Coca-Cola sign at King's Cross, Thom meandered and hesitated. He wasn't sure what to buy. He'd decided to cook something special for dinner that evening. Craig would appreciate it after his journey back from Melbourne. And, more to the point, it might soften him up. Thom had resolved to tell him about Morton sooner rather than later.

Eventually, he chose the ingredients for a sea bass dish. He thought about getting a bottle of Champagne but decided that was overkill.

He was on the escalator back up to the street when his phone rang. At the top, he dropped his bags to see who was calling and answered.

"Hi Jerome."

"Hey, mate. Have you got a sec?"

"Sure."

"I'm just wondering if you've got time to meet me and Sinead this afternoon. We need to talk to you, urgently."

Thom was intrigued. This sounded like an exciting development.

"Okay. I just need to drop my groceries at home. Should I come to your office?"

"No," Jerome said quickly. "Can you meet us in Hyde Park in about thirty minutes? By the fountain?"

This seemed odd but Thom didn't question it. "Fine. See you then."

Thom arrived at the park having walked from home. He made his way to the fountain down an avenue, which looked Parisian with its overhanging fig trees.

He wondered why Jerome and Sinead wanted to meet him here rather than at their office. Still, it added to the sense of urgency and high drama. His mind turning to his blog, he decided to be unabashed about calling in favours.

He spotted Sinead and Jerome in the distance. They were both dressed in black, wearing sunglasses and carrying takeaway coffee cups. Neither smiled as he approached.

Jerome greeted him first. "Thanks for coming, mate." His voice was flat, unenthusiastic. The triumph of the night before had clearly worn off.

"So, what's going on?" Thom asked, disconcerted by their low voltage.

Sinead nodded at Jerome, signalling that she'd be the one to tell him. She inhaled deeply, clearly about to impart bad news.

"Rob Morton's been released from custody. Without charge. He's returned to his duties and..."

"What?" Thom's mouth dropped open.

But Sinead ploughed on. "*And* we've been told to destroy the file we've got on him. The paper records, all the recordings. *Everything*."

"But he's on tape saying he killed TJ Hickey. I don't get it."

"That's just it, mate." Jerome spoke in a withering tone. "*That* story he told you about TJ Hickey. It's total bullshit."

He made it sound like it was Thom's fault.

"How do you know?"

"Because Rob Morton was nowhere near the scene that night. He was at Paramatta police station doing a presentation. That's more than twenty kilometres away. It's all on CCTV."

Sinead added: "We've checked everything. There's just no way that story can be true."

Thom was now even more bewildered. "It makes no sense. Why would even he say it?"

"Because he wanted to discredit us," Sinead told him. "And he's done a bloody good job. His hot-shot Federation rep reckons we've victimised him. And the frigging Police Minister, of all people, agrees!"

Jerome pulled a face. "They weren't happy about us using a civilian either."

Thom saw Sinead give Jerome a pointed look from behind her sunglasses.

She then took a sip of her coffee. "They always attack our methods. It's the low-hanging fruit."

"But what about all your other evidence?" Thom asked.

Sinead shrugged. "As far as the powers-that-be are concerned, it's worth jack shit. They're more interested in investigating *us* now. And that means I'm going to be up to my eyes writing reports so we can cover *our* arses."

There was a note of rancour in her voice. Once again, she glanced meaningfully in Jerome's direction.

Jerome responded with a hint of defensiveness: "Morton's known *for ages* we're onto him. *Someone* must have tipped him off."

Another possibility occurred to Thom. "Do you remember when we met for coffee that Saturday? You know that he was following me, don't you? He'd have seen us."

This was clearly news to Jerome and Sinead.

Jerome lifted up his sunglasses. "Well, you haven't told us *that* before," he said accusingly. "When did you know?"

"Not until afterwards. When I left the coffee shop, I heard someone creep up behind me on the street. And then, I was knocked out cold. And a few hours later, I woke up in a motel room with him."

Sinead stared incredulously. "Oh my god! Why the fuck didn't you tell us?"

"I thought you knew."

"Er no." Sinead rolled her eyes, exasperated. She then peered at Thom in concern. "Did he do anything to you?"

"Not really." Thom frowned as he thought more about this. "Well, he tried to throttle me when I said something he didn't like. Apart from that, he just vanished and left me alone in that motel room for hours and took my clothes. It was more psychological torture than anything."

"Jesus," breathed Sinead.

Jerome gazed into the mid-distance. "Morton's been one step ahead of us the whole time," he said almost admiringly. His eyes shifted back to Thom. "It would have helped if we'd known, mate."

"I'm sorry. It just didn't occur to me."

They stood together, for a few moments, in a resigned, weary silence. Meanwhile the fountain gushed noisily in front of them. The park was busy with people eagerly heading towards their weekends.

Thom had a disturbing thought. "What am I going to do?"

"What do you mean?" Sinead looked at him queryingly.

"Well, Morton knows I was part of all this. What if he wants revenge? Am I going to get any protection?"

Jerome sucked in his lips and shook his head. "We're not going to get resources for that. So, we're *all* going to have to watch our backs."

Sinead tried to offer some reassurance. "The important thing is not to panic." She sounded like she was trying to compensate for Jerome's bluntness. "It's possible Morton will just leave you alone. He might even think you've done him a favour."

Thom wasn't sure she understood the gravity of the situation. "That's really not something I want to second-guess."

"Look, Thom." Sinead's voice had a firmer edge now. "Just try to keep your head down for a few weeks. You'll be fine. If you see anything strange, give us a call."

Thom found this advice completely useless. Morton wasn't the sort of man to give warnings, and she knew that. Besides, what would they do if he did call them? Not much, he suspected.

Jerome looked at his watch. "We've got to go" he told Sinead.

"Well, it's been good to see you, Thom." Sinead gave him a small, sorrowful smile. "Take care of yourself."

"Will do" Thom murmured.

Jerome raised his hand in farewell. "Yeah, see you around, mate.".

Watching Jerome and Sinead walk away, Thom felt discarded, disowned, and abandoned. He realised they were in a lot of trouble themselves. And to them, he was now a liability. That was why they hadn't wanted him to go to their office.

He had a bleak, dreary, walk home, bedevilled by dread and failure. He was beyond apprehensive about having to tell Craig. Before he'd gone to the park, Thom had envisaged regaling him with a sensational adventure story. But what he now had to tell him made him look naïve, foolish, and duplicitous. Imagining the scene, he already felt stung by the cold contempt of Craig's inevitable response.

When Thom let himself back into the apartment, he saw that the sliding door out onto the balcony was open. Craig must have got home early. But his briefcase wasn't in its usual place. Looking down the hallway, Thom saw the bedroom door was shut. Perhaps he was in the shower.

Thom was already wondering when to tell him about Morton. He was divided between getting it over with and delaying for as long as possible. Deep in thought, he wandered over to the balcony doorway for a fortifying breath of evening air.

As he looked out towards the horizon, with a soft breeze fluttering in his ears, he briefly fantasised about stopping time altogether. Behind him, he heard movement as Craig came back up the hallway. Thom waited a second before turning to greet him. When he did, he gasped in shock. It wasn't Craig standing in front of him; it was Rob Morton. Somehow, he'd got into the apartment.

Seeing Thom's reaction, Morton let out a noise that was somewhere between a guffaw and a cackle. He charged at Thom, lifting him off the floor, and carried him out onto the balcony. Thom's legs banged against the balustrade as Morton hoisted him over, dangling him four hundred feet above certain death.

Thom tried to scream, but he didn't have enough breath in his body. Wheezing and panting, his forehead was clammy with sweat, and his eyes and nose ran. He tried to grab onto Morton, but his hands were too shaky. His entire body had dissolved into a gloopy matter he could no longer animate.

A sadistic smile spread slowly across Morton's face. "Well, it's been nice, babe. But you know what they say about pride before a fall."

Thom tried to speak. He'd have begged for his life if he could. Morton was watching him closely, savouring the raw fear.

At that moment, there was a flicker of light and shadows, behind Morton, from inside the apartment. Someone was in there. And then, Thom saw Craig step out onto the balcony with his right arm outstretched. He was holding something which he pointed at Morton's head.

"Put him down, mate," he said calmly.

Thom realised it was a gun in his hand. In front of him, Morton turned his head and stared at Craig with what looked like defiance.

But Craig kept his cool. "Gently does it," he urged. "Come on now. Don't make me pull this trigger."

The detective looked back at Thom, perhaps weighing up his options. It felt like an eternity. Thom didn't trust him not to release his grip.

To his surprise, Morton grimaced apologetically. "I wasn't really going to drop you, babe. I was just messing."

With that, he pulled him back up over the balustrade and helped him down. Thom immediately collapsed onto the floor and a wail escaped from his mouth.

Ignoring him, Craig, with his gun still levelled, ushered Morton towards the doorway. "Get inside and stay where I can see you. Don't move too fast."

Thom pushed himself up onto his hands and watched. Morton gingerly walked backwards into the apartment, shepherded by Craig.

"Keep going" Craig said as Morton neared the front door. "Now stop right there."

Morton paused for his next instruction. Craig just stared silently at him for a moment. Then, without warning, he swung onto his left leg and karate-kicked him twice in the stomach. The detective groaned and staggered back, clutching his abdomen. As his breath returned, he lifted his head and snarled.

"You wouldn't fucking do that if you didn't have that gun in your hand, ya prick!"

Craig was impassive. "Try me. Anytime."

Morton pulled himself slowly back up to standing and he smirked knowingly: "Does your little boyfriend..."

Craig raised his gun. "SAY ONE MORE WORD AND I'LL BLOW YOUR FUCKING BRAINS OUT! Now get the fuck out my house."

The detective edged towards the door and opened it. "This isn't over," he hissed.

He let himself out, slamming the door behind him.

Outside on the balcony, Thom lifted himself off the floor and dragged himself back into the apartment. He flopped onto the couch and stared out at the balcony, without speaking. Craig just stood and watched him.

Eventually, Craig broke the silence. "Are you going to tell me *what the fuck* has been going on?"

There was a pause before Thom responded. "Of course, I will," he murmured distantly. He turned to face Craig. "But I really want to know what exactly it is you keep a gun for."

Chapter Thirty-One

CRAIG GLOWERED AT THOM. "NEVER MIND ABOUT THE GUN! I want to know what that cop was doing in my house."

Thom was feeling equally truculent. "But I *do* mind about the gun."

"You've got more to explain than I have."

"Now *that* is debatable."

They were locked in a standoff with neither wanting to yield. Eventually, Thom decided to strike a bargain.

"Alright. I'll go first. But I still want to hear your side of the story."

Craig nodded reluctantly and slid onto the couch, putting the gun down on the coffee table.

Thom started at the beginning. He told Craig how he'd met Morton, how he thought he'd be a useful source. Craig didn't seem surprised that the detective had turned threatening. But his eyes widened when Thom told him about the connection with Lars.

And he was visibly astounded by Sinead and Jerome's investigation, especially Thom's part in it.

"Let me get this right," he said trying to comprehend Thom's story. "The cops recruited you as some sort of undercover mole?"

"Pretty much," Thom confirmed. "And it all went to shit. As you just saw."

Craig shook his head. "Just why? Why did you have to get involved?"

Thom looked downwards. "Because I felt sort of responsible. Lars was in a really bad way after seeing Morton again. And Cady came over here to talk to me because she was worried. She thought he was going to have a relapse."

"You should let Last Chance fight his own battles," growled Craig.

"It wasn't just his battle, was it?" Thom said sharply. "And there was a chance to get some justice done for once. I couldn't just turn my back."

Craig frowned at him. "But what about us? All this shit has been going on and I've known absolutely fuck all about it. You know, I feel like we lead parallel lives."

"Yeah well, you can complain about that when you've told me why you keep a firearm."

Craig sighed with an air of forbearance. "I've had it for years."

"I've never seen it."

"Well, you wouldn't have."

Thom folded his arms. "But why do you have it at all?"

"It was given to me," Craig told him. "When I first moved to Sydney. *You know* I worked as a security guard before I started the pool business. Sometimes, I had to stay overnight on construction sites. There were some pretty rough characters around, so my boss gave it to me for protection."

Thom's eyes shifted to the coffee table, and he surreptitiously studied the weapon. He was no expert, but he didn't think it looked twenty years old. Still, he no longer had the will to pursue this any further.

"Can you just get rid of it, please? Now."

His eyes met Craig's.

"Alright."

Craig stood up, scooping the gun off the table, and stepped towards the front door to drop it in his briefcase. Then, he went into the kitchen to get his car keys.

He called out to Thom. "Were you planning to cook tonight?".

The subject of dinner, mundane as it was, seemed incongruous to Thom. But the normality of it was a blessed relief.

"I *was*. But I'm really not in the mood now."

Craig came back out of the kitchen. "Me neither. I'll pick up a takeaway on the way home. Is there anything you want?"

"I really don't mind. Whatever."

"Righto. See you later."

After Craig went out, Thom stayed on the couch processing the last twenty-four hours. Plucking up some courage, he pulled his phone out to call Lars. He wanted to talk to him before Craig returned.

Lars picked up. "Hey."

"There's something I need to tell you." Thom launched straight in. "They've had to let Morton go. He *made up* that story about TJ Hickey. He wasn't anywhere near on the night."

"What?" mumbled Lars, confused. "Why did he say it then?"

Thom didn't answer straightaway. But in the silence that followed, he could tell Lars had worked it out for himself.

"I'm sorry, Lars," he said eventually.

"It's not your fault" Lars told him. He sounded flat and defeated.

Thom was equally despondent. "I don't know what else to do."

"There's nothing else you *can* do. Jesus, Thom. You've got to stay out of Morton's way. There's no fucking telling what he'll do."

"What? Like try to throw me off our balcony? He's already done *that* today."

"Whoa!" cried Lars. "What the fuck?"

There was a part of Thom that enjoyed Lars' reaction. With quiet relish, he elaborated further.

"He was here in the apartment waiting for me when I got home. And fuck knows how he got in. He had me dangling over the edge, outside, and he was going to drop me off. But Craig came home and stopped him."

"Fucking hell!" Lars was agog. "What did Craig do?"

"That is a story in itself," Thom said wryly. "Are you around at all tomorrow? I could tell it to you then."

"Yeah, sure. I'm working at the restaurant in the afternoon. But how about coffee at 10am? We can go to that place on Abercrombie Street?"

"Sounds good." Thom was looking forward to offloading. "See you then."

About half an hour later, Craig came home. He was carrying his briefcase and the paper bag with their takeaway dinner. He smiled shyly, as though he and Thom had just made up after a row. They unpacked the cartons onto the coffee table and settled down in front of the TV. The subject of Morton wasn't mentioned. Thom was struck by how relaxed Craig looked, settled in his chair, with his feet up on the table.

"I don't want any more secrets between us, Tommo," murmured Craig.

"Neither do I."

They were now cuddled up in bed after switching their bedside lamps off. Thom lay on his side with his head tucked onto Craig's shoulder. He was feeling drained but restless.

Craig ran his fingers through Thom's hair. "And I don't ever want to see you in that sort of danger again."

Thom lifted his head. "What if Morton comes back?"

"He won't" Craig insisted.

"How do you know?"

"Because I'm going to fix this."

With that, Craig gently pushed Thom's head back down onto his shoulder.

Thom still wasn't reassured. "But how?" he probed.

"I have contacts, Tommo."

"Well, what are *they* going to do?"

"Let me handle this my own way," Craig said quietly. "No more questions."

He tapped his fingertips against Thom's head, in a light, rippling motion.

"Alright." Thom allowed himself to relax, inhaling the scent of Craig's faded aftershave. He relished the warmth of his body and the feeling of being safe. But as he drifted off to sleep, he felt a spasm of unease. This man with whom he shared a bed, his lover and protector, was mysterious and unknowable.

"But you've always known he has a past!" protested Lars.

"Yes," Thom conceded. "But the operative word is *past*. And that gun of his makes me wonder."

They were sat outside the coffee shop, near Lars' house.

Lars rolled his eyes. "Look. If Craig hadn't shown up with the gun, you'd have been splattered. You know that old saying about gift horses and mouths, don't you?"

"Hmm. I suppose you have a point." Thom took a sip of his coffee.

His attention shifted briefly to the street around them, with its terraced houses and Eucalyptus trees. Nearby, a man with dreadlocks waited patiently while his dog sniffed a phone box.

Thom put his cup back down on the table. "I just feel like I don't really know him sometimes."

"You know everything you need to," Lars reasoned. "It's pretty clear he'd kill for you and he'd die for you. What more do you want?"

"You're probably right. But there are a few things I can't help wondering about him."

"Yeah well, sometimes it's best not to overthink stuff. Not all questions have to have answers."

Thom snorted. "How very profound. You're quite the sage today, aren't you?"

"Ha!" exclaimed Lars. He then looked meaningfully at Thom. "Don't take this the wrong way. But the problem isn't that Craig's past has caught up with *him*. It's that *yours* has caught up with *you*."

Thom felt this was a dig. He knew Lars had reason to be disgruntled. But *he* wasn't to blame.

"That's not fair, Lars. I just did what I was asked and..."

"I know!" Lars interjected. "I'm not getting at you. I know there's a whole other game being played here. And that reminds me, have you seen this?"

He reached into his canvas bag and pulled out the *Sydney Morning Herald*. He unfolded it and pushed it across the table to Thom.

Thom picked it up and saw the headline: 'Honest cops victimised by corruption probe."

"It's about your mates at the Police Integrity Commission," Lars told him. "*They're* being investigated."

As Thom read it, his mouth dropped open. The story implied the Commission had gone rogue and targeted decent police officers. There were dark hints about the pursuit of personal grudges.

"This is ridiculous," he hissed. "It sounds like a Police Federation press release. There's no impartiality."

Lars shrugged. "That's the mainstream media for you."

Thom gazed down at the paper. "But they should be better than this, surely?" He shook his head despairingly. "Otherwise, what's the point?"

An idea suddenly took form in his mind.

"You know what," he said looking back up at Lars. "*I'm* going to write about what happened to me, about the investigation. And I'm going to publish it on my blog."

For a moment, Lars just stared at him in disbelief. "You *are* kidding, aren't you? After everything that's happened?"

"*Because* of everything that's happened," Thom stressed.

"I think...you're actually crazy. Aren't you scared? Because you *should* be."

"No. No, I'm not. Because yesterday, I was dangled four hundred feet in the air, and I lived to tell the tale. So, I don't think I can feel fear anymore."

Lars raised an eyebrow. "It's your funeral."

Soon after, Lars had to go to work, and so Thom took the train home. On the way, his phone buzzed when he had a text. His heart lurched when he saw it was from Rob Morton, but he forced himself to read it in the carriage.

'Sorry about last night. I was just letting off steam. Stay out of trouble. xx.'

Thom wondered what this really meant. He couldn't decide whether it was a joke or a threat.

Chapter Thirty-Two

"He's just playing mind games with you," Craig assured him. "Try to ignore it."

In the bedroom, Thom stood back and watched as Craig stripped off the bedsheets for the weekly laundry. He'd just arrived home and had told him about Morton's text.

"Well, I'm not going to be intimidated," Thom insisted.

"I'm pleased to hear it, Tommo." Craig scrunched up the sheets, dropping them on the floor. "How was Last Chance this morning?"

"Good, I think. He seems to be back to his old self."

"Good."

Craig smiled distractedly, making no further comment. Thom sensed he was waiting to tell him something.

"And how was your morning?" he asked, trying to prompt him.

"Alright." Craig nodded and paused before going on. "I spoke to my contacts earlier."

"Oh. And?"

Craig cleared his throat and sat down on the mattress. "There's something we need to talk about, Tommo."

"*Okay*." Thom sank into the space next to him on the bed and looked at him expectantly. "What did they say?"

"They said...we should just get the hell out of here right away."

"Right away?" Thom was nonplussed. "I'm sure you don't literally mean today, do you?"

"No!" Craig chuckled. "I was thinking more the next three to four weeks. How do you feel about that?"

Thom took a sharp intake of breath. "I don't know. I suppose it's probably for the best. But I'm going to have to leave my course though."

"Well, you can transfer credits from your uni, can't you?"

"I guess. But what about your franchise? What are you going to do with that?"

"I'm going to try to sell it to one of the other brokers. And I've got a good opportunity tomorrow. There's a charity polo match on the North Shore which Property Boomers are sponsoring. I'm going to show my face there and I thought you could come with me?"

"Why not?" shrugged Thom. "I've never been to a polo match before."

Thom really wanted to ask Craig about his "contacts". Who were they and what did they know? And why the urgency? Still, he resisted the urge. As Lars said, some questions didn't need answers.

He was still determined to write his blog post. This time, he would be upfront with Craig about it, although he hadn't decided *when* to tell him. No doubt Craig would be furiously resistant, and they'd have an almighty great row. But, after recent events, Thom decided it was a storm they could weather.

The following afternoon, Craig and Thom drove out to Richmond for the charity polo match. Before they left, Thom had spent ages trying to decide what to wear. In the end, he'd settled on a long-sleeved black shirt with jeans and his Adidas trainers.

As they crossed over the Harbour Bridge, Thom thought about broaching the subject of the blog. He wanted to get it out of the way, so it wasn't hanging over him. Still, it seemed a shame to spoil a nice afternoon by putting Craig in a filthy mood. He wondered if he should leave it until they got home, but he couldn't make his mind up.

It took them nearly an hour to get to Richmond and he spent the entire journey quietly ruminating in the passenger seat. He became more and more anxious. The peaks of the Blue Mountains appeared on the horizon when they neared the polo club. By this time, Thom could no longer contain himself.

"There's something I need to tell you," he blurted out. "You're not going to like this."

He turned to look at Craig's profile, watching him for his reaction but there wasn't one. His eyes stayed fixed on the road.

"I'm going to write another blog post."

"Uh-huh," Craig muttered. "What about?"

Thom braced himself for the explosion. "I'm going to write about the investigation. Into Morton. Any my role in it."

Craig said nothing and swung the jeep into the driveway down to the club. Thom took his silence to mean they would argue about it later.

They parked the jeep and got out in a field that had been commandeered as a car park. In the adjacent meadow, there were several marquees, each with their own corporate sponsor. Dozens of people mingled in the enclosures outside as if they were at a wedding.

The galloping of horses' hooves could be heard in the near distance. Behind the marquees, a small group of spectators were stood in front of white railings, watching the polo. Thom and Craig made their way across the grass, and through the throng, towards the Property Boomers marquee.

Craig glanced around them at the other guests. "It's a pretty nobby crowd," he observed to Thom. "These people are like the high society of Sydney."

Thom privately thought they all looked like lotto winners, but he didn't say anything. He noticed that Craig had his shirt sleeves rolled down, hiding his tattoos. He realised that Craig might be feeling self-conscious here.

Inside the marquee, there was a line of tables draped in white linen, with food and champagne. Behind them, young, enthusiastic waiting staff stood attentively. Craig took a couple of champagne flutes from a tray and gave one to Thom. Feeling inexplicably thirsty, Thom drained most of his straightaway.

They went outside into the enclosure because the marquee was virtually empty. Craig, barely touching his champagne, looked around for people he knew. Thom was about to suggest they go and see the match when Craig spotted someone; a thickset, middle-aged man with glasses who was marching past them.

He intercepted him. "G'day Duncan."

The man stopped and looked at him blankly.

Craig offered his hand. "It's Craig Huatare. We met last week at the sales conference. In Melbourne."

Recognition dawned on Duncan's face. "Ah yes, Craig!" He grinned and slapped him on the back. "How're you going, mate?"

"I'm good, thanks." Craig gestured to his side. "This is Thom."

Duncan turned to Thom and shook his hand vigorously. "Good to meet you, Thom." Peering at his face, he added "I hope you don't mind me saying, mate, but you don't look anything like your dad."

Thom's lips parted in surprise. He was about to disabuse Duncan of this notion when Craig hurriedly interjected.

"I'm actually relocating back to New Zealand. And so, I'm selling my franchise. Are you looking to expand at all?"

Duncan smiled noncommittally. "I'm always open to it. What are your annual returns like?"

Craig began reeling off figures and percentages. Thom tired of the conversation very quickly and excused himself to get another drink.

When he went back into the marquee, the waiting staff were far less attentive, and were quietly chatting amongst themselves. Thom cast a furtive glance in their direction before picking up a glass of Champagne and downing it. He looked around again to see if he'd been observed, but he thought not.

He put down the empty glass and picked up a full one to take outside. He was feeling distinctly light-headed because of the Champagne and the sunshine.

Stepping out into the enclosure, he saw that Craig and Duncan had been joined by a couple: a slim, blonde woman of indeterminate age and a tall swarthy man in his forties. She was wearing oversized sunglasses and a shift dress.

"This is Thom," Craig announced when he went over. "Thom, this is Nicki, my area manager. And this is her husband, Ian."

Thom had often heard Craig speak about Nicki, admiringly.

Nicki offered him a firm handshake. "How're you going, Thom. It's great to meet you at last." She smiled warmly. "Craig has told me heaps about you."

"You too," Thom replied. "I like your sunglasses. Very Jackie O."

He cringed inwardly when he heard himself say this. He realised he was drunker than he'd thought.

But Nicki seemed amused by it. "That's exactly who I who was channelling," she laughed. "Jackie O. I have to say that your sunnies are pretty cool too."

Craig pointed at Thom's glass. "How many of those have you had, Tommo?"

Thom turned his face towards him, with his eyebrows raised imperiously. "Just the one" he lied. He turned back to Nicki. "Honestly, he makes me sound like some lotto winner type. You know, the sort who gets totally plastered on free Champagne."

As he said this, he made a point of looking at the crowd around them.

Nicki's smile tightened. "Nothing wrong with enjoying a drink or two."

Craig looked at him pointedly. "Just not too many eh, Tommo." There was a hint of warning in his voice.

Thom rolled his eyes. "That's the sort of thing *my dad* would say to me."

He'd meant this to be light-hearted, but he could hear he sounded snippy.

"Wait." Duncan pointed at Craig and then at Thom. "You two *aren't* father and son?"

Thom let out an unguarded shriek. Craig looked mortified. And Nicki and her husband persevered with forced smiles.

"No." Thom smirked. "We're *really not*."

"Oh," Duncan mouthed as he realised. "I thought it was strange you've got totally different accents."

Thom finished the rest of his Champagne. "I think I need another drink. Nicki, would you like me to get you one too?"

"That would be fabulous, thank you." Nicki gratefully handed him her empty glass.

Thom went back into the marquee. Everything seemed to be almost swimming around him now. When he returned, he decided he should talk less.

Nicki seemed pleased with her replenishment. "Bless you."

As she talked business with Craig and Duncan, Thom sipped his drink, and made no effort to follow the conversation. The afternoon felt increasingly dreamlike as more Champagne bubbles went to his head. He heard an eruption of cheers from the distance when something happened out on the polo field.

Meanwhile, Duncan was talking agitatedly about next year's mortgage rates. "It's the same old bullshit," he complained. "The regulator says one thing. And the government says something else."

Hearing this, Thom couldn't stop himself jumping in. "That's what governments do. They are masters of sophistry and double-speak." He knew he was slurring but carried on. "It's like everyone knows police corruption is *rampant* in this country. And that's why they set up the Police Integrity Commission. But it was on the strict understanding that it would do absolutely bugger all."

This was greeted by a leaden silence.

Nicki's eyes widened. "Wow! I wasn't expecting the conversation to get so *political*."

Craig laughed awkwardly. "Thom *is* very political, I'm afraid. And he's had far too much to drink. I think we should be making a move."

He put his hand on Thom's back and began to steer him away.

Thom felt like he was being marched off in disgrace. But he didn't remonstrate. Despite his inebriation, he wanted to salvage *some* dignity.

Nicki stepped forward to see them off. "Well, thanks for coming boys. And Craig, feel free to give me a call tomorrow."

"Will do." Craig raised his hand in an embarrassed half-wave. "Great to see you all."

He propelled Thom out of the enclosure.

Thom, his vision blurring, focussed on putting one foot in front of the other. He realised, as they were leaving, that they hadn't seen any of the polo.

Back in the jeep, Craig fastened his seatbelt. "Proud of yourself, Tommo?"

"Should I not be?" Thom mumbled. His eyelids felt heavy.

Craig stared out of the windscreen and shook his head. "God knows I'm used to your crazy ramblings. But you seriously didn't do me any favours back there. What got into you?"

"Do you even have to ask?" Thom retorted, more alert now.

Craig ignored this and started up the engine, reversing the jeep out of their parking spot. They drove back out onto the main road in silence. Before long, Thom felt compelled to speak.

"Do you know what I'm sick off, Craig? I'm sick of the lies and the hypocrisy. And I'm sick of this bullshit double game everyone's playing. No wonder there hasn't been any fucking justice for TJ Hickey. I'm going to write this blog post and I don't care who I fucking offend."

He was jolted in his seat when Craig suddenly pulled over. He braced himself to be angrily yelled at.

"Just shut up and listen a moment," Craig hissed. "I *want* you to write your blog post."

"What?" Thom was dumbfounded.

"*I said,* I want you to write it."

"Are you serious?"

"Totally." Craig raised his eyebrows. "Why? Did you *want* us to have a fight about it, Tommo?"

"Not really." Thom was still confused. "What's made you change your mind?"

Craig chortled. "Don't worry, Tommo. I haven't become a lefty. It's to give us some breathing space until we're out of here. We need everybody to think you're just a crank nutjob. A conspiracy theorist. That way, Morton will figure it's not worth bumping us both off."

He restarted the engine.

He added, "Your little performance today will have helped."

Thom didn't argue. As insulting as Craig's remarks were, his reasoning had an undeniable logic.

Chapter Thirty-Three

Ellen smiled sardonically when she saw him. "Oh hello, Bubbles. Have you come to entertain us with more of your amazing stories?" She gestured behind her. "Archie's in the back."

Thom had arrived at the Aspire office just as she was leaving. Already, she'd made him feel ridiculous like he'd been exposed as an unreliable fantasist. She walked off into the afternoon leaving the door open.

Stepping inside, Thom paused before going through to Archie's office. He was apprehensive about seeing him. By now, Archie would know that Morton hadn't been charged. He probably thought Thom had invented the whole thing.

Perhaps he sees me as a "crank nutjob" too.

He found Archie sat at his desk with the door open, immersed in paperwork. He hovered outside in the tiny corridor, clutching the book he'd lent him.

Eventually, the pastor looked up. "Young Thom. What can I do for you?"

"Hi Archie." Thom went in, holding up the book. "I've just come to give this back."

He put it down in front of him on the desk.

"Thanks, mate. Did you enjoy it?"

"Very much. I found it very enlightening. And it challenged my perspective too."

Archie looked back down at his paperwork. "Well, that's good, mate."

Thom watched him for a moment as he pretended to busy himself. Then he broke the silence.

"Look, Archie. About Friday..."

"I saw Rob yesterday," Archie cut in. He lifted his head to meet Thom's gaze. "You should know he's in a pretty bad way."

"Bad way?"

Thom was incredulous. What could Morton possibly have to be in a "bad way" about.

Archie nodded. "Yeah. He told me what's been going on between you two. And I have to say, it explains a lot."

"Going on between us?" A horrible suspicion formed in Thom's mind.

Archie looked away briefly, clearly embarrassed. "Look, it's not my place to judge you, Young Thom. Because what you and Rob do together is your own business. But take it from me, your...*other* mate will find out about it eventually."

Thom was too astounded to respond. He'd expected Morton to have *a* version of events lined up for Archie. But not this.

Archie carried on. "You know, I was pretty shocked to see Rob like that. Because he doesn't show his feelings easily. I remember when he was fifteen, I had to take him to the emergency room with a broken nose. He'd been hit in the face with a cricket ball. I tell you, the kid didn't make a sound."

"But he's not a kid anymore," Thom heard himself murmur.

"No," Archie conceded. "But all this has really got to him. He knows he got too heavy with you by trying to make you leave your boyfriend. And he shouldn't have threatened to tell him. But mate, you haven't exactly been an angel in all of this."

Thom wondered if there was any point trying to set the record straight. But looking at Archie's face, he decided there wasn't.

Archie shook his head wearily. "You know, Young Thom, you're not a bad person. But you have *this need* to create drama. And it makes me wonder if you're just not very happy. I think you need to look deep inside yourself and ask why."

Sat in front of Archie, unable to tell the truth, Thom assumed Morton was simply deranged. But when he thought about it later, he realised the detective had very deftly cast him as a manipulative hysteric.

"That's almost as bad as trying to throw you off the balcony," Lars said the next day.

He and Thom were stood by the library lawn, drinking takeaway coffee just before Holly's seminar.

Thom laughed. "Worse. But what if he said any of this to Craig?"

"Craig knows you better than that," Lars assured him.

Thom swallowed a mouthful of coffee. “Well, you’d think. Especially as we’re now so intertwined. And that reminds me, I need to talk to Holly afterwards.”

“Really? What about?”

“Programme Credits. I want to see if I can transfer to a university in New Zealand.”

“But I thought you were staying here until next year, when we graduate.”

“We *were*. But Craig wants us to leave Sydney by the end of the month.

Lars looked shocked. “Whoa! I wasn’t expecting that.”

“No, neither was I,” Thom said ruefully. “But after everything that’s happened, it seems like a good move.”

“Is it what you want?” Lars asked probingly.

Thom gazed out at the lawn. “I don’t know. I don’t really feel it’s a choice anymore.”

“Well, you’ve got your reasons,” Lars sighed. “But it’s going to be weird without you. You’ve been like my wingman for the last couple of years.”

Thom smiled. “Is that your way of saying you’re going to miss me?”

“No,” Lars replied, determined not to be sentimental. “You’re replaceable.”

Thom started work on his blog that afternoon. Sat at the kitchen counter, he opened Craig's laptop and revisited his last post. He saw it had had over a thousand hits, which was respectable but not spectacular. It had attracted fifty-odd comments offering praise, criticism, and much in between. Some of the contributions were erudite, but many were just profane.

It took him a couple of hours to write fifteen hundred words about his mission to ensnare Morton. He left out names but included the detective's false confession. When he finished, he reread it and came up with a title - 'Good Cop, Bad Cop: The Day I Went Undercover for Anti-Corruption'.

He'd finished editing when he heard the front door open. Craig had come home from work. Thom felt relieved not to have to keep the blog a secret from him this time.

Craig dropped his briefcase and came into the kitchen. "How's it going, Tommo?"

"Good." Thom turned around. "I'm just about to publish."

"Let's have a look." Craig peered over his shoulder and read the opening paragraph. He nodded approvingly.

"That should do it."

Do what? Tom wondered.

He stared apprehensively at the screen and took a deep breath. "Okay, here goes."

He pressed the 'publish' button, dispatching his work out into the cybersphere.

"Well done, Tommo." Craig began unknotting his tie. "I'm going to get changed and go out on the bike. Maybe head up to Watson's Bay. Why don't you come with me?"

Thom, to his surprise, found the idea strangely exhilarating. He wouldn't usually be enthused about riding on the back of the Harley. Not remotely.

"Hmm. Do you think I should? You know what I'm like on that thing?"

"Yes, I think you should."

"Alright then." Thom shut down the laptop. He realised he hadn't needed much persuading.

Half an hour later, they were cruising along the ocean road in the early evening sun. Thom found he'd lost his fear of falling off, and he didn't cling as tightly to Craig. Today, he felt a sense of release.

He and Craig careered past the Art Deco mansions with their views of Sydney Harbour. As they rode up towards the Catholic school, in its gothic splendour, the lights turned red.

While they were waiting, Thom suddenly had this uneasy feeling. Looking sideways, he noticed a car – a bottle green Mercedes. It had sidled up next to them. The car had darkened windows so he couldn't see who was in it, and its engine vibrated with threat. He wondered if he was imagining things. But he could tell Craig felt it too because he twitched beneath his leather jacket. As soon as the lights changed, they took off. Still, the car stayed far too close.

They were soon stopped by another set of lights and the Mercedes continued to stalk them. Thom resisted the temptation to look at it. His helmet felt stuffy as his breath had become heavy with anxiety. He sensed the driver was pursuing them, intent on harm.

He squeezed Craig to try to warn him. When the lights turned green, the traffic began moving again. Just after the school, Craig abruptly swung off the main road into a sloping side street. The Mercedes followed behind them.

Craig accelerated, making the bike judder. In response, the car sped up. Its front bumper clipped their back wheel. And they nearly skidded out of control.

"Fucking hell!" gasped Thom. "They're trying to ram us!"

Craig quickly regrouped, pressed down, and kept going. He got them further away from the car and swerved around a corner down to the bottom of the street. There, he stopped the bike in front of a narrow walkway to the beach.

The Mercedes ground to a halt a few feet away, with its engine still running. Whoever was inside was watching them from behind their opaque windscreen.

Craig turned his head to face the car and raised his middle finger. Then, with a defiant roar, he and Thom tore down the walkway. It was just wide enough for them.

"WOO-HOO!" Craig howled, clearly enjoying himself.

They rode across the empty beach, creating clouds of pale dust in their wake. The horizon, above the ocean, was dominated by the city skyscrapers.

It occurred to Thom that they shouldn't really be there. Not on the bike. But he was beyond thankful to have shaken off their pursuer. Before long, they found an exit and rode all the way home.

"What was that all about?" Thom said as they dismounted in the carpark. "Do you think it's anything to do with the blog?"

Craig was dismissive. "Nah. It was just some sad fuck with a Mercedes and no sex life."

Thom wasn't convinced. When they got in, he decided to check out the reaction to his blog. He was sure it was the reason they'd been chased by the car, whatever Craig said.

He logged on and scrolled down past his bio. He steeled himself up to read hundreds of crushingly vituperative comments. But all his posts had vanished. And in their place were dozens of photos. The first one was of a naked man crouching in front of another.

What the fuck!

Craig came into the kitchen at that moment. He saw the screen and cackled.

"Are you looking at porn, Tommo?".

"No," Thom murmured. "I'm not." He looked up at Craig, bewildered. "They've hacked into my blog."

Chapter Thirty-Four

THOM DECIDED TO DELETE HIS BLOG THERE AND THEN.

"What else are they going to hack into?" he said to Craig as he hammered away at the keyboard. "My medical records?"

"I'm sure it's nothing to get riled up about, Tommo," Craig ventured. "They've obviously decided to have a laugh at your expense."

He peered over Thom's shoulder at one of the images and let out a guffaw.

"It's probably just their way of telling you your blog sucks. *Literally.*"

He laughed again.

Thom pursed his lips. "Hmm. I'm not sure I share their sense of humour."

"That's because you don't have one, Tommo."

"Shut up," Thom muttered. He clicked on the mouse. "There. That's done."

The blog was finally expunged from the cybersphere. He felt like he'd battened down a hatch and protected himself against further infiltration.

Craig was still stood behind him. "Happy now, Tommo?"

"*Happier.*"

The next morning, Thom got into the lift, with his towel draped around his shoulders after his gym session. He was going back up to the apartment. His workout had been invigorating, clearing his mind of the blog. He'd slept well too.

Letting himself back in, he almost walked into Craig who was just leaving.

"Ah, Tommo." Craig was clearly pleased about something. "Good news! I've got a buyer for the franchise. I'm meeting them today."

Thom raised his eyebrows in surprise. "Really? When did this all happen?"

"I've just had a call from Duncan, who we met at the polo match. You know, where you disgraced yourself with your drunken ramblings..."

"Yes, I remember."

"Well, he knows someone who wants in, and he's put them my way."

"That *is* good news." Thom smiled impishly. "Maybe I should get blotto on Champagne more often."

Craig looked at him with mock disdain. "It was *in spite of* you not *because* of you, Tommo. Anyhow, if I seal this deal, we'll be out of here in a couple of weeks."

"Just like that?" Thom was disconcerted.

"Yep," Craig replied. "Just like that."

"But what about all our stuff?"

Craig shrugged. "I'll just hire a removals company. They can come in, pack everything up and ship it over to New Zealand. Job done."

Thom inhaled deeply. "This is all happening so quickly."

"I know!" Craig leaned down to peck him on the lips. "Exciting, isn't it?"

"Yes," murmured Thom uncertainly.

Craig regarded Thom's face before clasping his shoulder. "It will be fine, Tommo. You'll see."

Thom looked up at him. "I know."

They locked eyes for a moment before Craig pulled away.

"Righto. I should probably make a move. Big day ahead. What have you got on?"

"I'm going to be home late tonight," Thom told him. "I'm going to a masterclass on campus. Do you know Naomi Heaton? She writes for *the Melbourne Age*."

"Yeah, that annoying lefty columnist you like."

"Well, she's *giving* the masterclass. And the whole faculty's going to be there. Then, I'm going over to Lars'. Because we're doing a joint presentation next week. Apparently, I'll get some extra credits."

"Yeah well, make sure Last Chance doesn't get all the credit." Craig kissed Thom again. "See you later."

After the masterclass, that evening, Thom and Lars took a bus from campus back to Newtown. They talked about how underwhelming they'd found Naomi Heaton in person.

"Well, they say never meet your heroes," Lars mused.

Thom agreed. "She's absolutely nothing like her column persona. There just isn't the same spark."

Before they got off, Thom changed the subject and mentioned the offer Craig had had.

Lars shook his head in wonderment. "He doesn't hang around, does he?"

"Tell me about it. I can't believe it's happening so quickly. In fact, it probably won't sink in until we're actually *in* New Zealand."

"Far away from all this" Lars sighed, getting up as the bus came to a halt.

Thom shuffled out of his seat and followed him off. They alighted at the top of King Street and crossed the road.

It was starting to get dark. As they walked along the street, Lars stared down at his shoes, seemingly lost in thought. He looked back up and cleared his throat.

"I think Cady and I have another problem," he confided.

Thom thought to himself: *It was ever thus.*

"What sort of problem?" he asked.

Lars stopped outside a pub. "I'll show you."

Thom followed Lars through the main bar into the pokies room at the back. In there, it was quiet but for the whirring and the flashing lights of the fruit machines. When he'd first arrived in Sydney, Thom had been amazed at just how prolific gaming was, especially in the pubs and bars.

As Lars marched towards one of the machines, Thom realised Cady was sat in front of it, wearing a leopard-skin print coat. Her eyes were heavy with kohl. She was so entranced by the spinning lights that she didn't notice them arrive.

"Damn," she muttered to herself when the spinning stopped. She reached into her coat pocket to pull out some coins.

Lars touched her gently on the shoulder. "Hey."

She turned her head, slightly startled.

"Oh hi. What are you doing here?"

She didn't seem pleased to see them.

"We just swung by to say hello," Lars told her, his voice casual. "Thom's coming back to ours to work on the presentation."

Cady acknowledged Thom with a childlike wave. "Oh, okay. I just came in here to kill some time before work."

She said this with a hint of defensiveness.

"It's all good," Lars assured her. "What time are you due at the club?"

"9pm. I'm getting the ferry from Circular Quay."

"The ferry? What's wrong with the train?"

"I just feel like taking the ferry."

"Fair enough." Lars kissed her on the lips. "Have a good evening. And I'll see you back at home."

"I can't wait, baby," she murmured, visibly relieved to see him go. She turned her attention straight back to the fruit machine, dropping her coins into the slot.

Thom and Lars stepped back out onto the street.

Thom glanced sideways at Lars. "That was awkward. What's going on?"

Lars pulled a face. "It's her latest addiction – the pokies. She goes in there every day before work and blows a fortune. She thinks I don't know."

"Any idea why she's suddenly got hooked?" Thom probed.

"It's because of me, isn't it?" Lars sounded weary. "I know I've put her through some stress recently. What, with the dirty cop and all that shit."

"Well, she *was* very worried about you."

"Yeah, I know. And I'm not blaming her. But she's got an addictive personality and I'm worried it will spin out of control. It always does with her."

When they got back to Lars' house, they dropped their bags on the lounge room floor. Lars opened his laptop on the writing desk in the hallway. Thom pulled up a stool beside him, clutching a folder full of notes.

"Okay," Lars exhaled. "I thought we'd go high-tech and use PowerPoint. That will impress Heidi. You've done the reading, haven't you?"

Thom opened his folder. "Yep."

"Fantastic."

They set to work. But an hour passed without them making any progress. They poured over Thom's notes, debating what to use. Still, they couldn't even agree on what they disagreed on.

Lars stared despondently at the screen. "This is much harder than I thought."

They were interrupted when Lars' mobile vibrated on the desk. He stood up to answer it.

"What? Hold on." He started to pace up and down the hallway. "Cady, calm down! Your wallet? Well, haven't you got it with you? What? Don't yell at me!"

Even from where he was sitting, Thom could hear it was Cady on the other end, distressed and agitated. It seemed to be rubbing off on Lars.

"Alright, alright!" he cried. "I'll go and look in our room. Can you remember where you left it?"

He disappeared up the stairs with the phone pressed to his ear. While he was gone, Thom commandeered the laptop. They'd had a desperately unproductive evening. Still, he was determined to salvage something from it.

Lars came back down holding Cady's wallet in one hand. He was still talking to her on the phone.

"Don't stress. I'll get a cab up there. It's fine. I won't be long."

He hung up and turned his attention to Thom.

"Will you be okay here on your own for a bit? I've got to go up to Circular Quay because Cady needs her wallet."

"Yeah, sure," Thom shrugged. "But didn't she have it with her in the pub?"

Lars rolled his eyes. "Don't even go there." He looked at his watch. "I'll only be about twenty minutes."

Thom thought this was optimistic but said nothing. A few minutes later, a taxi arrived outside the house beeping its horn and Lars went out leaving Thom by himself.

Chapter Thirty-Five

In the event, Lars was gone for longer than he said. Thom, however, didn't mind. Left to his own devices, he easily turned his notes into bullet-points. Before long, he'd created enough slides for their presentation.

He was rereading his work, feeling pleased with himself, when he heard Lars knock at the front door. He'd obviously forgotten his key. Thom got up, mildly irritated, and went to answer it, pulling the door wide open. But the towering figure on the doorstep wasn't Lars.

"Hello babe," grinned Rob Morton.

Before Thom could react, Morton stepped inside and shut the door behind him.

Thom stood his ground. "What do you want?" he demanded.

He noticed Morton was dressed in his work clothes and carrying a sports bag, as if heading to the gym.

The detective put the bag down. "I just want to talk, babe." He motioned at the couch. "Sit down."

"No." Thom looked back defiantly. He was surprised how unafraid he felt.

"Don't be like that, babe."

Morton put his hand on Thom's shoulder, digging in with his fingers. He then lowered himself onto the couch pushing Thom down beside him.

He took hold of Thom's chin. "Look at me."

Thom glowered. But the detective had a flirtatious gleam in his eye.

He regarded Thom fondly. "You know, we've both been through a lot these last couple of months. Just *so much* has happened."

Thom ignored this and gave him a hard stare. "You hacked into my blog, didn't you?"

"Oh that." Morton sniggered. "I think I did you a favour, babe. You know, most people would rather look at pretty pictures than read boring articles."

"Boring was it?" Thom raised his eyebrows.

Morton beamed at him indulgently. "Don't get me wrong, babe. You're a very intriguing boy. But yeah - I hate to be the one to break it to you - your writing is pretty fucking boring."

"Well, it certainly interested *you* enough," Thom shot back.

"Nah. Everyone knows the PIC are dickheads. They'd have to be to get you to do their dirty work for them."

"Really? Then why not just leave the blog up there?"

Morton heaved his shoulders and sighed as if releasing a burden. "Because it's time to move on from TJ Hickey. *Nobody* knows more than I do about all the hurt it's caused. But we all have to heal. Raking up shit from the past doesn't help."

Thom was struck by the solemnity of his tone. "You almost sound like you mean that."

"Fucking right I mean it!" Morton exclaimed with mock affront. He became serious again. "Don't laugh, but tomorrow night, I'm speaking at a community meeting Archie's organised. And I'm gonna tell them that *change* needs us to forgive and to let go."

Thom made a sceptical face. "That's very profound. But maybe you should leave the homilies until *after* the inquest."

The detective chortled. "You're a spiky little thing, aren't you?"

"Do you think?"

Morton ruffled Thom's hair. "There's something you should know about me, babe. I *get* anger and loss. Because I lost someone too."

He left this hanging in the air, inviting the next question.

Thom took the bait. "Who did you lose?"

There was a sorrowful pause as Morton looked away.

"His name was Chrissy," he said quietly. "Short for Christopher. He was a beautiful boy but sort of crazy. Difficult."

He trailed off, staring ahead for a moment, as if lost in reminiscences He then turned back to Thom, with a small confiding smile.

"Would you like to see him?"

Thom didn't particularly, but he felt he couldn't say no. "Erm... okay."

Morton shifted onto his side to pull his wallet from his pocket. He produced the photo and handed it over.

The dog-eared picture Thom saw was of a younger Morton, smiling happily, outdoors. His arm was wrapped protectively around a slender young man with cropped blond hair, who was obviously Chrissy. Seeing him, Thom felt a peculiar, inverted *déjà vu*.

"He looks like me." His eyes flicked back up at Morton.

The detective moved his face in closer.

"Yes, he does." He gazed into Thom's eyes. "That's what I thought the second I saw you."

He traced his finger slowly down the middle of Thom's face, pulling slightly at his lower lip.

"You're so like him," he murmured.

With that, he leaned forward and pressed his lips to Thom's, kissing him with ravenous urgency. Thom pulled away, dropping the photo, but only after he'd let Morton's tongue slide into his mouth.

"Rob!" he protested.

"But that felt good," Morton insisted. "I know you've wanted it too."

Thom shook his head. "It doesn't matter if I did. It was completely wrong. Just like everything else you do."

Morton held up his palms. "Look! I'm just a bit emotional, okay. I don't talk about Chrissy much."

He turned away with a wounded expression and stared down at the floor. In the silence that followed, Thom wondered about the real reason for his visit. Maybe it *was* connected to Chrissy somehow.

"Rob, what happened to Chrissy?"

Morton swallowed before answering. He kept his eyes trained downwards. "Chrissy was fond of the junk. He had a habit. I guess you'd call him an addict. And it killed him in the end."

Thom felt a chill when he heard this. He regretted asking. One way or another, deaths by heroin seemed to follow Morton around.

"I'm sorry to hear that." He hoped, with these bland words, to close down the conversation. He just wanted him to go.

The detective turned back to face him. "It's all in the past, babe. I've dealt with it. The truth is, Chrissy was always a disruptive force in my life."

He paused, apparently struck by realisation.

"You know, now I think about it, *that* is the other way you're just like him."

His eyes hardened, and his mouth curled downwards.

Thom was unnerved by his sudden change of expression. He decided to try to placate him.

He kept his voice steady, not wanting to seem anxious. "I don't know what to say to that, Rob. But you have to understand, *I'm not* Chrissy."

Morton's furrow deepened. He said nothing.

Thom sensed he'd misfired. He decided to appeal to Morton's reason. "Look, I don't want to be rude, but I really need to get on with my work. Lars will be back *any minute*."

The detective snorted. "Not soon enough for you, mate."

He leaned over and unzipped his bag on the floor. Scooping up the photo, he dropped it inside and rummaged around. Thom was alarmed when he saw him pull out a syringe and a shoelace.

"What are you doing?"

The detective, totally silent, slowly sat up and rotated his body towards him. Then, he sprung on Thom, like a panther, pinning him down with his knee. Thom gasped in shock when he realised.

This is what he did to Ben.

Crushed by Morton's weight, Thom hammered away with his fists, but the detective was impervious to his blows.

"It's not gonna hurt, babe," Morton told him gently. "Now don't fight."

Thom's face reddened as he continued to thrash around beneath him.

Morton pressed down harder. "Hey, hey," he whispered. "Just go with it."

He gripped the syringe between his teeth as he rolled up Thom's sleeve and tightened the lace around his arm. Plucking the syringe from his mouth, he was about to inject him when the front door swung open. He dropped it in surprise and swivelled his head to see who was there.

It was Lars. He stood on the doorstep, agape.

"What the fuck!" he exclaimed.

Morton glared. His knee still on Thom's chest, and his eyes fixed on Lars, he reached out for the syringe.

Lars shuffled back, holding the door open.

"DETECTIVE SERGEANT ROB MORTON!" he hollered to the neighbourhood. "GET THE FUCK OUT OF MY HOUSE!"

The detective gave him a withering look and shook his head. "*Don't* be an idiot, mate."

Lars pulled his mobile out of his pocket. He held it up in front of him. "DETECTIVE SERGEANT ROB MORTON!" he yelled again. "IF YOU DON'T LEAVE MY HOUSE *IMMEDIATELY*, I'M CALLING THE COPS!"

Morton froze. "I am the cops, mate."

Looking unimpressed, Lars sucked in his lips and began dialling.

'Alright!' Morton snapped, conceding defeat. He pulled his knee off Thom's chest. "Just put your phone down mate. I'm outta here."

He sulkily flung the syringe into his bag and zipped it up.

Lars hung up and stood back against the door, watching the detective gather himself up. As Morton swaggered out, bag in hand, he stopped to eyeball Lars.

"No more chances for you, *Last Chance,*" he snarled. "See you later."

He jabbed Lars hard in the chest making him stumble. Then, unhurriedly, he descended the steps and headed off down the street. Lars straightened up and waited before stepping into the house, slamming the door shut.

"Fucking hell, Thom!"

Springing up, Thom swung his legs back onto the floor and ripped off the shoelace. He wiped his face with the back of his hand.

"Did you give Cady her wallet?"

Lars frowned. "Er...yeah." He then sucked in his breath and looked pointedly at Thom. "If I hadn't come back when I did..."

Thom gripped his knees and stared ahead. "I know, I know."

Lars tried to make eye contact with him. "Thom, that guy is going to kill you."

Thom opened his mouth to respond. But no words came out. He was trembling now. Lars observed him for a few seconds before sinking down onto the couch next to him.

"Look, I'm going to call Craig. He needs to know about this."

Thom nodded. "Okay," he murmured distractedly.

"What the fuck's happened?" Craig demanded, as he stepped into the house. "Is Thom alright?"

Lars shut the front door behind him. "Yeah, he's fine. He's just in the bathroom."

Lars hadn't gone into detail on the phone. He'd said just enough to convey a sense of crisis.

Craig looked at him queryingly, waiting for the explanation. "So, what gives?"

Lars took a moment to find the words. "I had to go out earlier. And so, Thom was here on his own. When I got back, I found Rob Morton about to give him a hot-shot."

Craig's jaw dropped. "Fuck!" he breathed. "What did you do?"

"Well, I made a shit load of noise and threatened to call the police. So Morton just got up and left."

At that moment, the bathroom door opened at the rear of the house. This was followed by Thom's footsteps as he came back into the lounge. He stopped in the doorway when he saw Craig.

Craig met his eye. "Tommo, how did he get in here?"

Thom flopped down onto the couch. "He just knocked at the door and pushed his way in. He said he wanted to talk."

"About what?" Craig probed.

Thom shrugged. "I don't know. He spouted all this...*psychobabble* about healing and letting go of the past. Then he started going on about his dead boyfriend. And that's when he tried to kill me."

Craig exchanged glances with Lars.

"I think I'd better get you home, Tommo."

When they got in the jeep, Craig banged the steering wheel.

"Fuck! I thought I'd got this under control."

Thom just looked at him and said nothing. He wasn't sure why Craig was so angry with himself, but he had little inclination to ask.

Chapter Thirty-Six

Back at the apartment, Thom let himself out onto the balcony for some air. Gripping the railing, he contemplated the night lights down below.

Craig had gone into the kitchen to make himself a hot chocolate. Before long, he came out carrying a steaming mug, and wrapped his arm around Thom.

"This is way more serious than I thought, Tommo. That cop is not going to give up."

Thom slumped his shoulders in resignation. "He's going to get me in the end, isn't he?"

"No." Craig pulled him closer. "No. he isn't. I'm going to make sure of it. But there's something I need you to do."

"And what's that?"

"Stay here," Craig implored him. "Don't leave this building without *me*. I will try to be around as much as I can."

"But what if he gets in again?" Thom fretted. "And how long can we keep this up for anyway? I can't exactly stay here forever."

"He won't, Tommo," Craig insisted. "It's just for a couple more weeks."

Thom wasn't convinced. "Maybe we should go to the police."

"You *know* we can't do that," Craig told him firmly. "Look. Let's just stick together and we'll be fine. Trust me."

Thom's resistance was wearing down now. "Okay" he agreed. He allowed himself to lean into Craig.

He didn't think Craig had *much* of a plan, but it was better than nothing. They might survive if only by running down the clock.

That evening, they just ate cereal and toast for supper. Afterwards, Craig switched on the TV to catch the news, but Thom was too preoccupied to watch himself. But later, when Craig lit the oil burner before bed, he found himself relaxing more than he felt he had a right to.

Thom was woken in the early hours by his phone ringing on the bedside table. Next to him, Craig also stirred.

His eyelids heavy with broken sleep, Thom reached out for the phone and saw it was Cady. He answered without lifting his head off the pillow.

"Hullo," he mumbled, barely awake.

There was a silence and then he heard Cady emit a sob.

"Oh my god, Thom!" She started wailing.

This made Thom sit up. "Cady, what's wrong?"

"It's Lars!" she cried. "He's in a coma!"

"What!" Thom gasped. "How?"

Craig's lamp snapped on, on the other side of the bed. He hoisted himself up to watch Thom on the phone.

Cady snuffled phlegmily as she tried to pull herself together. "When I got home from work, he was just lying there on the couch with a needle in his arm. He wouldn't wake up, so I called for an ambulance."

She let out another sob. "I think he's taken an overdose!"

"Oh my god" Thom murmured.

He remembered what Morton has said to Lars before he left:

No more chances for you, Last Chance. See you later.

"Cady, where are you?"

Cady sniffed again. "St Vincent's. Lars is in the intensive care unit."

Thom pulled at his hair as he tried to think. "Okay, that's a five-minute walk from my house. I'll come down."

After he hung up, he got out of bed and started pulling his clothes on.

"Did you hear all of that?" he asked Craig.

"Yeah, most of it," Craig replied. He leaned forward. "Does she know what he ODed on?"

"She didn't say, but it will be heroin, I guess." Thom paused. "Same thing Morton meant for me to OD on."

Craig raised his eyebrows and looked at him intently. "What? You think Morton did this?"

Thom nodded. "Yes, I do."

Craig threw off the bedsheets and swung his legs onto the floor. "I'm coming with you."

Thom was grateful for the company. Once they were both dressed, they grabbed what they needed – wallets, keys, phones – as they left. Taking the lift down to the foyer, smelling of abandoned slumber, they headed out into the night.

At the hospital, they navigated a labyrinth of corridors and stairwells, and followed endless signs. They found Cady alone in the relatives' room. She was wearing the same leopard-skin print coat Thom had seen her in earlier. The kohl around her eyes was smudged and her skin blotchy.

"Thank you for coming," she whispered hoarsely.

She'd clearly exhausted herself crying.

"How is he?" Thom asked.

Cady shook her head despondently. "They've done some tests, but they don't really know. He could have brain damage or liver damage. I had to tell them about his history with drugs."

"Well, they needed to know that."

"Yeah, I know," Cady sighed. She then looked at them pointedly. "Do you want to see him?"

Thom realised he was totally unprepared for this. He'd never even been inside an intensive care unit.

To his relief, Craig answered for them. "Sure."

Cady directed them to a partitioned bay where they found the comatose Lars. He was wired up to an apparatus of tubes and machinery, which bleeped intermittently. Around him, the smell of disinfectant was all-pervasive.

He looked disembodied and cadaverous. Thom and Craig stood back, regarding him wordlessly. It didn't seem to Thom as though they were seeing Lars at all. Craig, appearing to sense what Thom felt, squeezed his shoulder. As soon as they decently could, they went back to the relatives' room.

Cady's mood had changed by now. She was resentful and restless.

"He swore to me he wasn't using heroin again," she told them, with an air of grievance.

Thom realised she probably didn't know about the incident with Morton.

"Cady, did you speak to Lars again after he gave you your wallet?"

She looked surprised by the question. "Nope. I was working all night."

Craig pitched in. "Did everything seem normal to you when you got home?"

She frowned. "What do you mean?"

"Was there any sign that somebody else had been in the house?"

"No." She looked at them both in askance. "Why?"

Thom opened his mouth to tell her about Morton. But he stopped when he saw a glint of warning in Craig's eye.

This wasn't lost on Cady. "Wait! Do you think this has something to do with that cop?"

"It's a possibility," Craig acknowledged reluctantly. "But we don't know for sure."

"Well, shouldn't we tell the police?" Cady demanded.

"No!" Craig's response was decisive. "We haven't got enough to go on. If we're wrong, it will just make things worse."

Cady seemed discomfited by his vehemence, but she didn't argue.

Afterwards, when he and Craig were walking home, Thom was afflicted by guilt and unease. He felt they'd let Cady down. Instead of comforting her, they'd left her even more disconsolate.

He glanced sideways at Craig. "We should have told her."

"No, Tommo." Craig sounded weary, as if he'd had to repeat himself too many times. "We've got to handle this ourselves."

How? Thom thought.

Through the kitchen window, the greyness of the morning outside seeped in. Thom pressed down the plunger of his cafetiere and poured himself a coffee. He took his mug and his bowl of muesli into the lounge.

He had breakfast alone as Craig was still in the shower. Neither of them had slept well after getting back from the hospital. Thom had tossed and turned in the bed, managing only a couple of hours sleep. He sensed that Craig was similarly agitated.

Thom was on his second mug of coffee when a groomed and suited Craig emerged. Despite everything, he had a brisk, cheery air about him. He went into the kitchen to unplug his phone.

"Not going to the gym, Tommo?" he inquired, picking his keys up off the microwave.

"No," Thom replied. "I really don't feel like it."

"Oh well, you go often enough." Craig came out of the kitchen - keys and phone in hand. "Just so you know, I'm going to be home late tonight."

Thom raised his eyebrows. "Really?"

He had thought they'd be going back to the hospital together.

"Yeah," Craig yawned. "I'm going to this event at the Convention Centre called 'Find your inner mogul.'"

Thom was irritated. How could this even be a priority?

"I see. I expect it will be like all those other self-help events you go to - everybody giving each other massages."

Craig chortled. "Yeah, probably. But you know I like that sort of thing."

Thom didn't want his vexation to go unnoticed. "It's just that I was hoping to go and see Lars tonight."

"And *that's* exactly what I want you to do, Tommo." Craig fixed his eyes on him. "Go back to the hospital and keep Cady company. And stay there until kicking-out time. Then come straight home."

His instructions were unambiguously clear, but Thom was confused.

"I thought you said I should stay here and not go out. Unless you're with me, of course."

"I *know* what I said. But I'm asking you to do something different."

"But why?"

Craig motioned at him. "Come here, Tommo"

"What's this all about, Craig?" Thom probed.

"Come here, Tommo," Craig repeated.

Thom hesitantly got up and went over.

Craig cupped Thom's face in his hands. "I just need you to go with me on this," he murmured.

"And where exactly *are you* going?"

Craig smiled and tapped him on the nose. "I told you. I'm going to be at the Convention Centre."

Thom didn't believe this. He peered into Craig's dark eyes hoping to somehow extract the truth. But they revealed nothing.

"Alright," he muttered, giving up.

"Nice one, Tommo." Craig scooped up his briefcase. "See you on the other side."

With that, he kissed Thom on the forehead and disappeared out the door.

Chapter Thirty-Seven

Thom had a long, dreary day at home. He wasted at least a couple of hours watching daytime TV. Feeling slightly ashamed, he then vacuumed the lounge. After a sandwich lunch, he logged onto Craig's laptop. He meant to do some university work but, instead, found himself surfing the net. He thought of a website he wanted to revisit, and so he checked the browser history.

To his surprise, he saw the Aspire website listed at the top. This was strange because it wasn't *him* who'd been on there. In fact, he hadn't used the laptop for days. Then, he realised.

It must have been Craig.

Frowning, Thom clicked on the link, which brought him to an events page. Scanning it, he read some blurb about a public meeting at the Aspire office.

'How Can We Move On? – Chaired by Pastor Archie Henderson. Guest speakers include Rob Morton of the NSW police...'

This meeting was at 8pm that evening. Thom remembered Morton telling him about it the day before. But *why* the hell would Craig be so interested?

The hospital corridors were busy when Thom arrived. He ploughed through the evening rush on his way to the relatives' room. In there, he found Cady, standing by the window. She had someone with her: an older woman with an immaculate chestnut mane, and a cream trench coat draped over her arm.

As Thom approached, Cady introduced her. "Thom, this is Marsha, Lars' mother."

Seeing her close-up, Thom guessed Marsha was in her sixties. She looked tired beneath her carefully applied makeup.

She extended her hand, smiling warmly. "Thom, I've heard so much about you. It's lovely to meet you at last."

"You too," Thom replied, although he thought the circumstances far from lovely. He reached into his mind for some small talk. "Have you just got here from Canberra?"

"No, we flew in this morning. We're staying at the Four Seasons."

"Well, that's convenient," Thom said blandly.

"And expensive," Marsha laughed. "If we stay here much longer, we'll have to bed down with Cady."

"You'd be very welcome," Cady told her. "I'd even tidy the place up."

Marsha waved her hand dismissively. "Oh, I don't mind a bit of mess," she insisted.

Thom interrupted with a question. “How is Lars today?“

Cady and Marsha’s faces fell when he said it.

Marsha answered him. “No change, I’m afraid. We’re still waiting on the test results. My husband - Kelvin - is in with him now-”

She paused as the door behind them opened. “Ah, here he is.”

Thom turned to see Kelvin himself enter the room. He was a wiry, unassuming looking man, which was not what Thom expected. Everything Lars had ever said about his father conjured up someone more vigorous, more overtly powerful.

“Darling,” Marsha called over. “This is Thom, Lars’ friend.”

Kelvin crossed the room and took Thom’s hand. “Well, thank you so much for coming. We are extremely grateful for your support.”

“Oh, I couldn’t not be here - ”

Marsha interjected with a suggestion. “Why don’t we let Cady and Thom go and see Lars together? And we can take it in turns with them.”

“Yes, I think so,” Kelvin agreed.

Thom was struck by Marsha and Kelvin’s composure, and their consideration. He could easily imagine them at a diplomatic cocktail party. They’d be circulating, doing the rounds, putting everyone at ease. Even now, they were insistent on striking the right tone.

“They seem nice,” Thom observed.

He was stood at the foot of the bed in the intensive care unit. Cady had pulled up a stool next to Lars and was holding his hand.

"Oh, they are! They are like the best parents. And I totally love them." She sighed regretfully. "I just wish I could answer all their questions."

"Questions? What sort of questions?"

"Like... when did Lars relapse, and why *has he* relapsed?"

"Well, that must be hard to answer."

Cady shook her head wearily. "The truth is I just don't know. They must think that I'm totally oblivious, or I just don't care. *Or maybe* they think I'm hiding something."

"I'm sure they don't think that." Thom assured her.

"Hmm" Cady murmured, gazing at Lars. She squeezed his fingers.

To Thom, the patient in the bed was more absent than present. Cady started murmuring to Lars and stroking his hair. Thom felt uncomfortable, as if he were privy to an intimacy he shouldn't be.

Soon, it was Marsha and Kelvin's turn with Lars, and so Thom and Cady went back to the relatives' room. They were eventually told by a nurse that visiting hours were over. As they waited to say goodnight to Marsha and Kelvin, Thom invited Cady back for some soup. He'd cooked a vat a few days earlier

She smiled gratefully. "That would be wonderful."

Cady made herself at home, curling up in Craig's chair like a cat. Thom switched on the TV for her.

In the kitchen, he heated up the soup and found a bottle of chardonnay in the fridge. When it was ready, he took their bowls into the lounge room.

As he put her soup down in front of her, Cady straightened up and stretched out her arms. "All I want to do is watch some shit TV," she said sleepily.

Thom poured her a glass of wine. "Well, *McLeod's Daughters* is on in a minute."

They watched the show as they ate, and Thom made sure their glasses were continuously replenished. By the time the credits rolled, the bottle was almost empty.

Thom glanced at Cady when she yawned loudly. It occurred to him that she might not have the energy to take herself home. "You're welcome to stay in our spare room tonight," he suggested.

Cady folded her legs back up into the chair. "Thanks. That would be great if you don't mind."

"Not at all."

The news, which Thom wanted to see, was on next. Just as it started, Craig arrived home. He dropped his briefcase by the front door.

Seeing him, Cady raised her hand in greeting. "Hey Craig!"

Thom muted the TV.

"How was it?" he asked.

Craig came over to lean on the back of the couch. "Yeah, it was really inspiring, actually. It's given me heaps to think about"

Hearing this, Thom felt relieved.

So, he has been at the Convention Centre.

"Oh well, that's good." Thom gestured at the kitchen. "There's some soup left if you want some."

"Thanks, Tommo." Craig's eyes flickered between him and Cady, clearly about to ask the obvious question. "Is Lars any better?"

Cady bit her lip. "Not really," she replied despondently.

Craig seemed to be caught off-guard, as if he'd expected a different answer. "Well, I guess it's still early days. And I'm sure the doctors...."

He abruptly stopped mid-sentence and stared at the TV.

Thom turned to see what had seized his attention. Across the screen, a news headline was emblazoned: 'Sydney cop killed in hit-and-run'.

"What's this?" Thom muttered. He reached for the remote and turned the sound up.

They caught the tail end of the intro. The reporter was speaking over a shot of the Aspire office. "Detective Sergeant Morton had been due to speak tonight at a meeting in Redfern."

Then, a shellshocked Archie Henderson appeared when he was interviewed.

"We heard this bang," he told the reporter. "Like some sort of collision. And so, I came out here, and that's when I found Rob lying in the middle of the road."

His voice broke as he finished the sentence.

"Whoa!" cried Cady, clasping her hand to her mouth.

The report cut to a photo of Morton in his work attire: "Colleagues say Detective Sergeant Morton was a popular and much loved..."

Thom didn't hear the rest of this. All he could think about was that Morton was dead. Gone. Removed. Erased. He wasn't coming back. But *how* had this happened? And why? His focus quickly returned to the TV.

Onscreen, the reporter summed up. "There is a big question on everyone's lips tonight." He paused for dramatic effect. "Was this just a tragic accident, or was it something altogether more sinister?"

Thom's mind began whirring. He looked pointedly at Craig, whose eyes hadn't moved from the screen. Craig then turned to face him, his mouth an unyielding straight line. At that moment, Thom *knew*. In his mind, a conversation he'd had years ago, with Lars, began replaying like a video.

He and Lars were drinking coffee in the all-night café they'd frequented at King's Cross. Thom, still new in Sydney, had just met Craig. And he was desperate to tell to tell Lars all about him. Excitedly, he shared all he knew.

Lars' eyes widened when he heard about Craig's past. "What was he in jail for?"

"I'm not sure I should say...'"

"Oh, come on!" Lars protested. "You can't tell me something like that and leave me dangling."

"Alright. But if I tell you, it doesn't go any further," Thom said firmly.

"It won't!" promised Lars.

"Alright." Thom leaned forward and smirked. "He ran over a cop on his motorbike."

Chapter Thirty-Eight

The next morning, when Cady left, Craig told Thom they had to leave Sydney right away.

"But won't that look a bit suspicious?" Thom remonstrated.

He was taking sips from a glass of water as they stood facing each other in the kitchen.

"Not at all," Craig insisted. "Because we're going anyway."

Thom didn't find this particularly reassuring.

"And what if the police turn up and ask questions?"

"And what if they do?" Craig shrugged nonchalantly. "We just tell them the truth. *You* were at the hospital all night, *and I* was at the Convention Centre. It will all be on CCTV."

We certainly sound like we're trying to get away with murder.

Thom wondered how Craig could be so confident about the CCTV, especially if he'd been in Redfern. Then again, Craig hadn't even *said* he'd killed Morton. It was just this unspoken understanding between them. If Craig were now to tell him otherwise, he'd probably be relieved. He supposed he could ask him outright, but he knew he didn't want to hear the answer.

To distract himself, Thom went downstairs to the gym for his morning workout. Sitting on the bike, he pedalled away gently for the first ten minutes to warm up, watching himself in the mirror. He was determined to banish thoughts of Morton and of Craig from his mind. But even as he sped up, this proved impossible.

He reflected that he and Craig were well and truly in it together, bound to each other in ways he'd never bargained for. Thom realised he'd always known Craig had certain criminal aptitudes. If he was honest with himself, he'd found it enticing, at least in the beginning. Now, he wondered if he was in over his head.

Still, Thom was relieved Morton was out the way. The detective hadn't been merely dangerous. He was a mortal threat: snakelike, unpredictable, relentless. The only certainty was that he was about to strike. And Craig stopped him. Lars was right. Thom was lucky to have someone who'd go *that far*. The downside was having to share Craig's burden, his guilt. But maybe that was, in the end, what love was all about.

Thom pedalled even faster, hoping for an endorphin rush. He felt beads of sweat cascade down his forehead as his t-shirt got damp. He took longer, deeper breaths to keep his heart pumping.

If he had any twinge of guilt, it was for Archie not Morton. He'd seen the sadness etched onto the Pastor's face when he was interviewed on the news. He found the memory jarring because he felt he'd visited the grief upon him. And Archie deserved better. For him, Rob Morton would always be the brave misfit teenager he'd rushed to the emergency room, a lost boy who'd taken a wrong turn.

Perhaps he wasn't a million miles removed from Craig.

In his head, Thom heard Morton's words that evening in the motel room.

We're all dark in different ways.

At the Paddington Markets, traders were proffering their wares beneath pop-up gazebos. The Saturday crowds leisurely browsed the handmade candles and tie-dye t-shirts. Thom's gaze fell briefly upon them as he and Craig were sat at a table eating falafel wraps for lunch. The church tower loomed over the yard, like a reproach.

It had been Craig's idea to come here, for the sake of "looking normal". The night before, Thom had been panicked to see Morton was still in the news. The speculation about his death was getting more clamorous.

Thom chewed pensively on his falafel. He realised he must be looking distracted when he heard Craig speak.

"Look. Try not to worry, Tommo."

Thom wiped his mouth with a paper napkin. "What makes you think I'm worried?"

"Because I know you. *Anyway*, we'll be fine as long as we keep our cool."

Thom wanted to say *You're better at this than I am.*

"I've been thinking," Craig continued. "We need to sort the flights out on Monday – "

They were interrupted by Thom's phone ringing in his pocket. He pulled it out to see who was calling.

"It's Cady. I'm going to take this."

He answered, hoping it wasn't bad news. "Hi Cady."

Cady shrieked down the phone. "He's awake!"

"What?"

"It's Lars. He's awake. He came round this morning."

Thom put his hand to his mouth. "Fucking hell," he breathed. "That is just the best fucking news. How is he?"

"Oh, a bit groggy. A bit worse for wear. But apart from that, he's all good."

"Oh god, I'm so pleased." Thom had a surge of elation. "Listen, Craig and I are just at Paddington Markets. We could come over now."

"*Yeah.*" Cady sounded dubious. "The thing is, it's a bit early for visitors. Maybe you could swing by on Monday?"

"Yes, of course. Monday's good for me."

"Cool. See you then."

Thom cut in before she could hang up. "Cady! Does Lars know about... "

He tailed off, leaving Rob Morton's name unsaid.

But Cady understood perfectly. "Yeah, he does. And he's not exactly upset about it, trust me."

"I bet," Thom muttered.

After letting Cady go, Thom put his phone down on the table and exchanged glances with Craig. "Did you hear that? Lars has woken up."

"I heard, Tommo." Craig gave him a glad, contented smile. "See! I told you everything would come good."

"Yes, you did." Thom felt a dark cloud of foreboding had evaporated.

Craig scraped back his chair and stood up. He pointed to the remains of Thom's falafel. "Are you done?"

"Oh. Yes". Thom pushed the wrapper towards him, and Craig swiped it up to dump in a nearby bin.

As they made their way out, they passed the stall of a tarot reader. She smiled at them encouragingly. And Craig stopped to look at her price list.

"Shall we have a reading, Tommo?" he suggested.

Thom gave him a wry look. "I think I'd rather face the future when we get there."

On Monday morning, Thom went to the gym as usual. He came back to find Craig, sat in his towelling robe, busy with paperwork. His briefcase was open in front of him on the coffee table.

Craig looked up. "Ah, Tommo. Today's the day!"

"Is it? What's happening?" Thom wondered what he'd forgotten.

"I'm signing over my franchise." Craig seemed demob happy. "I've got a meeting in the city with that guy Duncan recommended."

"That's great news." Thom dabbed his forehead with his towel. "I'm just going to have a shower and then I'm going to see Lars at the hospital."

"Well, give him my best. I'm sorry I can't come with you."

"Don't worry," Thom replied. "There'll be other times."

He turned to go, ready for his shower.

"Tommo!" Craig called him back. "There's something I need you to do later."

"Sure." Thom turned around. "What's that?"

Craig put down his pen. "I want you to buy our tickets on my credit card." He looked at Thom intently. "Just go to the Flight Centre at King's Cross. And ask for Shane. He knows you're coming."

"Okay. Do you know what flights you want?"

"Just see what's available. But I want to be gone by the end of the week."

"End of the week," echoed Thom uncertainly.

"Yes, Tommo."

"That's very soon," Thom contended. "What about the car and the bike?"

"Easy." Craig leaned back in his chair. "I can get a quick sale on the car. And the Harley, I'll have shipped over. Which will cost the bloody earth, but it'll be worth it."

Thom sucked in his lips and nodded. "Sounds like you've got it all figured out."

Craig smiled, looking pleased with himself.

"There is one thing though," Thom added, folding his arms. "Where exactly are we going to live?"

"We've got two options," Craig told him, stifling a yawn. "We *could* stay with Mum for a couple of weeks. But I guess that might not appeal to you. If not, I know someone – a friend of Mike and Barbara's – who needs a house-sitter."

"Hmmm. Maybe the second option," Thom suggested. "I'd like us to have our own space."

"Alright. I'll call Mike today to fix it up."

"That sounds good," said Thom, glad to have this resolved. "Good luck with your meeting."

"Thanks, Tommo." Craig sat back up. "By the way, I'm not taking the car with me today, so it's all yours if you want it."

Thom pulled his towel tighter around his shoulders. "I don't *think* I will. But it's always good to have the choice."

Expecting a cool day, Thom wore his university hoodie with jeans and his Adidas trainers. He set off for the hospital, leaving by the back gate of the apartment complex. Stepping out into the autumnal sunshine, he smelt the crisp freshness of the morning air.

He walked quickly, positively bouncing through the streets, anticipating a joyous reunion ahead. He couldn't wait to see Lars, back in the land of the living, and join in the family celebration. Lars' awakening was a good portent for him and Craig, a sign that they were about to sail smoothly out of Sydney.

When he arrived, the hospital was noticeably quieter, more tranquil than last time. There were far fewer people darting about. He assumed Lars would still be in the intensive care unit and headed there.

As he approached the relatives' room, he saw Cady, with Marsha and Kelvin, through the glass. They were standing in the middle of the room talking to one of the doctors, a tall Chinese-Australian man Thom had met briefly before. They all looked stiff and tense, not at all what he'd been expecting.

What's going on?

It occurred to him he should go away and come back later. But he quickly dismissed the thought. When he gingerly opened the door and slid in, no-one turned to look at him.

He heard the doctor say: "I am very sorry for your loss."

What the hell does he mean?

As he watched on, like a bystander, Cady let out an anguished howl and buried her head in Marsha's shoulder. The older woman, shellshocked and staring upwards, absently patted her heaving back.

The doctor told them: "I'm going to leave you for a while. Let me know, when I come back, if there's anything I can do."

Kelvin just nodded.

The doctor tactfully withdrew, and Thom found himself face-to-face with Lars' father.

"What's happened?" he heard himself ask, sounding slow-witted even to his own ears.

Kelvin, visibly strained, replied with a forced patience. "Mark... I mean *Lars* went into cardiac arrest – about an hour or two ago - and died."

"What?" Thom gasped. "How?"

This had to be some sort of mistake, something reversible, something that could be undone. Surely, the doctors could revive Lars, resuscitate him, bring him back.

Of course they can't.

As the cold, hard truth began to sink in, Thom became acutely aware of the ticking of the clock on the far wall. Meanwhile, Cady's wailing sobs were getting louder as she was comforted by a distracted Marsha.

"I'm sorry to have to tell you this," Kelvin said to Thom, almost robotically.

"Sorry?" repeated Thom, his voice wobbling. "You really don't have to say you're sorry to *me*."

Kelvin swallowed as he struggled to stop his face from crumpling. "No," he whispered hoarsely.

He moved back into the centre of the room and wrapped his arm around his wife. They exchanged a look which betrayed a lifetime of intimacy. Cady, still rocking against Marsha, had quietened down.

Thom sunk into a chair and looked down at the floor. He realised Kelvin hadn't told him *why* Lars had gone into cardiac arrest?

He looked back up and surveyed the scene in front of him.

Was it because of Morton?

He abruptly sprung up out his seat in a state of agitation. "I'm sorry, I have to go out," he announced. "I *will* be back though."

Marsha and Kelvin looked mildly startled. But Cady didn't respond at all; she either didn't hear or didn't care.

Kelvin gave him a half-nod and mouthed "Okay".

Chapter Thirty-Nine

TEARING DOWN THE CORRIDOR, THOM TAPPED AT HIS PHONE trying to call Craig. He knew he shouldn't be using a mobile in the hospital. But there was no reception anyway. The only option was to go outside, and so he made his way back out to the main exit.

As he walked away from the building, his senses were assailed by the sunshine and car fumes from the busy road. Finding some signal on the kerbside, he called Craig only to go straight to voicemail.

"For fucks sake," he hissed.

He frustratedly tried again. Craig's phone rang out this time. But Thom just heard his greeting repeat itself.

"This is Craig Huatere. Sorry I can't take your call right now..."

"Craig!" Thom intoned with desperation after the bleep. "Can you please just call me back."

He hung up and stood clutching his phone as the traffic whizzed past. He decided give Craig a minute or two. Just as he was about to give up, a familiar looking car drew up alongside him. He quickly realised whose it was.

What the fuck does he want?

The passenger window wound down to reveal Jerome Thomson at the steering wheel.

"How're you going, Thom?" he called over, his voice friendly. "Have you got a sec?"

Thom shook his head, his jaw grimly clenched. "This *really* isn't a good time" he told Jerome reproachfully.

But Jerome wasn't deterred. "I need to talk to you. About Rob Morton."

"No, you don't," Thom muttered, turning on his heel. "That's all over."

Jerome shouted after him. "*And* Craig. We need to talk about him too."

Thom froze in his tracks. It was immediately clear to him Jerome knew *something*. But what? Whatever it was, he had to find out. He turned back around.

"What about him?" he said warily.

Jerome leaned over and opened the passenger door. "Get in" he instructed.

Thom didn't move.

Jerome tried cajoling him instead. "It's in your interests, trust me."

Reluctantly, Thom acquiesced and climbed into the car, slamming the door shut. He buckled up and folded his arms as Jerome drove off.

They traversed through King's Cross down to Rushcutters Bay. Thom sat in resentful silence the whole way. He wanted to berate Jerome for his intrusion, his insensitivity when Lars was... Lars was...

Jerome probably doesn't know about Lars.

Thom couldn't bring himself to tell him. He'd have to say it out loud, acknowledge it as a fact, make it real.

Jerome stopped the car at the edge of the park, from where there was a view of the yachts on the bay. He switched off the ignition and just stared contemplatively ahead offering no opening gambit.

This made Thom even edgier. "What's this all about?" he demanded.

Jerome sighed; he carried on looking out through the windscreen. "You know - the way Rob Morton died – I just find it really strange."

Thom shrugged before giving a breezily dismissive response. "I guess he had a dangerous life."

He had to be careful. He needed to say enough to keep Jerome talking, but not enough to be lured into his trap.

"True," Jerome agreed looking round at him. "But he was a bigger danger to you than anybody, wasn't he?"

"Well, *you* didn't help with that, did you?" Thom said accusingly. "But I'm sure he terrorised other people. He was *that* sort of man."

"No doubt," Jerome conceded. "You know, I studied him for a long time, trying to unravel his life. Get inside his head. And you were just like *one piece* of the jigsaw."

“I don’t understand why I was even on the bloody jigsaw,” Thom huffed.

Jerome smiled to himself. “No. Well, I couldn’t work it out either. At least not until I found the missing piece.”

“Which was?” Thom raised his eyebrows expectantly.

Jerome allowed a pause before replying.

“Craig,” he hissed. “*Your* boyfriend. I reckon it was *him* who killed Morton.”

He stared penetratingly into Thom’s eyes.

“I’m right, aren’t I?”

Thom had seen this coming and was ready. He kept his face neutral.

“You’re way off beam, I’m afraid. Because Craig was at the Convention Centre all night. There’s CCTV to prove it.”

“Oh yeah.” Jerome nodded as if acknowledging a good point. “We’ve already taken a look, and the CCTV totally checks out, like you say.”

“So, why are you wasting my time then?” Thom retorted.

“I want you to indulge me for a moment,” Jerome insisted, rapping his fingers against the wheel. “Just suppose Craig slipped out for a while. And he paid someone who looks like him - from a distance anyway - to sit in his seat while he was gone.”

It would certainly explain a lot.

Thom made a play of snorting in derision. “I would *suppose* you’re clutching at straws”

"But what if I have a witness who knows Craig, a business associate who was there that night. And they're prepared to testify the man they saw wasn't him?"

"Well, you obviously don't. Otherwise, you wouldn't be sitting here talking to me, would you?"

"Are you sure about that, mate?"

"Oh, I'm sure," Thom shot back. "You're not a homicide cop, are you? So why are you here? Well, I know why. You have fucked up big time, and you need to redeem yourself, to make amends. And you think I've got some sort of lead."

He watched for Jerome's reaction.

"Now I'm the one who's right, aren't I?"

Jerome glowered. "You're not as smart as you think you are."

Thom smiled ruefully. "Maybe not. But I'm smart enough to see what you're up to." He looked away and shook his head. "It's always about the internal politics with you lot, isn't it? Forget about justice or the truth because that's *not* what you care about."

"Whatever," growled Jerome.

For one acrimonious moment, he and Thom just glared at each other. Then Jerome recalibrated.

"Okay," he sighed. "Let's just say it wasn't Craig. That leaves *someone else* with a strong motive. So where were *you* that night?"

"What!" Thom cried. "This is getting ridiculous. You must know I was at the hospital. Apart from anything else, I can't even ride a bloody motorbike!"

"Motorbike?" Jerome's mouth dropped slightly open. "Who said anything about a motorbike?"

Thom cursed himself inwardly.

"Erm...I don't know. I must have heard it somewhere. On the news maybe."

"No." Jerome shook his head. "No, you didn't. The homicide boys think it *might* have been a motorbike. But that's just a theory they're working on. They haven't gone public with it."

Thom could feel himself turning a guilty pallor.

"So where did you get the motorbike from?" demanded Jerome.

Silence. Thom had no answer.

"Ha!" Jerome grinned triumphantly. "Busted!"

Thom wondered if Jerome was recording their conversation. But his reaction had been too spontaneous, too uncontrolled. Even so, Thom had said far more than he should.

He tried to row back. "It's just a theory," he blustered. "It doesn't mean *anything*."

Jerome regarded him like a predator slowly closing in. "You've just divulged to me you know all about this. That makes you an accessory. Do you know how much jailtime you could get?"

Thom, collecting himself, resolved to stay cool. "You'd have to prove it first, and you haven't got the evidence."

"Only a matter of time, mate," Jerome assured him. "But you have a choice in this. You can either go to jail with Craig or you can walk free. You just need to tell us what you know. It's up to you."

"Thanks," said Thom witheringly. "But I'll take my chances."

"Yeah? Well, you might change your mind when you see the whole picture."

"The whole picture?"

Thom knew Jerome was trying to play him, but he still wanted to know what he meant.

Jerome stretched himself out in the front seat. "*Everything* comes back to that missing piece of the jigsaw. We didn't know why Morton was interested in you. But he wasn't. *Craig* was."

Thom frowned. "That doesn't make any sense. Craig and Morton didn't even know each other."

Jerome peered at him curiously. "You really don't know, do you?"

"Know what?" Thom had this creeping sense of unease.

"*They* knew each other," Jerome insisted. "Your boyfriend and Rob Morton went *way* back. They had their own little criminal enterprise."

He smirked as he waited for this to sink in.

"Bollocks!" spat Thom. "Craig's a legitimate businessman. He built swimming pools for fucks sake."

"Yeah, he's *mostly* legit. But that didn't stop him laundering Morton's drug money. And his pool business was like the perfect cover."

"You're lying."

"I'm not."

Thom didn't want to entertain any of this, but there was something in Jerome's tone he found persuasive. He sucked in his breath and exhaled as he tried to think.

"Okay. Let's say this is all true. What was in it for Craig?"

"It's all pretty simple really," Jerome yawned. "If anyone gave Craig any trouble, Morton took care of them."

Like that Mongrel Mob guy who turned up.

Jerome added "Craig *really* didn't want you chasing the TJ Hickey story. So, he got Morton, his old buddy, to scare you off."

Thom felt his blood cool. "This is complete fantasy," he muttered to himself.

How the fuck does Jerome know all this?

It was true Craig hadn't wanted him writing about TJ Hickey. But the idea he would involve Morton...

"Look," Jerome snapped. "You need to see for yourself." He turned, reached towards the backseat, and dragged across a leather bag. Opening it, he rummaged around inside and pulled out a phone. He held it up.

"We found this when we searched Morton's apartment. After he died."

He pressed the phone into Thom's hand. "It's all there. Just scroll up".

Thom looked down at the screen. Straightaway, he saw that Craig and Morton were not the strangers he'd thought they were. In fact, they'd had been texting each other for months. Appalled but desperate to know more, Thom read one of their early exchanges. He soon understood *he* was its subject.

Morton told Craig: 'He didn't say much when I gave him a ride home. Cool customer your boy. But I'll keep an eye on him'.

'Thanx mate,' Craig replied.

Despite being forewarned by Jerome, Thom was still shocked to see *them* discussing *him*, in cold hard type, like this. Checking the date of the text, he gleaned it was sent the day Morton picked him up at the bus-stop.

Thom wanted to be sure what he was seeing, and so he clicked on another message. In it, Morton wrote: 'Had coffee with him down at Coogee today. Hes definitely fishing for something on tj hickey. Think I scared him off for you'.

This was a reference to the detective's thinly veiled threat by the cliffs, which it now seemed Craig was behind. Thom wondered what else he'd orchestrated.

Scrolling up, he read Craig's reply, sent on the evening they'd had a row and Thom stormed off.

'It didnt work," Craig complained to Morton. 'Check out his blog'.

The detective got back to him the next morning. 'Holy shit mate that boy is outta control. If you like I can take things up a level. Wont be 2 heavy. I promise'.

Thom knew Morton meant snatching him off the street.

'Go 4 it,' Craig urged.

The detective updated him a few days later. 'I just gave him back his fancy new trainers. You wont hear another peep about TJ Hickey'.

Craig was appreciative. 'Gr8 work mate' he told Morton. 'Let me know when you next need a favour'.

After this, there was a long gap in their messages. But weeks later, Craig texted Morton again. His tone was decidedly hostile this time.

'What the fuck were you doing in my house?!'

Thom realised he'd sent it after Morton broke in.

The detective responded swiftly. 'Your little boyfriend has been working for the PIC mate. Did u know that?? Their trying to take me down. I wasnt really gonna chuck him but we have a BIG problem'.

Craig snarled back. 'I'll sort it. Now stay the fuck away from him. Or I will fuck you up'.

His belligerent warning provoked fury from Morton.

'Don't fucking threaten me u prick. You need to get him under control mate or its out of my hands'.

This was the last message between him and Craig.

Clutching the phone, Thom dropped his hand to his lap. He gazed out the windscreen, stunned and disbelieving. His attention settled momentarily on a passing jogger. Everything around them - the park, the yachts, the people - felt unreal. Like a fabrication designed to deceive and manipulate.

Beside him, Jerome affected sympathy. "I know it's a shock, mate. But you had to see this."

His words washed over Thom, who was reliving the day Morton invaded the apartment.

What was that cop doing in my house?

Craig's question reverberated around Thom's brain. He should have realised then. It was just so obvious that Craig already knew Morton. How else would he have known he was a cop?

A dark thought occurred to Thom, and he turned to Jerome. "Why did Morton try to kill me?"

Jerome seemed hesitant.

"He was ordered to."

"Who by?"

"The wrong people," Jerome told him. "They didn't like your blog."

He gestured at the phone. "It's all there if you want to know more."

"I don't."

"Fair enough." Jerome looked at him beseechingly. "Look, mate. It's absolutely shocking the way Craig's played you. You know, he's a born criminal and he can't be trusted. *So please*, don't screw up your own life over him."

Thom leaned back in his seat. "Okay. What are my options?"

"Just tell us everything you know," Jerome pleaded with him. "If you do that for us, we can arrange immunity from prosecution."

Thom pondered this. "I just need a moment to think."

"That's fine, mate," Jerome replied. "Take all the time you need."

Thom, still holding Morton's phone, unfastened his seatbelt and slowly let himself out. Stepping onto the grass verge, he crossed over to the wall in front of the bay. He leaned over and stared down, deep in thought, at the waves lapping below.

It only took Thom a few minutes to decide what he had to do next. And he knew it couldn't be undone. He turned back towards the car and made eye contact with Jerome, who gave him a gentle, encouraging smile. Thom half-nodded in response.

Then, he swung around towards the bay, raised Morton's phone into the air and flung it into the ocean, where it plummeted to the depths.

Jerome, startled by this, sprang out of the car. "HEY!" he yelled, with all the might of his lungs. "What the fuck! That was evidence!"

Thom began walking away with his eyes fixed ahead. Jerome followed, apoplectic and flappy.

"Why did you *do* that?" he cried plaintively. "I don't get it. What's going on, mate?"

He seemed desperate for some sort of answer. "C'mon, talk to me!"

He was almost cantering to keep abreast. "Are you covering for Craig?" he demanded. "Is that what this is all about?"

His frustration gave way to fury as Thom sped up, ignoring him. And his face contorted into a vengeful snarl.

"YOU ARE IN SO MUCH SHIT!" he bellowed.

But he still got no reaction from Thom, which made him even madder.

"I'M GONNA PUT YOU IN JAIL!" he screeched, totally losing it. "Do you know what happens to boys like you in jail? They get *gang-raped*!"

Passers-by were now openly staring. Jerome stopped, giving up chase as Thom receded further into the distance.

"DID YOU HEAR THAT?" he shouted. "YOU'RE GONNA GET FUCKING GANG-RAPED! I'M GONNA FUCKING MAKE SURE OF IT!"

His threats, for all their violence, missed their mark. Thom just carried on walking, preoccupied and oblivious to the world around him.

Chapter Forty

"Let me get this straight." Shane in the Flight Centre looked sceptical. "You want to go to London *today*?"

Thom was sat in front of him, purposely expressionless. "That's right," he replied, trying to sound matter of fact.

But Shane was still dubious. "It's just I thought you were going to New Zealand. That's what Craig told me anyway."

Thom attempted a patient smile. "There's been a change of plan."

"Really?" Shane made no effort to hide his askance. "Any particular reason?"

Thom wanted to tell him it was none of his damn business. But he had to say something else. "Family emergency," he improvised.

Shane's eyes glinted, as if he'd understood. "Oh, okay," he nodded. He seemed reassured. "I'll see what I can do."

He leaned down to squint at his screen. "So you're going on your own?"

"Yes."

"And when are you coming back?"

"Erm..." Thom looked away and shook his head. "I'm not sure yet. I'll just to play it by ear."

"Let's go for a one-way ticket then," Shane decided.

His hands darted busily across the keyboard as Thom watched on. But his weary sighs suggested a fruitless search.

"Nothing there," he muttered. His face suddenly brightened. "Oh, just a sec."

He turned his screen towards Thom and jabbed at it with his pen.

"There's a seat on a Qantas flight leaving at 6pm. It's going via Hong Kong."

Thom seized his chance. "Perfect," he said quickly.

"But it's in business class," Shane added.

"Fine. I'll take it." Thom wondered if he was pushing his luck.

Shane raised his eyebrows. "It's gonna be expensive."

"That's really not a problem," Thom assured him.

He just hoped that Craig's credit card would stretch far enough.

Still, Shane seemed pleased to have a result. "Cool," he breezed and began tapping in Thom's details. "It's an electronic ticket. And you have to check in by 4pm."

Much to Thom's relief, the transaction went through without a hitch, and he was able to leave soon after. He stepped out of the shop, closing the door behind him, and looked up towards William Street. From here, he could see his apartment building looming over. He stood for a few moments in the doorway, steeling himself to go back there. For just one last time.

Thom was cold and shivery with nerves when he got in. He was really going to do this. He glanced around to see if there was any sign of Craig. But there wasn't. He was glad because it meant he could just take what he needed and go. And he didn't have long.

Zipping down the hallway, he went into the bedroom and slid open the wardrobe. He pulled out his passport and his old rucksack and tossed them onto the bed. Peering back inside, he tried to decide what else to take. But his mind wouldn't focus on the task.

For fucks sake!

Frustrated with himself, Thom slammed the mirrored door shut. He was then confronted by his own face. He was struck by how pale he looked and how drawn. Behind him, he noticed Craig's navy bathrobe, the one he always wore, draped over the back of a chair. He turned to look. Even from where he was standing, he could smell Craig on it – a smell he'd come to associate with home.

He realised, in that moment, he didn't want to go. Not one bit. But Craig had given him no choice.

"Fuck!" Thom hissed and banged the mirror with his fist.

He took a breath and looked back at his reflection.

The truth was inescapable: Craig had lied to him and manipulated and betrayed him. Just like Jake had. All this time, he'd been taken for a dupe, an idiot, a fool as he was deceived by a pretence of love. In his mind, Craig appeared in front of him, sneering contemptuously.

"Fuck you!" Thom snarled back. A tear of rage slid down his face. Convulsed by his own fury, he started pummelling the mirror.

"FUCK!" he screamed. "FUCK!" His blows got harder and harder. "FUCK YOU! FUCKING HELL! FUCK!"

He slammed his left hand into the glass again, and it cracked. When he felt his hand stinging, he realised he was bleeding.

"Oh Christ," he whimpered. "For fucks sake."

He ran into the bathroom to run cold water over his wound, picking away tiny shards of glass. Luckily, none of it had embedded in his flesh. The blood clotted after a minute or two.

Back in the bedroom, he sat down on the bed, feeling calmer. He allowed himself a moment of contemplation, sinking deep into the mattress. It would be easy enough to stay put. He could just let Craig explain everything away.

But he knew that *really* wasn't an option, however tempting. He'd never be able to believe a word Craig said ever again. More to the point, he was now embroiled in a murder. He had only one chance of escape from this mess, and he had to take it.

His eye fell on his rucksack. But he couldn't bring himself to think about packing.

And so, he decided he would take nothing. The flight back home was already paid for; he didn't even need money. If anything, the less he was encumbered with, the better.

He hauled himself up, grabbed his passport and came out of the bedroom. Stopping by the kitchen, he swiped Craig's car keys off the microwave. The only way he was going to get to the airport was by driving himself.

Before he left, Thom looked around over his shoulder and bit his lip. Then he quickly exited, closing the door behind him.

Inside the jeep, Thom put his passport on the dashboard and buckled up. He started up the engine. Driving out of the underground carpark, he found himself worrying about the traffic. It was a surprisingly mundane thought.

As it was, he had quite a smooth run out of the city. Looking in the windscreen mirror, he saw the apartment building shrink into the horizon behind. It occurred to him that Craig might now be home and have realised he'd gone. But Thom couldn't let himself dwell on it. At least he'd left his phone back there, so it wasn't as if Craig could call him.

The route to the airport was straight and linear, like a corridor. As he got nearer, overhanging signs with aeroplanes appeared, and the cars in front slowed right down. Before long, Thom had stopped, waiting for them to clear. Glancing at the clock, he saw he was on time, and relaxed.

He allowed his eyes to close for a moment and his mind to wander. Then, it hit him.

Lars is dead.

Thom gasped as his eyes flicked open. The realisation was cold and sharp, like a blade. Lars was dead because of him and Craig. It was they who'd pulled him back into Morton's orbit, sealing his fate.

"Oh God!" The cry escaped from Thom's mouth, and he clasped his hand to his face.

He'd said sorry to Kelvin when he was at the hospital. But "sorry" wasn't enough. It never could be. Thom then realised that he hadn't, in the end, gone back like he'd promised. He hadn't even said goodbye to Cady

A wave of grief suddenly erupted from him, consuming his whole body, and he heard himself howling. His vision was blurred by a torrent of tears and the wound on his hand reopened. He bled tiny red droplets onto the wheel. In front of him, the traffic started moving again.

Many hours later, he woke up on the plane, wrapped in an airline blanket. At first, he didn't know where he was. He lifted his head to see the darkened cabin with his fellow passengers in various states of slumber. And he remembered. He dropped back down onto his pillow.

He thought about the trouble he'd had getting through departures. He'd arrived at the airport in one hell of a state. Then, he saw the headline about Morton. If that hadn't made him edgy enough, he was stopped by the police. He'd expected them to cart him off there and then. But they didn't. Whatever their suspicions, they hadn't made the connection.

Thom decided he didn't want to think about this anymore. He needed to sleep. He closed his eyes and rolled onto his side and took deep, calming breaths. Everything began to swirl around him.

Tommo!

That was Craig's voice he heard calling, in his head.

"No," he murmured. He turned over, determined to banish Craig.

As he drifted off again, he was visited by a memory; a pleasing one. Lars and Cady had thrown a party at their house when Charlotte was over. It had been a drunken, rowdy affair. They'd all been there – him, and Craig, and Charlotte with her backpacker friends.

Early in the evening, they ran out of alcohol. And so, Lars announced he was going to the bottle shop for reinforcements. Pointing to Cady and Thom, he demanded they went with him to help.

In his mind's eye, as if he were a bystander watching on, Thom could see the three of them, in silhouette, against the pink Sydney sunset. They were walking down the street, with Lars in the middle, carefree in a moment of happiness, gone forever.

Chapter 41

Wellington, New Zealand – January 2014

The plane begins its descent and I look out the window. My first impression of Wellington is of mountains and trees. But there are buildings too, dotted like spring dew on the craggy surface below. We're flying over the coast towards the ocean, as if we're going to land in the water.

Eventually, I spot the narrow runway, which seems cut adrift from the shore. The plane circles it for what seems like an age. I can't believe we're really going to land down there, but we do. There is the inevitable bump as the wheels meet the tarmac.

When we taxi in, I see the outside of the terminal is emblazoned, like a theme park. My god, they're big on *Lord of the Rings* here. The plane stops rolling, and the seatbelt sign snaps off.

Disembarking doesn't take long. Wellington only has a domestic airport. And so, I don't need to show my passport or wait by the carousel. Not that I have any baggage with me anyway. Inside the terminal, the Middle-earth theme carries on.

I find the cab rank outside, beyond the sliding doors. The drivers are standing by their cars, chatting amongst themselves. They exude the languor of an unrushed, early Sunday evening. I catch the eye of one of them; a tall wiry guy, about 60. He smiles welcomely.

"Where to, my friend?" he asks. His accent isn't local.

I give him the address.

"No problem," he says gesturing at his vehicle. "Get in!"

The inside of the car is very tidy and smells of air freshener. I fasten my seatbelt.

He starts up the engine, making conversation. "Is it your first time in Wellington?"

"Yes," I reply.

He glances out to check nothing's coming. "You here on vacation? Business?"

"I'm here to see an old friend," I tell him.

The truth is my old friend isn't expecting *me*. But I don't mention that. In fact, I'd prefer to stay off the subject altogether.

And so, I try to divert him with a question of my own.

"Have you lived in Wellington long?"

"Twenty-two years," he replies, his eyes fixed on the road as he drives off. "I came from Egypt. I've been very happy here."

Great, I think. *You can tell me all about it. Then we won't need to talk about me.*

It's a good way to deal with curious people, I find; get them to talk about themselves.

Before I can encourage him to elaborate further, he jumps in with another question. "So, what is it you do for a living?"

He certainly takes an interest in his passengers.

But I'm happy enough to share. To a point. "I work for a newspaper."

"Ah!" He's positively intrigued now. "Are you a journalist?"

"Not exactly. I'm a sub-editor. That means I check the work of journalists."

He seems impressed. "That must be an interesting job."

"It has its moments."

Again, I haven't been entirely candid. It's true that I'm just a glorified proof-reader. My job has a certain cachet because I work for *the Guardian*. But there's no glory or glamour in it. That's reserved entirely for my journalist colleagues. All I do is rearrange their words and impose neatness and order. I find it quite satisfying, and it does pay the bills.

Having just said all of that, *I am* here in the Antipodes on an assignment of my own. And the paper are paying. A few months ago, I surprised my boss by pitching an idea. I didn't think he'd go for it, but he did. Tomorrow, I fly back to Sydney for the first time in a decade.

I have a reason for going there *now*. The tenth anniversary of TJ Hickey's death is coming up, and it's been on my radar for a while. A few years ago, the Australian government apologised to the Stolen Generation. Ever since, I've been wondering how this was received in Redfern. After what happened, could "sorry" *ever* be enough? There is a story to be told, and I want to be the one to tell it.

When I first mooted the idea to my hipster boss, he seemed sceptical. Or maybe he just didn't expect to hear it from me. I'm not exactly known for my ambition. Anyhow, I found the video of my BBC interview online. And we watched it at his desk.

Upon seeing the younger me, my boss shrieked "Fucking hell!" and chortled.

That was all the convincing he needed. He signed off on everything that week.

Before I left London, I lined up my interviews in Sydney. The first is with Holly Mailman, who's now a professor. She's very high-profile these days and gets lots of media gigs. She seemed friendly enough when I emailed, but I'm not sure she really remembers me. Still, I'll find out soon enough.

My conversation with the taxi driver has already dried up. A slightly awkward silence has fallen between us. But I'm not in the mood to fill it. He's driven us out of the airport onto a motorway. There are tatty bungalows and factories on either side. After the flight in, I'd imagined something more scenic.

Strapped in the front, I flex out my shoulders; they're a bit stiff after sitting on the plane. I should make some effort to talk. But I just want to retreat into my own thoughts. I have a busy schedule ahead in Sydney. A lot of work has gone into organising it; many hours of research.

Well, I say research. It really involved a great deal of Googling. It's amazing what you can find out about people – people from your past - by going online. But you should prepare yourself though. That's how I found out about Archie. He's dead. He was carried off, suddenly, by pancreatic cancer a couple of years ago. People's tributes to him were not so much heartfelt as heartbroken. I'm not surprised. He'd have left an unfillable gap.

There's one person I've never been able to find out *anything* about – Cady. I have since realised that I knew virtually nothing about her. Just her first and last names. And I'm not even sure *they* were real. They've produced nothing online. It's like she doesn't exist and never has.

She might be dead. Or she could be married with kids in the suburbs. I can't see *that* somehow, but who knows? I've realised, however, that I don't actually *want* to see her. And I have this intuition she would feel the same. I wonder how long she grieved for Lars. I wonder if she blamed me – still blames me - for him dying. God knows what we'd say to each other now.

To say I'm conflicted about going back to Sydney would be an understatement. It's not totally without risk either. They still want someone for Rob Morton's murder.

The case remains, technically, open. About a month after I left, the police questioned a forty five-year old man. But they soon had to let him go. Craig clearly managed to confound them. It's possible, I guess, that they could yet try to pin in on me.

Still, I'm not hugely worried. Too much time has passed. I doubt Jerome Thomson, for example, would be motivated to pursue me. He's now a rising star in the state parliament. Turns out his political ambitions weren't just a cover story. Some think he could even be the first Aboriginal Prime Minister. He got out of the police force just in time, before all the scandals hit.

As you can see, I've kept my eye on Sydney from afar. And it seems to me like the ghost of TJ Hickey still haunts Redfern. He has become, to borrow Holly's phrase, more symbolic there than real. They have memorial events for him every year.

The inquest finished soon after I left, and the coroner delivered a verdict of accidental death. He absolved the police of any blame. Which is utter bullshit. I've thought about this *a lot* over the years. I don't think the police *meant* to kill him. But they sure as hell don't deserve fucking exoneration. Their self-interest triumphed over justice. And everybody knows it.

I suppose I should have let all this go, consigned it to the past. Believe it or not, I tried. I really did. After I left, I moved back to London, and I made new friends, and I threw myself into a job. I was determined to put Sydney behind me. I told myself it was just one chapter of my life. And I wasn't going to be defined by it.

Then, I tried to forget them, every single one of them – Craig, Lars, Cady, Morton. I pushed them into the recesses of my mind. The problem was they just wouldn't stay there. They kept flickering back into my thoughts. If anything, as time has gone on, they've haunted me more and more. Sometimes, when I'm out, I think I see one of them, out of the corner of my eye. I end up doing double takes at strangers. In quiet moments at work, I go on Google Street Maps. And I look around Sydney again. It's like I'm back there, walking along those familiar streets, and I can almost feel Craig in the sunlight around me.

The taxi is snaking through a hilly suburb. You might call it affluent, but that wouldn't cover it. The sprawling Colonial mansions sit grandly behind iron gates. My driver must be quietly wondering who it is I know here.

Looking out, I'm impressed by how well Craig has done for himself. He now lives in this enclave. And it *is* him I've come to see. I am, as I said, turning up entirely unannounced. We have not seen nor spoken to each other since the day I left. I haven't even seen a photo of him online.

He never did get in touch, which surprised me. When I first went back to England, I stayed with my parents for a while. Every time their phone rang, I was convinced it would be him. Surely, he'd want some sort of explanation. Or, if nothing else, the money back for my flight. After Facebook became a thing, a few years later, I thought I might get a message, or even a friend request. Still, I don't think Craig does social media.

I've managed to glean a few things from the internet though. It looks like he didn't hang around in Sydney long before he came back here. These days, he runs a construction company which hoovers up government contracts. He must have made an absolute fortune. Charlotte jokes I should have stuck with him after all.

It is a good thing that Charlotte *can* now joke about Craig. I needed to tell *somebody* what happened – with him, with Morton. But it's such a dangerous thing to share. I don't trust people easily. In the end, it had to be her. She is not only my twin; she's the only one in my life who knew Craig. She might understand in a way nobody else would. Even so, it's a terrible secret I've burdened her with.

Mind you, she's been maddeningly inconsistent about Craig over the years. In the beginning, she was emphatic I did the right thing, getting away from him. She told me he was a control freak, and I'd been gas-lit. But more recently, she seems to have changed her tune. She actually said, just like Lars did all those years ago, that I was "lucky" to have someone that protective. She insists with great sagacity that "love is complicated".

I suppose she feels family life has given her perspective. She's no longer the dreadlocked backpacker camper vanning it around Oz. Soon after she got back, she married her edgy boyfriend from school. He used to be like the Kurt Cobain of Lymington. But at some point, when I wasn't looking, he morphed into a respectable lawyer.

Charlotte's words of wisdom are always well meant. They're just not always that helpful. And sometimes, they're quite the opposite as I found out a few years ago. By then, I thought I was done with Sydney, and I had exorcised all my ghosts. That was until Charlotte threw an almighty great curveball.

It was just before Christmas, and she'd come up to London to do some shopping. We'd arranged to meet for a drink in a wine bar in Mayfair. She arrived late, dragging her Selfridges bags behind her.

"Sorry, darling!" she trilled, as she approached the table.

"Don't worry," I smiled. "It's not as if I was expecting you to be on time."

She sat down and we ordered a bottle of Sauvignon Blanc. We quickly drank it as we talked about the things she'd bought, and her kids, and my job. Before long, we were mildly tipsy from the bitter wine. We got onto the foibles of our aging parents. And ended up shrieking with laughter.

Charlotte dabbed at her eyes with a paper napkin and topped up our glasses.

She then looked at me pointedly. "So, is there anyone special in your life at the moment?"

"Erm, no." I was a bit taken aback by the question.

"What happened to that doctor you were seeing?" she asked.

I shrugged. "It just sort of fizzled out."

"Wouldn't you like to meet somebody?"

I took another glug of wine. "I suppose I would. But it's difficult."

"*What's* difficult?" she probed.

"I dunno," I sighed. "Trusting people, I guess. You know, after what happened in Sydney."

"I thought you said you were over that," she said, frowning slightly

"I am," I insisted. "I just wasn't feeling it with the doctor."

Charlotte leaned forward, a sure sign she's about to dispense advice. "Well, you know what I think the problem is, don't you?"

I rolled my eyes. "No. Please, tell me."

She waited a second before replying. "*I think* you've always been looking for another Craig."

"No way!" I cried, nearly spitting out my drink. "Are you serious? Do you think I have some sort of betrayal fetish?"

"But you don't really know that's what happened, do you?"

"Sorry, what?" I put my glass down on the table, dumbfounded.

Charlotte looked hesitant, as if uncertain of my mood. "I've been wondering about this recently. And I'm just not sure that what you *think* happened is what *actually* happened."

I shook my head uncomprehendingly. "What do you mean?"

"Well, you remember those texts you were shown by that detective – Jerome, wasn't it?"

I snorted. "I could hardly *bloody* forget."

"Are you sure they were from Craig?"

"*Of course* they were from Craig!" I insisted, still perplexed.

"But are you absolutely sure?" Charlotte persisted. "Did you see his number?"

"I saw *his name*."

"Just his name?"

"Yes," I replied impatiently.

"So, you don't know they were from *him*, do you?"

I then saw what she meant. As realisation dawned, my mouth slowly dropped open, and I stared across the table.

Charlotte continued. "I'm not being funny, darling. But has it occurred to you the texts might have been fake?"

"Fake," I echoed in a distracted murmur. "Why?"

The answer had already formed in my mind, but Charlotte spelt it out anyway.

"Well, those anti-corruption people *really* wanted you to talk. And you've said yourself, they're a dodgy lot."

"Oh my god," I gasped. "Why would you say this to me *now*?"

Charlotte regarded me with a wary sympathy.

"I don't want to upset you, darling. It's just that this has been gnawing away at you for years."

For a moment, we sat in silence as I regrouped.

"Okay," I said, after taking a breath. "If Craig was so bloody innocent, why didn't he ever come after me?"

Charlotte smiled sadly. "You'd really have to ask him yourself."

We are now coming up to the sloping street where Craig lives. His house is further up.

"Can you stop just here?" I ask the taxi driver.

"Here?" He looks surprised.

"Yes, please."

He slows to a halt, leaving the engine running. I fumblingly pull some notes from my wallet and bid him an awkward farewell. As I step out the car, the summer rays beat down on my sunglasses. I stand on the corner and wait for him to go.

When I turn around, I can see Craig's house. It's an imposing place with a turret and a surrounding porch. The front garden is hidden by a tall hedge next to a long driveway. As I look on at it, I feel cold and sluggish with nerves.

Charlotte thinks it's a terrible idea, me surprising him like this. And she's right. In fact, it's positively unhinged. But I'm doing it anyway. I have a question I need an answer to. And I will only know the truth from Craig's raw, unrehearsed reaction. I find my resolve and begin my trudge up the street.

The gravel on the driveway crunches beneath my shoes. On the other side of the hedge, there is a loud strumming sound. There's someone trimming it. I stop in my tracks and listen. It could be Craig. After ten years, and so much distance, all that might be separating him and me is some foliage. Still, it might be a gardener, or someone else entirely. I decide to try the house first.

I approach the front door, which is wide and solid, and peer through the glass panels. Inside, I see a crooked staircase at the end of a hallway. My god, this is a far cry from our apartment in Sydney. I rap at the door, making a resounding bang with the heavy brass knocker. But it produces no signs of life from within.

Even though I know that no-one's coming, I stand and wait for a few moments. Eventually, I turn away, hoping that it *is* him in the garden. If it isn't, I've missed my chance. It would never be worthwhile making this journey again. More to the point, I don't think I'd have the nerve.

I can hear the trimmer's still going. And so, I let myself into the garden through a little picket gate, quietly closing it behind me. I cross onto the terrace, and I see that there's a man, with his back turned, working below.

From here, I can tell it's him. It's Craig, in heavy boots and protective glasses, trimming that hedge. He hasn't heard me because of the noise.

He's definitely aged. That much is clear to me. The tattoos on his arms give it away. And his hairline has receded; he's going grey. It sounds absurd but I never thought about him getting older. Maybe I wouldn't have noticed if we'd stayed together. And we *could have* done, so easily.

I carry on watching him work. I'm impressed by the garden, which is deep and well-manicured. He must spend ages on it. I wonder if he still rides his Harley. I bet he does, and it's tucked away in the garage.

Any moment now, he's going to turn around and see me. I feel strangely calm though. I have no idea what his reaction's going to be, but I'm not afraid of it. All I care about is my moment of truth. I haven't come here just to ask about the texts. For the last ten years, I've been wondering if I loved somebody I didn't even know. Perhaps now, I can find my answer.

As I look on, Craig finishes what he's doing and switches off the trimmer. Lifting his glasses, he steps back and inspects his work. Looking pleased, he swings around towards the house, where I'm standing. He freezes.

His mouth drops open as he realises that he hasn't been alone after all. He staggers back slightly. Then, as he recognises me, something steadies in his eyes. He's shocked, but he's not that surprised I'm here. In the silence, in this garden, I'm certain of one thing: he's been waiting for this moment for as long as I have.

The End

Acknowledgments

I have heard it said that it takes more than one person to produce a book. This story has been whirring around my head for many years, but it has finally taken the form of a book because I've had help along the way.

The first person I should acknowledge, therefore, is Sumaira Wilson of SpellBound Books for seeing its potential and commissioning it. Her colleague, Nikki East deserves special thanks for her editing. This book, however, would not have been remotely publishable without the very sage advice given to me by Richard T Kelly, my mentor at the Faber Academy. For the arresting cover design, which I loved straightaway, I have Jem Butcher to thank.

Writing a novel can be rather a long, solitary process, so I am profoundly grateful to Caroline Walsh and Elizabeth Glassenbury. They went above the call of duty and read the first and second drafts as I wrote them. It was just the sort of encouragement I needed.

This novel grew out of a non-fiction article I wrote back in 2009 about TJ Hickey and the Redfern Riot. While researching for it, in Australia, I interviewed a range of local activists, experts and others. They are too numerous to mention here, but they have made an enormous contribution to this story. If there is just one other person I should acknowledge, it is TJ Hickey himself. His life and death had a profound effect on the city in which he lived.

My story is not his story, but he is an indelible part of the time and place in which it is set.

Printed in Great Britain
by Amazon

44899532R00202